I0665106

Tears of the Deflowered

SILENT NO MORE

by JJ Staples

JJ Staples

Defloweredlyric@gmail.com
Copyright © 2018, JJ Staples
All rights reserved, printed in the U.S.A.

All rights reserved.
No part of this book may be reproduced, stored in a
retrieval system, or transmitted in any form or by any
means—electronic, mechanical, photocopying, recording,
or otherwise—without the prior written permission of the
publisher, except with brief quotations embodied in critical
articles or reviews.
For permission or inquiries, contact:
[JJ Staples Enterprises, LLC
This is a work of fiction. Any resemblance to actual
persons, living or dead, events, or locales is purely
coincidental.
Second edition.

ISBN: Paperback 978-0-9864349-2-1
ISBN: Hardback 978-0-9864349-3-8

Cover Photograph by Shutterstock.com. Printed in
[Country]

Unless otherwise noted, Scripture quotations are taken
from the Holy Bible, King James Version ® (NKJV)
Copyright © 2982 by Thomas Nelson. Used by permission,
All rights reserved.

Published by: JJ Staples Enterprises 2025

ISBN: Paperback 978-0-9864349-2-1
ISBN: Hardback 978-0-9864349-3-8

Library of Congress Cataloging in Publication

Dedication Page

Tears of the Deflowered is dedicated in memory
and love to my grandmother, Etta S. Williams.
She taught me to love and trust God, among other things.
Her life was my example and blueprint for living a
Christian Life.

Table of Contents

CHAPTER ONE

Pain is Insane

Your blood pressure rises

Heartbeats increase

You weep

Sadness controls

It hurts

Pain is insane

Physical suffering

A pill won't cure

Mental confusion

True agony

It's misery

Pain is insane

Worry replaces peace

Your spirit dies

Trouble rules

Heartaches come

It's excruciating

Pain is insane

Nothing makes sense. Time freezes as passing seconds rush to a sudden halt. The brain endeavors to decipher whether the torment should induce temporary paralysis or instant death. Every cell in the whole body cries. Blood flows, mimicking a river cascading over large boulders. Each nerve ending collapses while igniting multiple sparks as they spiral down into the pits of sorrow. This is a real pain. Breath-stealing, muscle-contracting pain.

Officer Judith Nelson knows all too well about this type of agony. While she clutches the car door to steady herself, her legs buckle. Painstakingly, she sucks in the air and exhales through her puckered lips. Even though the task is difficult, Judith forces her body to maintain an erect pose resembling the stance of a soldier standing at attention.

Her jumbling reflections move with the velocity of a race car rounding dangerous S-curves. Trying hard, she wills herself to belay the forward mobility and reverses her thoughts to start from the very beginning of her latest case involving Charles Smith.

There was a domestic disturbance call in which she was the responding officer at the home of Charles Smith and his wife, Nicke.

This was the place where Judith first became enamored of a middle-aged African American woman, Lyric, who was visiting with Nicke when Charles unexpectedly arrived. His appearance caused mayhem to erupt. At the residence, Nicke was detaining her husband at gunpoint. The rage she exhibited stemmed from him being the perpetrator who abused and impregnated her daughter and his stepdaughter, Jada, six years ago. Jada, fourteen, gave birth to a son, Micah. The shocking revelation and well-kept secret made something in Nicke snap, and she was determined to seek retribution. With love, patience, and persuasion, Lyric, with the grace and presence of a sleek gazelle, was successful at subduing her best friend, Nicke, as Judith gawked in amazement. Something about Lyric's competent reactions made her seem like a kindred spirit to Judith.

Thanks to the efforts of both Judith and Lyric, Judith arrested Charles and carried him off to jail. With Lyric's intervention, she persuaded Nicke to spare his life. The stress from the confrontation, though, caused Nicke to fall victim to a cerebral stroke. After which, the ambulance transported her to the Trauma Center, where she battles to recover and live.

While still sheltered behind her car door, Judith continues to reminisce about the events of the case. She wishes for a 'ride or die' friend, such as Lyric. How blessed Nicke is to have a person beside her when her world was spiraling out of control. Does Nicke have any idea what she would give to have this type of woman in her life? For now, Judith dismisses the desirous friendship and settles for her official title as a servant of the people, sworn to protect and serve the public.

From the day she first met Lyric and Nicke, her duty and obligation metamorphosed into safeguarding Jada. Now, Judith must explain why neither she nor the judicial system could protect Jada from Charles' deranged actions.

Earlier in the day, Charles' mother had posted bond money for him, as she could not see her son behind bars. But his early release enabled him to pursue his neurotic interest in Jada.

Right now, Judith is unsure what else Charles has done to Jada as she awaits her backup and is left to question whether she has blundered as a protector, potential friend, or perhaps both.

The brisk midnight air hits Judith's face with a pore-closing smack. The full moon allows the retreating sun to ebb its way through the starlit sky. Windblown twigs gather about her feet as she huddles near her police car. Torn between rushing into David Austin's house, Jada's boyfriend, or waiting for reinforcement as protocol demands, she toys with her handheld radio as she weighs her options.

According to a caller from this address, "there are two people shot. Proceed with caution. Back-up is on the way," the dispatcher says.

Sirens blare in the distance as three partners' cars and the rescue squad rounds the corner, screeching to an immediate standstill. Her Sergeant bolts as he high-steps to Judith for her version. With their guns drawn, the other officers crouch as they approach the house.

Within moments, James (Jim) Maxey, Nicke's doctor, skids to an abrupt stop behind Judith's car. From the passenger's side, Lyric exits and runs to Judith, hoping for more information. As Judith tries to calm her down, she sees Charles' pickup parked at the curb. Years of experience remind Judith that his vehicle, in this location and currently, spells nothing but disaster. Without time to consider the consequences, Lyric is beside Judith, pressing for information. "I'm on my way inside to learn the specifics. I beg you to please remain calm until I have a complete report," Judith pleads. Trepidation about the outcome is evident in her body language as Judith turns, waving her arms and motioning Jim to restrain her unequivocally.

Lyric wiggles to free herself from Jim's clutches. To hold her still, he interlocks his hands around her torso. "You cannot go inside. The authorities must first do their job," he utters.

Once comfortable that Lyric will not impede her work, Judith is about to step away when a fellow detective converges on the huddle.

Everyone is attentive as he relays new intelligence along with his assessment. "There is a young black female who appears to have been gunned down by an older white man before taking his own life. A visitor discovered the homicides. The lady is much too distraught to give a statement. From what I can tell, the circumstances suggest a murder-suicide."

Before anyone can process this information, loud tire squeals announce David as his car screeches to a stop. Without turning the ignition off, he jumps out and gawks at several cops, EMS, and all the other commotion on his street. He sprints with the momentum of a peregrine falcon accelerating up the walkway. A cop snatches him in a tight bear hug before he reaches the front door. Kicking in midair, he fights to get loose. Out of breath and panting, he manages to govern himself enough to speak. "What is going on? This is my house, and I live here," he clamors. Unable to enter, he scuffles to free himself. He hurries toward Lyric and Jim, hollering, "What is happening? Tell me!"

After hearing the detective's account, Lyric is screaming as he approaches, "We failed to protect another child! The police, her family, her friends, and the courts failed her. When will this killing ever stop? Can anybody save our babies? Lord, have mercy. Please, Father, have mercy on us! Dear God, we need your mercy," she hollers until collapsing into Jim's arms, seeking to unearth protection from the suffering flooding her soul.

With his eyes widening, David yells, "Jim, is Jada dead? Is she hurt?"

Visibly shaken, Jim shrugs his shoulders. "Man, I am not sure what happened. Once they have a chance to assess everything, Judith will let us all know."

While wringing his hands together, David expresses his confusion. "I left her at the hospital with her mother. There is absolutely no way she can be in my house."

Lyrics lifts her head from Jim's chest. She swallows hard before saying, "She found a wrapped gift and came to your house sooner than expected. The size and shape of the box made her think you were going to propose."

"Well, I am----I mean--- I was," David stutters as he stumbles out his words. "I was going to ask her to marry me over dinner, but changed the timing to breakfast because she wanted to spend the night with her mother." He squints his eyes and scratches his head while he stands by, probing for more enlightenment.

"No, David, earlier Jim and I took her to her car, and we watched her speed out of the parking lot. The last thing we knew, she was on route to your house," Lyric states while gazing at the ground. Thump-thump. Her heartbeat slows to a steady rhythm as realization sets in. With both hands pressed against Jim's chest, she searches his eyes for the courage she needs. Because she is unsure of David's reactions, she turns, drifts next to him, and throws her arm on his shoulder. With her index finger, she directs his attention to the stationary blue pickup across the street from his house.

Jim realizes she is painting a vibrant and clear picture for David. What he is uncertain of, though, is how David will respond upon comprehending Charles is inside. Fearing the worse, Jim plants his body behind the man. With his legs spread open, he raises his arms, presses the palms of his hands against his back, and then plants his feet. The scene resembles one from a sanctified church.

David's eyes follow Lyric's pointer to the blue truck, which he does not recognize. Since pulling up to his house, he's been struggling to fit it all together, to make the puzzle pieces match, hoping to understand. First, a police car was double-parked in front of his house, and a squad car was stopped in his driveway. Next, he focuses on Lyric, wanting to ask, "How do you and Jim know where I live?" But his mouth fails to verbalize this thought. Instead, he skips past this as his mind reverts to the pickup. No matter how hard he tries to force the puzzle pieces, the slots are not the right proportions and do not quite fit. All he desires is clarity. While he struggles, he glimpses a red sports car. Incapable of keeping quiet any longer, he blurts out, "Why is Candy's car here?" The words roll from his lips as he tilts his head.

Now it is Lyric's turn. Dropping her left arm, she allows it to dangle. Who is Candy? After thinking for a second, she spouts out, "Do you mean your ex-girlfriend?"

"Yes, the red one is hers," David says, pointing.

With a snap of their heads, both Lyric and Doctor Maxey follow his eyes to the area he is denoting.

"And the one behind her belongs to Charles," Lyric adds, nodding in the same direction.

The trio stands in silence. Once learning the identity of the mystery vehicles, each maneuvers and backs away from the others in disbelief.

With her head lowered, a single tear rolls down Lyric's face while her body sways back and forth.

After watching and overhearing the exchange, Doctor Maxey repositions himself between them both and places his arms around their waists. He pulls them closer, creating a makeshift circle, as he tries to shelter and prepare them for what lies ahead.

CHAPTER TWO

A BOND NOT MEANT TO BE BROKEN

A seed growing inside of you

Made up of your DNA

The fruit of your loins

Nourishing on your placenta

Waiting to make its debut

Depending on you for life

Feeling your every move

Hearing your thoughts

Seeing you from the inside

While understanding your strife

***

Every day that I carried you

I talked to you

I sang a song of love

You nestled inside

Watching with a bird's eye view

We connected and became one.
Bonding together like glue to rubber
I am you and you are me
Together forever until life is done

On the hard hospital lounger in Nicke's room, Tianna, the daughter of Lyric, shifts from her left side to her right, trying to make herself comfortable. In need of a satisfying stretch to ease the crook in her back, she strives to remain still so that she won't wake anyone else. She gathers the too-small blanket over her shoulders, which exposes her feet to the chill in the room. The high-pitched tones from the heart monitor affixed to Nicke are a noisy reminder of the seriousness of her infirmity. To keep Nicke company is the assignment Tianna volunteered to perform. Though she will welcome the morning so she can go home and lie in her bed for some real rest.

In her half-asleep state, negative thoughts run haywire through Tianna's head. Although her eyes are shut, they jerk in a rapid saccade motion. She cannot imagine how Charles justified having sex with a minor, and even worse, his stepdaughter. What kind of sick person can molest their own family? Her breaths shallow and quick, as her mind reverts to when she and her sister/cousin, Jada, were fourteen years old. A picture of Jada, testing their sisterhood by swearing to keep her secret, emerges.

"We are sisters, and sisters are supposed to keep each other's secrets," she began. "I need to tell you something, but promise never to tell." Once Tianna agrees by nodding her head, Jada reveals that her stepfather, Charles, impregnated her.

Stunned by the revelation, she pleads with Jada to let her tell her mother. Distraught and threatening suicide, Jada refuses. Today, thinking back on that moment, it registers to Tianna that she should have notified an adult. Now, she does not believe Jada would have carried out her threat. Instead, she understands Jada used blackmail as a means of manipulation. Opening her eyes, she murmurs, "Maybe if I had not been terrified to tell, Nicke would not be hospitalized and fighting for her life." The guilt of her silence is overwhelming.

No matter how hard she twists and turns, staying asleep is next to impossible. A sliver of light from the corridor shines under the room door through her half-shut eyes. Fully awakened by the racket of her aunt squirming and groaning in the hospital bed, Tianna scrutinizes every movement, wondering if her aunt is uncomfortable or in pain.

Nobody but God, Tianna thinks while concentrating on the machines announcing the conquest over death, but thankful for Nicke's progression of no longer being comatose. What if this were my mother, rather than Jada's, fighting to recover from a cerebral stroke? Would I be able to endure her suffering? The salty trail of tears weaves down her face. She mumbles to herself, "Lyric Williams, I love you." Gratitude inspires and reminds her to make sure and show her mother appreciation the next time they are together.

Nicke's arms flew upward while her body jerked as a cow would after being shocked by a cattle prod. She utters, "No, not Jada, not my baby."

Realizing Nicke is dreaming, she springs up to grab her hand. "Auntie, wake up. It's me, Tianna. Are you having a nightmare? Do you want me to call someone for help?"

Still groggy, Nicke whispers, "Where am I?" With her eyes now open, she surveys her room. After answering her question in her head, she pats the edge of her bed, gesturing for Tianna to sit.

Without hesitation, she rushes to Nicke's side. "What's wrong? Are you hurting?"

"No, I want you closer to me," In a hushed voice, she asks, "Where are Lyric and my daughter? In my dream, Jada was being tortured. I pray she is unhurt." She mops her eyes while slurring her words, "Lift–the–head–of my–bed, please."

Unable to ignore the anguish, she wonders if she should get a nurse despite her aunt's assurances that she's okay. She ponders whether there might be a problem with her airway, as her speech pattern is breathy and labored. There are also accumulating puddles of water forming on her face, and her gown is dripping wet. "Are you sure you want your head raised?"

Brightness floods the room as Tianna flicks on the overhead light and downplays her anxiety with a jovial tone. "They are both fine. Mom and Jada left about an hour ago to go home. So, I guess you are stuck with me." She smiles while rubbing Nicke's hand as she attempts to replace worry with gossip. "In fact, I am going to tell you a secret. Your daughter went to meet her man. She found what appeared to be an engagement ring in a small wrapped box that David had left by your bedside. She thinks he is going to propose. But you did not learn that from me," she says, while pressing her index finger to her lips.

"Oh girl, I already know. Now, elevate this bed."

This time Tianna does as requested. Her eyes bulged as she jammed her hands around her waist. "Just who is your news reporter?"

Again, patting the side of her bed, Nicke motions for Tianna to sit back down. "My throat is still sore, and talking is challenging."

With the anticipation of finding out who enlightened her about the alleged proposal, Tianna teeters closer.

"This afternoon, David came to see me and asked my permission to marry Jada."

"Oh, he did," she laughs, pushing her for more. "What did you say?"

"I gave him my blessings, but after my dream, I am reconsidering my approval. What do you think about him? Is he a decent and honorable man?"

"From what I can tell, he is a kind man. According to your daughter, they are practicing celibacy." After a quick search for her feelings, she continues. "Well, I believe he is the right man for her. But just in case, I told him if he messes up, hell will be a paradise compared to my fury. I can tell you this, though: he is very easy on the eyes. He wears his six-foot muscular frame well."

"That does not mean anything. Look at your stepdad, Johnny. He is an example of a good-looking man, but he is still an adulterer," Nicke says.

"What are you saying?"

"Forget it."

"No, please tell me. Did Dad cheat on Mom again?"

"Honey, I am not suggesting anything. I am sorry. I should not be sharing Lyric's business with you."

This breadcrumb dropped by Nicke arouses Tianna's curiosity. "I must know, she demands. Recently my mother's head has been drooping and seems to weigh down. That is, except when she's around your attentive doctor." Tianna grins as she plants her seed, meant to pique Nicke's interest.

At first, Nicke dismisses her efforts to conduct an inquest about Jim and Lyric. The gnawing intuition, which is hollering that Jada is in danger is taking precedent. Thus, she persists with interrogating Tianna about David. "But again, is he the right man for my daughter?" The last thing she should deal with is the disappointment of another trusted person. Especially because she is still fragile and requires time to heal. "Charles stole my baby's innocence and her faith in adults."

She turns her head away from Tianna as the disturbing memories of her last entanglement with her husband replays in her mind. Frown lines appear across her forehead. Her reflections are disjointed as she bypasses the sordid story which led to Charles going to jail and landing her in the intensive care unit. For her, there is a bit of solace in him still being there. At least, for now, Jada is safe.

Changing the subject, Nicke says. "Speaking of attractiveness, Doctor Maxey is tall, dark, and handsome," she declares, trying to engage Tianna.

"How do you know how he looks? Did Mom describe him?"

"No, I saw him with my own eyes," she says, before snuggling under her sheet.

No one speaks for several minutes. The only sound is the machinery. Both their bodies are present but, their minds exit the room. The two of them encounter separate out-of-body episodes.

Nicke does her best to drift off but is ineffective at silencing the cries for 'help.' Pleas of distress cause her to toss and turn as she wrangles with the monsters of her nightmare.

The demon haunting Tianna is her commiseration for her mother's plight of an unfaithful husband.

"What are you thinking about Auntie?" she asks after dismissing her concerns and focusing on Nicke's.

Grateful for the intrusion, Nicke spills the horrifying details while her body is acting out the scene. Inside, her heart palpitates as outside her extremities shiver. "Someone took my baby's life. She was imploring me to help her, but an unknown person was holding me back. I fought to free myself, but both my feet and hands were tied. The man made me watch as he killed my daughter. There was nothing I could do to stop him."

"Wow, I can see how burdened you are. Do not stress yourself out over a nightmare. Are you sure you don't want me to notify the nursing staff?"

Not willing to open her eyes, she shakes her head, no. "Everything inside me screams that Jada is caught in some calamity."

Tianna works to lighten her concern. "If her man popped the question, I suspect he is the one needing help. She may omit the celibate agreement and is probably throwing something on him, which has him screaming in enjoyment."

Not up to entertaining Tianna's humor, Nicke purposely ignores her.

"Please stop worrying. Dreams can drive a person to overreact. Who you need to be concerned about is my mom. She left here with your doctor. I think he is sweet on her."

"Your mother is also attracted to him," she shares.

"How do you know so much about her life? I thought you were in a coma."

"I was, but I wasn't dead. Once I regained consciousness, your mother updated me on everything. I suggested she should drop Johnny and take up the debonair doctor."

"No, Mom is a committed, spiritual woman. I questioned their relationship, but they assured me their friendship is platonic."

"That was before Lyric learned about your father's adultery and their love child." Scared, she said too much; Nicke slaps a hand over her mouth to pull the words back.

Tianna gasps. She is curious about why her mother did not mention the latest episode. This woman is his second mistress. The first time, Tianna forgave him but now, despite what he or her mother says, she is through with him and his lies! How does a man repeat the same mistake? Now, she understands why he stayed out of town for so long and was not being candid about working. In reality, he is playing house with another woman.

Nicke feels the aftershocks. "Please do not let your mother know, I told you. These pills I am taking have me delirious."

"I won't tell her," Tianna assures her. "How could he fool around on my mom again? After his first affair, why did he not know and do better? Does anyone respect the institution of matrimony anymore?" To cover her anger, she covers her face with her hands. "You can bet I am going to get to the bottom of his unfaithfulness. Johnny will be sorry he ever cheated on my mother."

"Calm down, baby. Lyric can manage her own life. Divorce for any reason is equivalent to the death of a spouse. You just be there to support her."

"I will always be there for her." Powerless to stop the words, she belts out, "If he has another woman, Mom should get even as a single woman and be with Jim."

Nicke, privileged with foreknowledge of Lyric having sent divorce papers to Johnny, does not want to let this slip. She wiggles in bed as she scrambles to think of a way to reverse the conversation. "Tianna, enlighten me about this Dr. Maxey."

"I am not familiar with him. I know he is a Believer and promises not to disrespect my mother's marital vows. But now I hope he does."

"No, please do not wish for this. Your mother is a strong woman. Religion is important to her and is her source of stability. Because of her beliefs, she is a forgiving person."

"Hopefully she will not forgive Johnny."

"Tianna, you forgot to say 'Dad,' right?"

A quivering sound escapes, but Tianna censors herself before she responds. "No, I said as I intended. He lost the right for me to refer to him as my father."

While caressing Tianna's hand, Nicke's heart concurs. "Do you think it is too late to call Jada?"

"Yes, it is after midnight. I am sure your daughter has shut down for the night." She reassures Nicke but figures when she drifts off again, she will phone Jada.

Afraid if her friend did not pick up her telephone, she would be further agitated.

The room is silent, with only the faint ding of the therapeutic devices. They remain silent for several minutes.

"Tell me more about your dream."

Nicke closes her eyes. "There is nothing more to say. My baby was murdered."

"Don't give life to those bad images passing through your mind. Jada is fine. Why not try to get some rest?" Without waiting for a reply, Tianna lowers Nicke's bed and turns off the light.

"I guess you are right. I am exhausted."

After pulling the bedding around Nicke, she kisses her cheek and says, "Goodnight," then returns to her makeshift bed.

While sitting there, Tianna's mind is still plagued by her stepdad's extramarital folly as she struggles to let go of her hatred. She is pleased Dr. Maxey is with her mother. A part of her evaluates whether to phone her older sister, Tasha, and relay the newly found Scoop. In place of that, she decides on a cup of coffee. Quietly, she eases the door open and tiptoes out of her aunt's hospital room. Kicking open the door to the refreshment center helps to channel her outrage. "Dad, I mean Johnny, how did you do this again?" she grumbles to herself. Once she secures her drink, she makes a split-second determination to dial her stepfather. One touch on her cell phone selects the only person responsible for the heartache.

"Hi, Tianna," Johnny greets her with astonishment. "Is your mother all right?"

Without restricting her aggression, she fires a retaliation shot. "How do you think she is doing?"

There is silence on the line. With her hand on her hip, Tianna takes a sip and preps for his comeback.

"Well, I guess things are rough for Nicke and Jada given everything they endured."

The diversion is clear to her, but Tianna addresses his statement. "Jada is dealing with a lot but, her new man,

David supports her. Aunt Nicke is not quite ready to go home, but she is improving."

"That is great news. Tell your mother I will call her later." Mindful he is trying to get her off the phone, Tianna denies him the satisfaction of avoiding an explanation for why he hurt her mother. Though cognizant he is not forthcoming, she still pursues the matter.

Outside, she locates a secluded seat where she sits to kick off an in-depth powwow. "Dad, when did you speak with my mother?"

"I—I, talked with her last night," he stutters. Baffled by where her line of interrogation is heading, He senses he should only impart what is asked adding nothing more. He readies for an inquisition, understanding she will be both the judge and his jury. The last verbal exchange, he recalls with his wife, caused him to convulse from her emotional breakdown. His head moves in a continuous left to the right rotation. He wonders how he could be so dumb to screw up the lives of so many people. Not only did he mistreat Lyric, but he also brought an innocent child into this drama. How can he explain this to Tianna when he cannot decipher his actions? "Where did you say your mother went?" He inquires, as he gazes out at the stars, exploring a way to erase his foolish decisions.

At first, Tianna is indignant about Johnny's question. She makes a fist until her red fingernails dig into the flesh of her palms, and she takes a deep breath before snapping, "I didn't say."

Johnny detects the return of resentment in Tianna's voice. Until now, he was unsure if she knew of his indiscretions, but judging by her attitude, he is confident she is a ticking bomb about to explode. Now what? Once again, he opts to retreat before he triggers detonation. Only this time, he elects to hang up. "Tianna, it is past my bedtime, and I have an early morning meeting. Tell your mother to phone me in the morning."

"I'll be sure to tell her when she gets back from her date." The words shoot off her tongue like an arrow aimed straight at his heart. *How do you like tasting your own medicine, Mr. Casanova? Did you believe my mother could not attract someone other than you? A beautiful 'all woman' who is blessed with choices.*

Without affording him the opportunity to follow up on Lyric's whereabouts, Tianna adds, "Rest well." She smirks as she ends their call. Rising from her seat, she skips back to her aunt's room while marveling at injuring him with her words. She was so intent on making him pay for his behavior; she remembers she neglected to call Jada.

After peering at Nicke and confirming she is still sleeping, she calls. The phone rings four times before going to voicemail. "Hey girl, please cut that man some slack and text me when you receive this message. Your mom is upset. She dreamed about you," Tianna whispers before the beeps acknowledge the recording ends.

Longing for a hot shower and missing her bed, she tries again to stretch out in the uncomfortable makeshift bed. There are only six more hours before daylight. Just as her eyes close, she is disturbed by a buzzing noise. Jada, she thinks before answering only to hear a dial-tone. She scrolls through the phone log and realizes it was Johnny. Delighted by the hang-up call, she beams.

***

Johnny was so glad he hung up before Tianna answered. First snorting through his mouth, then his nose, he paces. Afterwards, he phones his wife, but her voicemail picks up. "What type of rendezvous is she at this time of night?" Johnny poses to the atmosphere. Tears develop, but he clears them away as he whacks his hand on the nightstand. "Ouch, I will not lose my Lyric." A judgmental spirit overtakes him as he battles to conquer the voices in his head. She is supposed to be religious. One asks, "How long has this been going on?" Another one comments, "Probably since Donna entered your life." He falls across the bed desiring to silence the noises but to no avail. "I know she is not in love with this man," he retorts to the utterance. "Lyric loves me. All I can do is go home and try to win her heart back by giving her some attention." The voice of doubt replies. "Man, you blew this. You don't deserve a second chance."

He rolls over and hugs his pillow, acquiescing his betrayal may not warrant another stab at marriage. "What is wrong with me? Why would a man with everything throw Lyric away for another woman who is desperate to be with any employed man," he outcries. This is the first time he considers Donna pregnant to trap him.

As he dissects their affaire d'amour, he receives a call. One ring and he answers, "Lyric, where have you been? Who is the man you went out with?" Without stopping for feedback, he blabs. "Baby, I am sorry. I do not want you to leave me. Let's work this out. I don't want us to be over. I love you." He stops talking to grant his brain a moment to catch up.

"What! This is not your pitiful wife. I am Donna. You do remember me, don't you? You know, your baby's momma," she barks in disgust.

"Oh—Oh—why are you phoning me this late?" Johnny stammers out in a voice sounding like a young child.

"You are saying one thing to me and another to Lyric. Which one is it?" She demands.

Resorting to avoidance, Johnny laments, "You are right. I am confused. My stepdaughter said Lyric is out with another man. After learning this, I was enraged with jealousy. What I'm telling you is that I need some time to sort this out. Can we take a break until I am sure?"

Donna pulls the phone from her ear. Frustration causes her blood pressure to rise. An unfulfilling audible exhalation is released. "Johnny, what is there to think about? You said you want your wife." As she transfers the receiver from one ear to the other, her fight dissipates. "If you and Lyric want to pretend to be with each other, that is between the two of you. I will step out gracefully." The inflection in her voice calms. "Go, Johnny. Get out of my life and don't come running back if she does not want you."

The words she spoke dance in Johnny's head. "I am not saying I do not love you," gulping as he forges ahead. "We had a child together. I guess I am astounded to know she is already dating before the ink is dry on our divorce."

"Johnny, tell me why you became involved with me if you wanted Lyric? Furthermore, if you are in love with me, you would not care if your wife were with someone else. The only other scenario is that you are not devoted to either of us. I think you are a selfish bastard who insists on wanting your cake and eating it, too. Perhaps you are keeping us both around in case you might want a different variety or so we can share a piece with you."

"That is not true, Donna. You knew I was married before you agreed to become tangled up in my world. Your pregnancy was your way of trapping me."

She shrieks, shouting, "You dirty dog! I did not conceive our son by myself, and you did not have to stay. We had options which you refused to consider." Her voice cracks and softens to a whisper. "Please, go back home to Lyric."

Johnny forms an excuse before beginning where he left off. "I'm sorry. I should have said nothing about my son. I love him and you. I am just tired and distracted." He pauses while looking out of his hotel room at the Statue of Liberty. To him, the icon represents freedom. Only instead of seeing the copper torch-bearing lady, her face is replaced by a portrait of his soon-to-be ex-wife. He picks up the official-looking manila envelope from the desk. He fingers the flap but cannot bring himself to review the contents. Since being served earlier in the day, he's only had the strength to read the title, 'Petition for Dissolution Of Marriage.'

Without commenting, Donna slams the phone down.

Click. "Hello, are you still here?" He studies his iPhone. Johnny throws the court documents under his bolster. He drops on his bed, being sure his head hides the papers containing the end of his marriage. *Is she divorcing me for the man she is spending time with?* He deliberates just before drifting off.

CHAPTER THREE

YOU OWE ME

Couldn't depend on you

What else could I do

Took matters in my own hands

You failed to understand

Left me alone to fight

I tried to be polite

But that didn't work

Had no other choice but to go berserk

I came to you for help

Where else was I to go

But you did not believe me

So, I had to protect myself

Now you owe me

Charles announces to himself, "Thanks, Mom, for getting me out of jail. There is no way I can spend another second in that hell hole with these pitiful criminals. It's about time she protected me," His mind overflows with cogitation of his past and future endangerment awaiting him as he drives down the street.

When did my life turn this complicated? He asks himself. The smell of yeast and butter loosen in his sub-conscience as he slips back to a time of his youth. The harsh voice of his mother chastising him and his baby sister, Jackie, while at the breakfast table rings in his ears. "Get your arms off the table and sit up straight. You're acting like pigs eating from a trough." In his memory, the stinging sensation from a backhand to his face is as fresh now as when he was a boy. "Where are your manners, boy? How many times must I tell your stupid ass how to behave in my house? You are just as uncouth as your crazy father," his mom rants. He remembers how his mother's handprint on his white skin branded a beet red outline.

Ever since I exposed Uncle George for touching me, she has hated me. Why did she not believe me? Her brother was a creep. Both physical pain and psychological grief consume him during his stumbling down the street of remembrance. He grips his anal sphincter muscles and expels a grimacing moan. "All she had to do was listen to me the first time I told her." He hollers into the silence.

Still, even as an adult, Charles can again hear his uncle through the lifetime scars and nagging flashbacks of his unspeakable childhood assaults. "Boy, you know you enjoyed the games we played. Now, lay in this bed and give me some more. If you share this with anyone, I will tell everyone you are gay."

With the words ringing in his head, Charles' body barrels to attention as he examines the passenger's seat of his car, expecting to see the man who violated him. The sounds seemed so real and current; his entire body is shaking at the realization that it's just a memory. He dries his hands on his pants, leaving a spot that soaks through to his skin. "No matter what he said, I am not a homosexual. I married a woman and fathered a son." The desire to free his mind from the dolorous thoughts makes him shake his head several times. Still, the visions continue to manifest regardless of how tight he fastens his eyes. The recollection of his uncle's sexual coercion led to him being assaulted. Many nights he tried to fight him off but to no avail. How he yearned for his mother to protect him, but she would always defend her sibling. The abuse continued for several years until he realized no one would assist him. To prevent another moment of defilement and humiliation, he decided to take matters into his own hands.

It was the night of the usual binge drinking for George. He'd soon be famished and insist his nephew cook him something to eat before accompanying George to his den of perversion. This time, though, Charles was adamant to stop his uncle once and forever.

Summoned, as expected, to fix his dinner, Charles complied without any resistance. This was the day he had planned for, and now was the time to carry out his elaborate scheme. Charles took the ground meat from the refrigerator. Once he was sure no one was watching, he retrieved a previously hidden Maxwell House can from under the sink. The lid was dislodged, revealing the millions of fine, crushed pieces of glass. He combined these pulverized fragments into a beef patty, careful not to cut himself. He fried the hamburger and smothered it with green peppers and onions, along with three strips of bacon. Upon completion, he constructed George's plate, being precise to soak the bread with plenty of ketchup. Unflappable and unfazed, he detached from his feelings and relished in the fatal consequences that ingesting glass would have on the gastrointestinal tract of his hapless victim.

George stumbled to his place setting and almost tumbled over, cursing the chair for moving. Liquor reeked from every pore in his body, sending a definite message that he was beyond inebriated. He grabs the food, cupping the burger with both hands as the grease and condiments run down his arms. The lack of coordination caused the first attempt at biting his sandwich to fail. The second attempt was successful, as he stuffed over a quarter of a portion into his mouth and swallowed it without chewing.

He attacked the meal with such enthusiasm; Charles felt a smile grace his face. With every bite, revenge danced in his eyes as he awaited the effects. After the last mouthfuls are gobbled down, Charles sneered.

A gag launched George into an uncontrollable coughing spell. He began writhing in pain as the glass severed his innards. A combination of blood and Heinz left a crimson red path as they dripped from the side of his mouth like a slow, leaky faucet. "TIMBER," Charles shouts with excitement, as George topples down resembling a cut oak tree. Just before his eyes gyrated to the back of his head, George glared at his nephew, begging for help.

Instead, Charles stepped over him, retched his throat with a falling guttural sound, then hawked the collected phlegm in George's face. "Die," he mutters without looking back as he shrugs and shuffles to his room, pausing only long enough to wipe the red mixture of both blood and ketchup from his shoes. With one jump, he flung his small, framed body on the bed and turned the television to a John Wayne cowboy movie.

The next morning, Charles is awakened by screams. He heard his mother bellowing from the kitchen,

"George, wake up! Get up! What happened? Charles, call 911 and tell them to send an ambulance."

He peeks into the kitchen, where his mother is crouched down next to her brother. Without stopping, he dials the emergency number and reports in a concise voice, "My Uncle George is dead on our floor."

The operator asks how he died, and Charles states, "he was drinking and must have choked on his vomit."

She asks his age.

"I am fourteen years old."

"Then may I speak with a grown-up?"

"Mom, the lady would like to talk to you."

Charles, while perched on the couch, observed that his mother was out of breath and sobbing as she hustled to the phone and was begging for immediate help, confirming the address before slamming down the phone. When she glanced over her shoulder, she observed him with both hands holding his head up and his elbows resting on his knees. There were no explicit expressions on her face before she whirled around and began badgering him for information.

"What happened here last night?"

Without changing his posture or intonation, he answers. "How am I supposed to know? I was in my bed."

"What do you mean, you do not know? He was fine before I left for work."

After sitting back, Charles replied. "He did what he does every Friday night; got drunk and passed out."

"George did not blackout. He is dead," she roars.

"I gathered that," he counters with sarcastic emphasis.

"Boy, don't make me whip the skin off of you. That was my brother and your." A knock on the door interrupts her sentence.

Charles glides to the door and swings it wide open. With no inflection, he says, "Come on in."

His mother cuts her eyes towards him, her glare promising to gut him like a pig as soon as they're alone. She leads the police officers and the medical professionals to the kitchen.

Charles followed them but took an unexpected detour to his room. Unconcerned with the investigation, he curled up on the bed and tried to engross himself in a game show. But even the TV wasn't loud enough to drown out the conversation in the kitchen.

Viola cooperates with the officers—she tells them George was diagnosed with stage four cirrhosis and liver failure.

The paramedic says, "Oh, so this is why his skin is yellow. He has jaundice." He explains that in the veins leading to the liver, the blood might back up and create a blockage. The vascular vessels can then burst. He suspects this was the case here. The attendant then asked Viola if she wanted an autopsy performed.

Charles peeped out of his room in time to observe his mother pulling on the corner of her tee shirt and then shifted her weight from one side to the other before answering. He hears her reply, "No, that will not be necessary. We all knew this was coming." She weeps bitter tears.

As the paramedics cover the corpse and push the remains past a second room, the door is ajar and Jackie, Viola's eight-year-old child, emerged. It appears she slept through everything until now. Wiping her eyes and trying to focus as the stretcher is wheeled in front of her. She jumped like a jackrabbit. "Mommy, what is happening?"

Viola rushes to her frightened daughter and takes her hand. "Your Uncle George has gone to heaven," she wails.

Stepping back to await Jackie's response, all Viola receives is a sigh from her daughter and a blank facial expression. She is not clear if she is in shock or relieved by the news.

Once the authorities and the body leave the house, Viola beckons Charles. "Get into this kitchen and scrub up this mess. Jackie, you help him. I worked all night, and I am beat."

About to heed his mother's command, Charles watched as his mother walked around the large blood stain and made her way to the far counter. She removed the top from the Maxwell House can and jumped back when, rather than coffee grounds, she saw a powdery substance with tiny sparkles.

Charles snatched the can from his mother's grip. "Momma, I will brew some." He ran to his bedroom and concealed the can under his bed. After returning, he secured another can from the pantry and scooped the granules out. Trembling a bit from the close call, he knocked over a cup while filling the basket with water. As he brushed the sweat from his brow, he circumvented Viola's piercing eyes, watching his every move. Next, he prepared the bucket with hot bleach water while still being careful not to allow eye contact. After grabbing a rag, he disinfected the tile floor to remove the bodily fluids of the deceased. A sense of circumvented invaded his whole being. George can hurt no one else again unless they meet him in hell.

While cleaning, Charles studied his mother waddling down the hallway and following the bloody footprints to his bedroom door. It is clear that she was hunting for the reason he lied about not knowing what happened to his uncle. This evidence proved he was aware of more details than he admitted.

Turning on her heels, she shouts, "You are a liar and may even be a murderer! After you are done in the kitchen, get your butt in this hall and clean my carpet. I better not see any residue in my house, or I am going to kill you the way you took George out."

He freezes. Not sure whether he should run out of the apartment or hide inside, the thought of his mother knowing he was responsible plagued him. How did she figure this out? Unsure, he falls to his hands and knees. Unable to breathe and choking on the fumes, he scrubbed harder and faster until his knuckles were raw and bleeding. He dared not leave any traces of his filthy uncle.

***

Honk, Honk, Honk, the blaring sound of a car horn brings Charles back from his life as a child to adulthood. He rolls the car window down and sticks his middle finger up at the driver behind him. "This is not New York. I will move when I am ready. I am the one in a hurry," he bellows.

"I have been driving around for the last couple of hours, searching for Jada. No one will ever stop me from being with her. I love her, and she loves me. Now that she is old enough for us to be together, no restraining order can prohibit me from being with my family. I will do whatever I have to do to be with her, including murder. For what I did to Uncle George, I am going to end up in hell, anyway."

As he closes the chapter on his abuse, his mind floats to when Jada delivered their son, Micah. Afraid then of what would happen if anyone learned of him impregnating her, he transports him back to the birth of the beautiful seven-pound little boy. Fear kept him from showing any emotions. He contemplated how much he feared his indiscretion would be revealed if the biracial baby was born with his blue eyes and white skin. To his delight, the newborn had gray-green eyes, curly, sandy brown hair, and a light caramel complexion. His features resembled the neighbor's boy, whom Nicke and everyone else assumed was the baby's father. Charles fell in love with the infant when he first held him in his arms. Now, six years later, he will learn the truth. If he cares for me as his grandpa, he will surely accept me as his dad. We can be a family. Once I persuade Jada to go away with me, we will leave with our son and never return to anywhere in the state of Texas.

While he exits the expressway, it occurs to him that at his courthouse proceedings, Jada was with another man. He wonders if they were intimate lovers. His blood boils as he imagines her in the arms of another man. Beads of perspiration form on his face while his eyes squint close. He clenches his teeth together, then strikes the steering wheel with a powerful fist. "Damn," he yells as he creates heated friction from rubbing his hand back and forth on his thigh in an endeavor to alleviate the self-inflicted pain. He repeats, "damn it, damn it, that hurts." His words are unleashed through a creamy white foam that gathers in his mouth. He sucks the inside of his cheeks, trying to collect enough liquid to swallow and moisten his parched vocal cords.

The throbbing subsides, and he replaces his anger with questions. Why did Jada bring her boyfriend to court? How could she tell everyone I am Micah's father? What if Jada refuses to be with me and chooses that other man? As the questions pop into his head, he dismisses them one after the other with an affirmation and a resolution. I will take them all out before I concede to anyone stealing my woman and my son from me. I have waited a long time to have them, and no one will prevent us from being together! "Even unto death," he declares to the universe, "can keep us apart." The antipathy Charles reveals forces his body to shudder while he concludes it is all or nothing.

Stomping on his brakes, he stops for the red light he notices at the last second. Once still, he unlatches the glove box and checks to make sure his .44 automatic weapon is loaded and ready for whatever awaits them.

After the signal changes and he accelerates, he tucks the gun in the front band of his jeans. "I am equipped for my life, either here on earth or standing beside Uncle George in the pits of hell. Whichever, as long as Jada and I are together," he rants.

CHAPTER FOUR

CANDY'S MASTER PLAN

Stop, think, and make a plan
Study, strategize, and do all that you can
Move, work, and never stop
Hinder, prevent, and strive to be on top
Refuse, block, and push all doubt away
Go, get, and fight for what you want today

Worry, fret, and reap what you sow
Fight, battle, and refuse to let go
Win, lose, or perhaps a tie
Nothing beats failure but a good old try
It's not important if you can
It only matters that you work and have a plan

With Whitney Houston's song, 'I Will Always Love You' blasting from the speakers of her red sports car, Candy harmoniously sings along. She belts out the melodic tune while imagining her debut on the television program, The

Voice.' While bobbing in time to the beat, she feels the bass as it rattles the top of her convertible. Her mind traveled to a previous conversation with David when he told her he was going to ask for Jada's hand in marriage. Even though she pleaded and confessed her love, he rejected her. In fact, after her confession, he physically ran away and left her standing alone in the hospital corridor. The music ends as she lowers the sun visor and stares into the mirror. How can I win Dave back? When she fluffs her long, straight black hair, the gold chain with a diamond pendant around her neck catches her attention. Approximately nine months ago and about the same time she ended their relationship, he gave her the necklace. With this symbol, he pledged his forever love. Unable to take her eyes off the gift, she allows herself to recall when she first opened the box. Although appreciative, she did not want to be tied down but assumed in a year or two, she would be ready. Never once did she ever consider he would be the one unavailable; much less engaged to be married. Every time they broke up, and she wanted him back, all she had to do was to have sex with him. He was too weak to resist her advances. The more she gave him, the more he wanted. She used this knowledge to seduce him back into her clutches when she grew tired or bored with her latest conquest or fling. Each time he accepted her back but not now. She knows he'll be faithful and will treat this lady as his queen. What she did not expect was that he would replace her and her dream of destined marital bliss. She always believed the role of Mrs. Austin belonged to her when she was ready for it. Now an intern in her last year of residency, *how complete her world would be if he were her fiancé. Rather, he is planning on asking that girl, Jada, to become his wife.* She throws the stethoscope draped around her collar on the rear seat. She whispers, "Dave, I love you. Please, come back to me." Despite what others would say is defeat, she will not accept. Instead, she strategizes and plans her next moves. Figuring out he ran because he was afraid of giving into her persuasion. A cunning smile graces her face. "Jada is clueless of the extremes I will risk taking back what and whom I want," she conveys to her reflection. While rifling inside her purse, she searches for the key to David's house. I knew this duplicate would come in handy. Thankful she is always prepared; she considers the bag in her trunk for impromptu overnight stays with male suitors of her choosing as she speeds out of the parking lot. The luggage includes toiletries, six-inch high heels, and an alluring black lace teddy and thongs. Her body twitches and her eyelids flutter as she pictures her five-foot-eight-inch and very toned caramel colored body in the sexy apparel. Convinced of his becoming powerless to turn down her voluptuous shape, she strokes her curves and gloats. I just might skip the lingerie and lay in his bed nude. The image causes her to giggle out loud.

Candy looks at her watch, noticing it's 9:45 PM. Surely, he cannot be home yet. He said he was going to the mall to purchase her engagement ring. According to him, his girlfriend is spending the night with her mother. That means the obstacles are removed and will allow me to execute my trap. Hoping to arrive at his residence before he returns, she speeds up above the posted speed limit.

The house is dark when she pulls up, with only the motion sensor light from the garage shining. A long Cadillac is parked a few doors down and seems to offer a safe hiding spot. To conceal her personalized tags, she backs close enough to contact the bumper. She grabs her backpack and runs on her tiptoes to the front door, resembling a cat-burglar attempting a break-in. A turn of the key unlocks the door just as she spots a blue pickup driving slowly past the house. She sighs with relief that this is not David. Fearful of getting caught, she rushes inside. After entering, she drops her bag and hurries into the front area, flicking on the low wattage lamp. She finds several candles and distributes them around the living room and dining room. Afterwards, she arranges the tea lights in the shape of a heart. Once they are all lit, she twirls around to revel in her creation, reflecting off the glass dinner table. The beauty causes her to smile as she inserts a CD for some smooth after-dark music. Next, she enters the primary bedroom to prepare the final touches, which she is sure will invite David to join. Even though the temperature outside is seventy-two degrees, she flips the switch to the see-through fireplace in the lowest setting. A yellow hue casts about the room. Hopeful of the designed ambiance, the assurance of a mood conducive to lovemaking is complete. She steps back with folded arms and relishes in the aura. Satisfied with the romantic scene created, all she has left to do is to grab the champagne, shower, and dress.

Upon glancing at her watch, she calculates she has about fifteen minutes before his arrival. A dash to the bar and she snatches a bottle of Cristal with two lead crystal flutes. The glasses produce a ringing, ping sound as they inadvertently clink together. She pours the drinks and sets one on each of the bedroom end tables. A trail of her clothing is left behind as she strips and abandons it. Once the water is hot enough, she darts in and lathers while splashing water everywhere. She is in and out within five minutes. Bath and Body Works' signature scent, Twilight Woods' lotion, is applied from her face to her feet. Enthused by the timely accomplishments, her chest tightens as perspiration rolls down between her breasts. Just as she is reaching to turn off the light, the squeaking sounds of a door opening grab her attention. *Oh well, that settles it. I do not have time to put on my negligee. Besides, David will not be able to withstand this naked body.* She beams with delight as she surveys her shapely figure. With trembling hands, Candy fumbles with the light dimmer and jumps into the bed and tucks the cover over her head, being careful not to expose any identifying parts. She wonders how she will unveil herself. Should she jump up or perhaps stay hidden until he slips in beside her? Remaining still proves to be difficult as she anticipates his touch, but she manages to remain silent, revealing only a silhouette.

CHAPTER FIVE

SHE'S MINE

In life sometimes

we want what we cannot have

We know this but refuse to accept the facts

We think we can control another person

Because our needs are more important than theirs

In life sometimes

We try to possess people like objects

We will stop at nothing to get what we want

We think we can force them to accept our desires

Because we give them a label,

they must comply

In life sometimes

our wants and needs are not what we think

nor are they what we can and should have

Sometimes it is just life

Earlier that day, Charles had followed Jada to the house he is now slowly driving past. He glimpses a woman nearing the front door. "Great, I am in luck. That looks like her." His spine tingles as a warm sensation travel through his limbs. An adrenaline rush takes over his body accompanied by a burst of energy which balances the hysteria but amps his respiration. He searches for Jada's car or the blue BMW she drove. He spots an older Cadillac and a red sports car, but figures Jada's car is stashed inside the garage. Four times he circles the house before stopping and peering through the windows. He cannot determine if anyone is moving around. What he does learn is the once bright foyer is now advertising a low flickering seductiveness which radiates throughout the house. He guns the motor as he rounds the corner. "I will not tolerate that guy partaking of Jada's oasis of ecstasy. She belongs to me. I am the only one allowed to plant my seed inside her." As he spouts his rage, he softens when his imagination relives entering her. The sensations of warmth and excitement flooded his loins. He struggles, going back and forth between the dichotomy of arousal and anger.

Lost in a world of turmoil, he lacks the concentration needed when maneuvering a car. A Fleetwood darts in his path, requiring him to slam on brakes. "Stupid ass, watch where you're going," he yells before almost striking the red car parked behind Charles when wheeling into the vacated spot. After shutting the engine off, he redirects his attention to the house. Still not clear if there is any motion inside, he abandons the car and moves to canvass the neighborhood without being seen.

He crouches behind the row of Wintergreen Boxwood hedges which line the property and affords excellent concealment from passersby. The touch of the equalizer holstered in his waistband assures him if required; he is prepared to take Jada by force. He trails the green fencing to the back of the home. Like a ballerina, he ducks and dodges. Determined, Charles tiptoes to the interior door. His only choice is to face his competition head-on. Once again, he caresses his handgun as he sneaks onto the porch. Shielded by the back of the Tuscan column, he collects himself and calms his nerves. After reaching for the handle, he turns the knob. To his delight, the door is unlocked. Cautiously, he pushes the wooden barrier open and peaks inside. Each of his senses heightens as he creeps into the obscured lighted home. No talking is heard. A whiff of sweet vanilla permeates his nose and spawns into an instant aphrodisiac. He sidesteps and shuffles to burrow himself behind a four-panel room divider boasting a panorama view of Chinese scenery. For a second, he hesitates to admire the artistry of the hand-carved, gold bamboo and trees inlay on the screen. Masked behind the partition, he deliberates if he is in the right home or not. His eyes dart from room to room when they fixate on an 8x10 framed photograph propped on the mantel. The picture confirms he is indeed in the correct place. He recognizes the male as the same man who escorted his beloved to his court proceedings. He studies the photo and notes the sophistication, attractiveness, and youth of David. Not wanting to compare but helpless to not to, he juxtaposes David's attributes to his own. He is black, tall, possesses a mountain of muscles and the image of a Mandingo King. Whereas, he is white, short, and a senior man with a bulging belly. Love, he deducts, is more important than beauty. Not confident if Jada will agree, his blue eyes narrow and his lips sealed together. In place of focusing on how he stacks up against David, he shakes his head, forcing his brain to return to his present mission. I must be vigilant about how I weave her back into my life. My future with her depends on me getting this right.

Charles peeks out from his hiding space and detects a light shining under the master bedroom door. Straining to listen, he can hear water gushing through the plumbing system, signaling someone is taking a shower. A voice whispers in his head to wait until the house is quiet and everyone is asleep. Even though he develops a scheme, a tinge of unease flips his course. The thought that if he delays entry, this will allow time for another man to penetrate the mother of his child, overrules this initial strategy. Now, he decides the time to make his move. With perspiration building around his upper lip, he goes to where he presumes the couple is located. He leans against the wall, resting his back and head. From the elastic band of his pants, he removes his gun and disengages the safety lock. With his eyes fastened, he pulls the hammer back. A clicking noise intermingles with the love song. He pauses for several minutes as he contemplates his next move. Assured there is no longer any movement on the opposite side of the door; he opens then eases the entry closed after him.

The candlelit room flickers, casting a yellow hue on the discernible furnishing muting their colors. They introduce an aureate and blend with the walls and ceiling. Already sexually stimulated, he is aroused further by the silhouette of a small frame laying in the extra-large bed.

Is it Jada? While he resolves if they are alone, his eyes survey the room, and he searches for someone. A naked body springs from underneath the covers as he approaches. At that second, Charles realizes she is not his beloved. Startled, he jumps back, trying to figure out who the mystery woman is before him. His mouth flies open, and his eyes bulge as he brandishes his firearm at her. "Who are you?" Charles demands her while she is staring at him and fumbling to conceal her nakedness.

With her arms wrapped around her knees and cuddled close to her chest, she appears calm. Candy's mouth falls open, but no sound emerges. All she can fathom is the man has a magnum directed at her. Frightened, she scours the room for a comparable weapon worthy of challenging the one pointed at her. The only viable solution is the expensive Cristal champagne bottle. In a soft and weak voice, she sings out. "Who, who are you? What are you doing inside my boyfriend David's house?"

Before responding, he tilts his head to an angular position, and his eyes squint. He repeats, "David, your boyfriend, I understood this role is being played by someone else."

With her fear thermometer boiling on high alert, her tone changes from fearful to arrogant. "Not for long, because I am the one for David. You better get out of this house before he comes home."

"Where are he and Jada?" Charles asks.

"Jada," she echoes as she wrinkles her nostrils. The fact that he is aware of Jada and her relationship rules out the original concerns of whether the stranger standing before her is an intruder or a sexual attacker. "He will be home any second and will not be happy to know you are with his unclothed girlfriend." She flings her legs to the side, edging closer to the best available object in which to defend herself.

While watching her reposition, Charles leaps back into defensive mode, his right leg leading. His arms extend as he holds his piece with a two-handed death grip. Charles stares into her eyes. His heartbeat races, and the stimuli from the anticipation of the unknown present an icy chill as he endeavors to hide his trembling body. "I thought they were a couple. Who are you?"

"My name is Candy," she states while glancing toward a potential skull-crushing tool. The number one concern was to avoid spooking him and causing his firepower to engage either unintentionally or intentionally; she freezes in place. I must move from defense to offense, or this fool may put a bullet in me. By capitalizing on her female assets, she starts a plan to strike back. To expose her bare breast, she releases the cotton bedding. A twist of her torso to the side, the arching of her back, and the caressing of her 38Ds is her reenactment of a triple X-rated movie. Her head lowers as she bats her eyes and maintains a lingering look. Next, she sticks her index finger in her mouth and licks her freshly manicured fingernail.

Wow, her boobs are enticing with extra-large areola around her 'standing at attention' nipples. Charles rocks back and forward, trying to deny his desires. But he is ineffective and draws into the allure and web of her body. How could any man be capable of resisting her body?

Gingerly, she stands, revealing her completely nude body. Her arms crossed behind her back. While as she is sitting on the corner of the bedside table disguising her surprise ambush tool, she closes her eyes and expels a fake moan. With her legs gaped open, she awaits Charles' reaction.

Fixated on the perfectly groomed heart shaped bush, it is welcoming and invites him to come inside. He slides one hand down and caresses his nature. No longer able to suppress his desire, his body reacts to the aesthetically pleasing sights in front of him. Taking advantage of the opportunity, with one hand he gropes her full bosom, then touches the hairy covering surrounding her garden. He loses control, and his enclosed mound prematurely melts. With his eyes shut, he groans with euphoria.

Just as Candy is about to reveal the minuscule and only safeguard at her disposal, the creaking sound of an exterior door startles them both.

Behind her back, she grips the neck of the bottle, but she must verify who entered the house.

The disturbance impels Charles backward. *It is him*, he gathers. *Now David is going to pay. He stole Jada from* me. *Plus, he is also involved with this other woman. Jada will understand why he had to die.* A pivot move has him pointing at the entrance.

Candy clenches the concealed bottle to save David. With the speed and velocity of the 'Shanghai Trans-Rapid' train and all the strength she can conjure up, she swings, aiming for his head. But before she can make contact, he spins around.

CHAPTER SIX

GOING TO GET HER MAN

When a woman loves a man
She will do all that she can
To keep him in her grip
Refusing to let go of their relationship

If that love fades away
She will plead for him to stay
She will even lie and connive
Trying hard to revive

Revive what they once had.
No matter how good, no matter how bad
All she knows is what she requires
Winning his love back is all that she desires

As Jada turns the key to start David's car, she rolls the window down and bids Lyric and Dr. Maxey farewell. After waving, she says a quick prayer while fleeing out of the lot. "God, please keep my mother secure," she whispers. A part of her possesses guilt for abandoning Nicke with Tianna, while the other is ecstatic about being on her way to see David. After finding the small gift box, she is sure he is going to ask her to marry him.

She travels back to when he left the hospital and how her antennas went up. At the time, she thought he was ditching her to be with another woman. Now she realizes all he wanted was for her to come back to his house for a special evening. "Wow, this is why after we parted from the courthouse, he told me he had errands to run," she says. With a chuckle, she weighs how blessed she is to attract a man who loves her.

Apprehension overtakes her excitement as she conjures up the last call she received from Charles. His words resonate in her head. "If I cannot have you, no one will." She presses the electric button, assuring her car doors are locked. "David will protect me."

On the expressway, she struggles with whether to stop past her house to pick up a few things that will complement the evening her man is planning. Abruptly, she exits the highway. "I WILL NOT be afraid to live! No longer will I permit Charles to control me."

Searching for Charles' pickup, she checked all the vehicles parked to make sure he was nowhere nearby. Once she was sure she did not see his truck, she backed into a nearby handicap space. Though I am parking illegally for safety's sake, this is a ticket I am willing to pay for if I must. She isolated her apartment key and rushed up the steps to her door, taking two at a time.

After slipping in, she scurries around, throwing a champagne bottle into a large burlap grocery sack. She retrieves a silver tray, several metal skewers, and a variety of fresh fruit. Once she grabs the utensils, she contemplates how to decorate the dish. The whole pineapple is placed in the center as she designs an arch with the remaining pieces. Each piece she intricately weaves to the other. The results take on professional characteristics. She admires her creation. *Yes, this colorful arrangement represents what David means to me. A rainbow of color is what he brought when my life was stormy, dark, and black.*

After the tedious work, she rests her head in her hands and her elbows on the counter. Tired from the hustle, she slows down and thinks through her next steps. Unable to keep her mind on a possible pending engagement, she allows it to slip into the depths of her deepest fears. What makes a grown man have sex with a child? She wonders? Charles must be sick to even think of deflowering me, his supposed stepdaughter. She quizzes herself. "Why did I accept him touching me? Why did I not tell a trusted adult?

Why did I believe he was in love with me?" Her stomach churns, and for a second, she thinks she is about to throw up. Gradually, she composes herself.

Perhaps I am not worthy of a man as wonderful as David. She rubs her shoulders, wanting to wash off the perceived dirt without the benefit of a shower. Though she endeavors to recapture her happy place, the interference by thoughts of Charles overshadows her mood. Where she once was rushing to make it to David's house, now she is reconsidering even leaving her apartment.

She shuffles to the living room, sits down on the couch and shuts her eyes. "Get it together Jada," she says. *Perhaps I should not go. I am supposed to be with my mother.* Fights of insecurity, her deserving of love, and her terror of Charles are swirling in her mind. *What if he hurts David while trying to force himself on me?*

She shivers as she remembers his recent attempt to rape her, which was interrupted by an impromptu visit from her mother and Lyric. With his potential volatility, she labors over if she wants to involve her man any more than he is already. These prior encounters with Charles convince her he is willing to jeopardize himself and his freedom to be with her and their son. The thought of him injuring David is unsettling and more than she is inclined to risk. This reason alone is enough for her to reject his proposal unless she is ready for him to be hurt or killed. By explaining her fears to David, her gut says David will not let her go. So, instead of telling the truth, she will use the excuse that for now, her life is far too complicated. "I care too much to gamble with his mortality just for my happiness." After Charles's trial and hopeful conviction, she will then reconsider.

Until this happens, she must break up with him to keep him safe. She bawls as the agony of letting David go sinks into her soul. Tears overflow, rolling down her cheeks and dropping off her chin. She expels a gut-wrenching howl. Her body folds as she wraps her knees with her arms and settles into the fetal position. Sobs linger until their sounds dissipate to silence, even though her lips continue to shake. Once she stops wallowing in sorrow, her mind persuades her extremities to move and do what she can no longer deny has to be done.

Jada collects her belongings and snatches up the festoon platter. On her way out the door, she grabs a paring knife and shoves it into her pocket.

En route to David's house, she rehearses how she will decline his offer of marriage. Upon being satisfied with her explanation, her heart pleads its case. It thumps out a Morse code, relaying how foolish she is if she ends their relationship. The beating vessel also reminds her of his ex;

Candy is hanging around in their background just waiting to steal him back. Both the heart and the brain argue their points until she arrives at her destination. Met with the flickering light through the front room window of what appears to be candles, Jada creeps into the driveway. Smiling, she decides he is conjuring up a surprise evening. After picking up the garage remote, realization snaps as she questions how he knew to expect her. Their last communication was about her coming in the morning for breakfast. She checks her watch to see it's 11:15.

She lingers in the car, fighting the suspicion that perhaps he is entertaining another female guest. Neither Jada's heart nor her brain prepared her for the possibility of him cheating. With her hands trembling, she gathers enough courage to enter the home. A fluff of her hair and a swipe of her lipstick stall her entry and provide the necessary time needed.

Once content with her appearance, gingerly she steps to the interior door. Hesitating with her hand on the nob, she asks her Heavenly Father for his help and guidance. After turning the doorknob, she walks inside. A veil of fear engulfs her being, while the fast thumping in her chest never ceases. Each knee knocks against the other as she drags one foot in front of the next. Once making her way from the mudroom into the kitchen, she glances around, noticing the lit candlesticks and soft music. Her eyes dart through each area to soak up the scene. Straining, she tries to listen to any conversation, but to no avail. Still not sure who or what she is going to find on the other side of the closed door, she maneuvers toward the primary suite. Holding her breath, she grips the handle to push the aperture open.

***

Bang—Bang—Bang, Charles extricates three rapid-fired bullets from the gun's chamber as he instinctively or perhaps mistakenly engages the trigger. The vigor of the 44 caliber recoils and thrusts him to the floor, while the echo of the deafening blast lasts for several seconds. What did I just do, he questions. His hands tremor like a person struck with a condition of advanced Parkinson's disease. After inhaling, the stench of cordite laced with sulfur overtakes him. As he lifts the gun to his face, he inspects the iron, questioning what caused it to fire. Out of the corner of his eye, a beautifully undressed lady is slumped over on the bed. A sense of mortification engulfs his entire body.

His body is as frigid cold as a corpse, and his blood drains from his face. Unable to comprehend how a single action can snuff out someone else's existence or deal with the consequences of murdering someone, he plunges to his knees. His mother once likened him to his dad. She told him he was his father's son, a no-good sperm which never should have been fertilized and permitted to be born. For years, Charles set out to disprove her. Now, given his recent actions, he accepts she is right. The marriage to Nicke, a black woman, was wrong. But not because of her race, but because he was retaliating against his mother for not protecting him as a boy.

For the first time, he is remorseful and willing to accept responsibility. There is an admission of being a pervert and of molesting his stepdaughter. I am worthless and mentally sick and have been for quite some time. The world would be a better place without me. "Jada, please forgive me for the pain and hurt I inflicted upon you," he mumbled. With this apology, he places the muzzle deep inside his mouth and fires. A loud but muffled sound blares as a cataclysm of red blood mixed with fleshy fragments of his life explodes through the self-produced entry and exit wound. The once whole living human being is now shrapnel splattered over the wall and flooring.

***

Just as Jada touches the brass knob, she hears the second set of thunderous ear-shattering booms (POW–POW–POW) ring out, causing her to drop to the floor.

After distinguishing the loud firecracker-sounding blast, Jada loses touch with her surroundings. A high-pitched ringing sound lingers. Her breathing labored as her entire life flashes before her eyes. There is a gasp of pain intertwined with grunts of suffering. "I'm shot," she cries out, then agitates her head from one side to the other as she ventures to skyrocket back to reality. Simultaneously probing for an entrance wound, she pats and beats herself like someone trying to extinguish a fire. After concluding the shots did not strike her, she tackles, standing with the help of the nearest wall. Who would shoot inside David's house? Oh, Lord, please do not let David be dead. He is supposed to ask me to be his wife. She collapses against the surface, knocking a signed 'Ernie Barnes' collectible painting off the wall. The distressed wood framing and glass shatters, sending a piece of the glass into Jada's leg. She jumps at the sudden noise, and the initial cut rattles her nerves. She stares at the gashes as crimson colored plasma pools in her shoe.

The thought that David may lie on the other side of the door, still battling for his life, propels her into motion. A swell of agony engulfs her body. What if Charles is on the other side of the door waiting for me? Will he kill me too? Should I call the police first? The questions pop into her head like kernels of popcorn in hot grease. If there is a possibility of rescuing him, she determines the risk is worth taking. While reciting a quick prayer, she limps to the main suite. After rotating the doorknob, a quarter inch at a time and as quietly as possible, she peeks in through a crack in the door. The faint lighting makes it almost impossible to see.

Immediately, she is confronted with a metallic smell that reminds her of an old toolbox. Salivation from her tastebuds senses copper, as though she is sucking on a penny.

She shoves open the door and hunts for the light switch. Her hand brushes the intercom panel. A hunched-over figure in the bed is camouflaged by what she hopes is red wine. Her rational mind insists it's a woman and not just a bundle of bedding, which her irrational self yearns to believe. "No, this cannot be another woman in David's house." Transfixed, she gawks until she can no longer deny the pile. Not only does she admit she is staring at a motionless, naked woman, but also at one whom she recognizes.

With the vigor to produce white spots manifesting under her lids, she kneads her eyes. As she flips on the lights, amplified in front of her is her boyfriend's past, Candy. Sprawled over his bed and saturated with blood, the once vibrant being is now unmistakably dead. "Who killed her? Why is she not clothed? Where is David?" Jada stammers. Goosebumps cover her skin. Her legs wobbled like Jello, plunging her to the floor. The effects of carbon dioxide exceed her body's production and provoke her to overbreathe. To hold her rapidly beating heart inside its chamber, she clutches her chest. "This is a nightmare. Will someone please wake me up?" She drops her head and closes her eyes. Confident, when she opens them again, she will be at her house and in her room. This time, when she opens her eyes, Jada detects a second person. The Caucasian man is drenched in claret red blood, missing the fleshy parts of his head, with chunks of brain matter splattered on the white drywall. Repeatedly, her eyes fluttered shut. This sequence repeats over as they try to forestall the gory images. Burned flesh penetrates through her nose. The setting speaks of hate and rage. "Charles," she hollers from the top of her lungs.

The room spins as the sensation of being clobbered by a hammer creates a throb inside her head. She gags, followed by retching noises filtered from the previous work of her digestive organs. She salivates several times, swallowing the excess liquid and trying to prolong the inevitable. But the half-digested mixture of food, spit, and gastric acid makes a quick exit up her throat and out of her mouth. The vomit disregarded her silk blouse or linen shorts, nor did it spare her hanging curls or David's carpet.

"Lord, have mercy, please," she begs as she crawls backward, hurling herself away from the terrifying sight. All the while she is moving, she yammers, "Oh my God! Oh my God! Oh my God!" Greeted with intense burning, first in her left palm, then her right, from colliding with the sharp glass of the shattered artwork, she continues scooting regardless of the pain. Warmblood spurts from the piercings. Through the suffering, she discovers an obscure corner of the family room. After barricading herself between the wall and the end table, she sobs uncontrollably. The noise in her head subsides as her memory reconnects with what a person should do in a situation like this. She rummages for her cell until she recalls she left it in the car. Looking around, she sees the house phone on the table. Thankfully, it is within arm's reach; she stretches until the tips of her fingers can snatch the handset from the cradle. There is an overwhelming instinct as she clenches the receiver to her forehead, deciding whether to dial her mother and beg for reinforcement. While traveling back to age twelve, she whimpers, "Mommy, I need you. Charles has hurt me. No, Dad, please stop." Out loud, she cries until realizing her mother did not protect her then, and still cannot. Today she does what she should have done then—dials 9—1, 1.

"911, what is your emergency?" the operator asks.

Jada sniffles into the headset but is incapable of vocalizing anything.

The operator restates her question with more force. "May I help you?"

In a low, whispered voice, "Send the police. A man and a woman are dead." Jada uses every portion of her stamina to convey her request before dropping the phone in her lap. She can still hear the person asking for additional data. Even though Jada wants to respond, she is unable. Instead, she draws her knees to her chest and waits. "Where is David?" she ponders while dissecting the gruesome facts. "Why was Candy in David's bed undressed? They must be intimately involved." She embraces her upper body with her arms and sways back and forth. Though she tries to block the visions, incomplete fragments flash in her consciousness. She has more questions than explanations.

"How did he know where David lives? Did Candy shoot Charles, or did he murder her?" Jada lifts the telephone, still lodged inside the cocoon she tried to make with her body.

"Miss, the police are here. You are safe now."

Detecting a bam–bam sound against the front door, she tries to move in that direction, but she is weighted, as though being held by a one-hundred-pound load that impedes any progress. Her mind hollers, run, but her legs and arms do not cooperate. "Help me," her lips mouthed, but no sound was released.

Three officers bolt through the unlocked door with their guns drawn. Still garnishing his firearm, one officer advances to Jada while the other two advance through the house. They probe through the kitchen and shout, "All clear," until rendering every room secure except the bedroom. Once entering, one yells, "We have two deceased– a black female and a white male."

Upon receiving this information, the police officer detaining her turns and says, "Miss, can you tell me what happened?"

The connection between her brain and mouth temporarily breaks.

"Please, I recognize this is painful, but there are two people dead, and you are the only witness." In a much harsher pitch, he asks, "What is your name?"

Still powerless to speak, she rocks faster in her cradled position with her head upward, studying his face. A glassy, far-out gaze reveals in her eyes.

The evidence shows that she is confused, but he will not holster his Glock until she is vetted. He examines the areas near her, looking for a weapon or an indication of her identification. "Miss, are you the one who dialed 911?"

"Yes," she replies. Her body's mobility slows, resembling a rocking toy horse losing momentum.

One officer runs out of the house to give a precursory report to his superior, Judith Nelson. Surrounded by two men and one woman, he intrudes and reports his findings. To this, the unknown lady beside him howls.

To join her comrades, Judith walks away from the group. Wedged into a corner, she locates Jada. Her hands and feet are covered with blood, but she is alive. Stooping to be eye level with her, she relays in a hushed tone, "Jada, this is Officer Nelson. We are here to help you. How did you receive your injuries?"

Recognition of the person talking causes her to look up and comb the policewoman's face. With the release of her legs, she stops moving. In Jada's mind, she restates the question asked before inspecting her lacerations. As a trail of her blood puddles on the hardwood, she lingers in silence.

"David and Lyric are outside. They are standing by for a status. The quicker I can interview you, the sooner I can reassure them," Officer Nelson says.

"Aunt Lyric, Aunt Lyric," Jada echoes, reaching up like a baby begging to be lifted from the floor.

"Yes, sweetheart, Lyric is here, but first I must know what happened." Officer Nelson turns to her subordinate and tells him to fetch the paramedics. She is losing a lot of blood. "Jada, we need to have you bandaged and checked over. I will be back."

Judith heads to the bedroom, where the amount of carnage causes her hands to tremble from such gruesomeness. Now, it is apparent why the young woman is distraught. Though not much different from the many others she's witnessed during her career, this crime scene has an emotional effect. While she gazes from Candy to Charles, she grapples with ascertaining the reason. "The woman on the bed is named Candice. I am not sure of her last name, but she is the owner's ex-girlfriend," she explains to the investigating detective.

A member of the Forensic team says, "The way she is lying here unclothed makes me question if they were still dating." He secures a picture of the body.

Judith considers the officer's statement. "The man there is Charles Smith. I am working on a sexual abuse case involving him and the young woman in the living room, Jada Jordan. The Judge issued a restraining order for him to stay away from her, but I knew he had no intentions to comply."

The Medical personnel are finishing bandaging their patient when Judith reenters the room.

"Sutures will be necessary to close her wounds, as will analysis for likely acute stress disorder," the paramedic says.

Officer Nelson bends down as she tries again to question her. "Can you tell me what happened?"

Jada shrugs her shoulders and whispers, "I do not know. I heard gunshots and discovered them dead. Candy's breasts were showing. Pieces of Charles's head were all over the wall." Sketches of her ordeal flicker in and out of her memory and bring forth an inconsolable crying spell. Struck by anxiety, she clenches her teeth while her other extremities flare, but cannot find freedom. Her nervous system short-circuits. Nothing said resembles English. "Snakes are crawling on me. Get them off me," she shouts while wedging deeper in the corner and fighting off the elongated, legless creatures she imagines.

The attendant attempts to de-escalate the apparent breakdown by gingerly lifting her from the floor and placing her on a stretcher. "We must transport her now," one says. They set an oxygen mask on her face.

Ahead of them, Judith blazes. "Jada is inside," she shrieks while trotting to Lyric, Dr. Maxey, and David. "There are some cuts and bruises, and she is in a bit of shock, but she is alive. They are transporting her for treatment. All things considered, she will recover."

"Thank you, Lord," Lyric screams while running to the gurney. "Are you injured?"

The EMT pushes her back as she tries to wrestle a hug. "Ma'am, we need her in the ambulance stat."

"Can I accompany her?" Lyric pleaded as she grabbed the front of the rolling cart.

"Yes," he replies in a rushed tone.

David speeds over to Jada and caresses her shoulder. "Baby, I am here with you. I am so sorry for whatever is going on here. I will see you when I can. Soon."

In a move that surprises all watching, Jada turns her head and refuses to acknowledge him. "Lyric, I will meet you after we finish here," Jim announces.

"Sure," she mumbles.

"What is going on? Can I go inside my house? And why are they stringing yellow tape?" David asks.

Preparing to interrogate him, Judith holds his hand. "Walk with me to my car, " she tries to reassure him. David, perhaps you should allow Jada some time to process her feelings and call her in the morning. Lyric will take good care of her tonight."

Perspiration appears on his face as he gulps and then stamps his feet, "No, Officer Nelson, tell me."

Jim places his arm around his neck. "The important thing here is that Jada escaped serious harm. Calm down, son."

"Well, David," Judith starts. "We cannot be sure what occurred until we can get Jada's version. But first, it is essential to ask you a few things." She takes out her pad and pen and slides her horn-rimmed glasses on her face. She peers over the frame. "David, where have you been this evening?"

Tilting his head to the side, he replies. "What do you mean? I left Jada with her mother at about 8:15. From there, I went to the mall to pick up a diamond ring for her. On the way back home, I went to the grocery store so I could prepare a romantic breakfast. After shopping, I came home and found all this mayhem."

"So, you have not been home since you left this morning?"

"That is correct. Why do you ask? I am clueless about what is going on here." He turns as a body bag rolls out his front door. "Who--"

"Why would Candy be here?" Judith interrupts.

"Candy," he repeats. "I am not sure." He motions towards the red sports car. "That is her car parked across the street."

Without looking up to see where he is motioning, her head stays lowered, and she continues writing. "Yes, I know, but why would she be here?"

He shuffles his feet back. Probably, Candy stopped by to visit with me. Or, conceivably, she waited outside for me to come home. As David analyzes their last conversation, the purpose rushes into his head. "I ran into her as I was leaving Nicke's room. I told her I was going to ask Jada to marry me. She wanted to talk, but I was in a hurry to make it to the jeweler before they closed," he says. "Perhaps she hoped to persuade me to reconsider. Once she arrived and saw I was not here, I guess she hung out waiting for me." As he is speaking, he glances at Jim for backup, since he, too, is acquainted with Candy's spontaneous behavior.

Judith shakes her head no. "Unfortunately, she did not wait. Rather, she entered your home."

"How did she get inside?" he asks.

"This is also my question," she responds.

"I do not know unless Jada let her in."

Officer Nelson lowers her bifocals and interlocks her arm with his. "Both Charles Smith and Candy are dead," she blurts out.

He doubles over as though someone jabs him in his gut. "No, there is no way," he shouts in disbelief. "Why? How could this happen? Did Jada take their lives?"

His inquiry confuses Officer Nelson and causes concern that David would think she is the murderer. "Why would you ask if she did this?"

Shrugging his shoulders, he considers it troublesome to invest any energy into her line of questioning. Learning that Candy is dead is surreal to him. The tears flow like a faucet without a shutoff valve. His legs buckle, giving way to the fear of failure. "Are you sure?" he asks.

"Well, we must inform the next-of-kin, but first we need you to confirm a preliminary identity. But I must warn you; identification may be tough." Not waiting for his response, she glides toward the body, which is about to be placed in the vehicle. Then she signals for David and Jim to follow. She unzips the body bag and reveals only the head.

Both men lean down for a better look. There before them lies a woman with a purple hue to her skin. Her facial expressions are frozen, showing she has experienced horrific fright. A pungent scent of rotten meat laced with a tinge of sweet, cheap perfume radiates from the container. The two men nod in agreement. This beautiful and vivacious woman is familiar. Together they say in unison, "Yes, this is Candy."

Officer Nelson okays them to proceed with taking her to the morgue. Returning her attention to David, she studies his appearance. Through his body language, Judith reads the heartbreaking distress he exhibits. The once self-assured man she first met appears to be aging right in front of her. *I wish I could persuade him that things will work out fine, but judging from the drama that is unfolding, I believe his and Jada's lives will forever change.* She proceeds with instructing David. "I would urge you to sleep someplace else tonight." Judith checks her watch. The time is 1:45 AM. "Forensics will process the restricted area for several more hours. Once our work concludes, I suggest you hire a death clean-up company. You can research online or, if you would like, I can call a business and give them your number to handle the arrangements. Please try not to be present during the cleaning. Also, apprise your homeowner's insurance agent to determine if there is coverage for this type of loss."

With narrowed eyes and furrowed brows, he tilts his head sideways. "I do not care about having my house clean. My anguish is because Candy was murdered. Now, I have to let her family know. How do I tell them their daughter is dead?" For the first time since he and Jada became a couple, he admits he used Jada to get over the break-up with Candy. "Judith, I need to retrieve a change of clothing."

Before responding, she steps aside to grant Charles' mangled body, concealed inside a body-bag to pass.

Without saying a word, the three of them watch the loading of the body in the awaiting van. Each of them is caught up in their thoughts about the dead man.

"Regrettably, I cannot permit you to access now or allow any disturbance of the investigation. Your home is still an active crime scene," she says.

"Sure, that is fine with me. I trust you and your advice. What I need is some time to regroup."

Putting his arm around David, Jim asks, "Would you like a ride to the hospital?"

"No, I am driving Jada's car and can find somewhere else to spend the night." He pulls a keyring from his pocket. He touches the one to open Candy's house, which he forgot was still in his possession. When they split, she refused to take it back, telling him that anytime he was welcome. He smiles, remembering her, adding that he should always call first. He realizes he has just found the answer to where he will retire for the night. After thanking Jim and Judith, he bids them goodnight.

"I am also going to leave and check on Jada," Dr. Maxey says to Officer Nelson.

"Alright, I will see you after I wrap up here. Thank you for your help. Lyric is lucky to have found a friend in you." Playfully, she punches Jim and dances away before he has an opportunity to comment.

On the way to his car, he rehashes her words. He is aware she is teasing him about his relationship, but deep inside, he craves more from Lyric. It is difficult to resist her, especially since finding out she is filing for a divorce. *Johnny is one stupid man to let a woman like her go. If she gives me a chance, I will not make the same mistakes he made.*

CHAPTER SEVEN

SAVE ME

The weight of the world can weigh you down
First one thing, then the other
Before you can conquer this or that
Ready, set, here comes another

You try to prioritize the most important stuff
Juggling each and every task
Until your heart shouts, "take off that pretend mask
Stop right now. I've had enough!"

You are drowning in a heaping teaspoon of bad luck
One more swallow and you will choke
So, you laugh, you smile, and you try to joke
With your head up, you try to pretend that you're not
stuck

After you have done all you can, help me becomes your
plea
You raise your arms and reach for help
Finally realizing you cannot do this by yourself

Wounded, beaten, and defeated, you cry... save me

Lyric listens as the ambulance attendant calls in a report regarding Jada and prays the stress from this episode will not produce the same consequences on Jada as the previous confrontation with Charles had on Nicke's health. She cannot be sure. Even though her insides tremble, she rubs Jada's arm. All she can do now is make sure she is aware of her presence.

Despite the understood fact that touch is supposed to elicit some feeling or emotion, Jada does not respond. Her pupils enlarge while fixating on the roof, and while her body is withdrawn like a turtle hiding in its shell.

Troubled by the potential health impact on her niece, Lyric wonders how she will tell her about the events of the night. What will happen when she learns of Charles' killing both Candy and him? A part of her wants to call her daughter, Tianna, but she is afraid to arouse suspicion, as she is spending the night with Nicke. Desperate for advice, she considers calling her husband but remembers how Johnny started a new life with his girlfriend Donna and their son. *The only other person I can talk to about this is Jim. Although I am trying to keep my distance from him until*

my divorce is final, I need his help. I hope he will get here
soon.

The ambulance stops in front of the emergency room. Jada is unloaded and rushed into a triage room. A staff person approaches Lyric. "Are you a family member?" she asks.

"Yes, I mean no, not exactly," she stumbles. "I am a close friend," she explains while pointing toward the stretcher. "Her mother is a patient here and does not know about her injury."

"Well, I can try to get as much as I can from you, but technically, because of the HIPAA act, I can only discuss her prognosis with family or her designee. Do you know if she is allergic to anything?"

Lyric covers her mouth with her hand, trying to recall Jada's medical history. Since she cannot remember, she shakes her head no.

Curtly, the clerk asks, "No, there are 'no' allergies or 'no,' you do not know?"

Steam builds like a pressure cooker as Lyric suppresses her anger, trying not to explode. Once under control, she rolls the chair away from the receptionist's desk, retrieves her purse, and struts to the waiting area. "Calm down, stay professional and do not permit this girl to make you say something you will be sorry for later," she cautions herself. Before switching away, she hears her call, "Miss, I need this information if I am going to check her into the hospital." The very impolite woman is overlooked by Lyric as she throws her head up and chooses to ignore her request. In an obscure corner, she spots a chair where she plops down and picks up a magazine. She thumbs through the pages, pretending she is interested in the contents.

The sliding doors open and same the attendants Lyric recalls seeing earlier are pushing two stretchers. Both are carrying the remains of Charles and Candy in separate black body bags. One man stops and engages in a conversation with the receptionist. While speaking, she reacts by grabbing her head and falling against the wall. The news of her death causes a disturbance, which Lyric surmises is because Candy was a Staff Resident Physician. *Everyone working here will soon learn she is dead. I hope none of them mention this around Nicke.* She tries to recollect if she saw reporters at the scene, but everything is a blur. Two people killed in the suburbs is a story the public would undoubtedly find newsworthy. *What if she or Tianna see this on the television before I have a chance to tell them?* It is best to prepare her daughter for the possibility, she decides.

After the first ring, she answers. "Sorry to call you this late, but we need to talk."

In a groggy voice, Tianna asks, "Mom, what is wrong?"

"Listen and please stay calm. Do not wake up your aunt. Can you step into the hall so we can have a private conversation?"

After moving out of her hearing range, Tianna grills her mother. "Is something wrong? Where are you?" She asks in a panicked voice.

"Calm down; I need you to meet me downstairs in the ER."

"Oh my God, what happened to you? Are you sick or are you hurt?" she cries. The pain in her mother's voice sends off alarm bells.

"No, I am fine. Just come down, and I will tell you everything. Please hurry." Lyric pushes the end button. Her hands shake as she tries to formulate what and how to tell Tianna the pieces she gleaned from the horrendous evening. The only intel for sure is that two people are dead, and Jada is injured.

The elevator opens, and Tianna runs to her mother. Without stopping, Tianna grabs her around her neck and the two embrace the way it's expected if a year or more has passed since they last saw each other.

"Mom, you are scaring me. Tell me what is going on?"

Lyric gulps before clenching her hand and leading her to the chairs on the rear wall, away from everyone else. With her head lowered, she shares, "Charles is dead."

Tianna slides back in her chair as the words register. "I am shocked, but please forgive me if I am not sorry, he is gone."

"That is not nice, nor is it what a Christian should say," Lyric chastises.

With Tianna's eyes bulging and lips turned up, she changes the subject. "Where are Jada and David?" she asks.

Before responding, Lyric takes Tianna's hand in hers and pats it as she attempts to prepare her for the disturbing news she is about to deliver.

"Mom, please do not tell me if something is wrong with Jada."

"Shush and sit down. I will tell you what I know, but I will warn you, I do not have all the facts yet."

Shaken, Tianna sits toward the edge of the seat and stares and concentrates on the way her mother's lips move.

To prevent her from interrupting, Lyric speaks at an accelerated speed as she recounts the events of the night.

Tianna falls backward. The last thing she knew was that Jada was going to David's house because she thought he was going to propose. "So, how did a pending engagement morph into two people getting killed?" With her eyebrows squeezed together, she studies her mother's face. "Can we see her now?" Without waiting for an answer, Tianna continues, "I am going to ask someone."

Lyric lifts her head, then uses her arm as a shield to block Tianna in the seat. "That clerk is not very helpful, and I do not want any additional problems. Earlier, she was rude to me."

"Oh no, please do not tell me she disrespected you," Tianna rants. Jumping to her feet, she stumps toward the sign-in area.

Lyric drops her head. She lacks the vigor to stop her and hopes she does not make a scene. The strength she once possessed seems to leak through the hole in her heart—no doubt created by Johnny's extramarital affair at a time when she needs him most.

The sliding doors open as Tianna nears the registration desk, stopping her in her tracks.

There is a near collision with the intake woman as she brushes past her, ensuring she is the first to greet Dr.

Maxey. Her attire and eagerness led Lyric to believe she must be in search of a physician to marry.

"Did you hear about Candy?" the young lady asks him while trying to catch her breath. With her hands on her waist, she awaits his response.

"Yes," Jim says in a disinterested tone as his eyes search the waiting room. He glances at Tianna and nods in greeting. Once he spots Lyric, he is transfixed as he struts towards her, calling her name.

The sound of Jim's voice sparks her into motion as she runs to him. They share a passionate hug and embrace as she snuggles into his firm grip.

Both the receptionist and Tianna, with their mouths open, watch the couple.

After releasing her, Jim caresses her face and pushes her hair back to examine every facial feature. A lone tear rolls from

her eye. He kisses the salty fluid as it reaches her cheek. Her response is the return of affection he prayed to have one day.

With closed eyes, Lyric buries her head in his masculine chest as his arms engulf her. This embrace is the security she longed for since their first meeting. *Oh, this is an intoxication better than any alcohol could ever accomplish. Johnny never made my heart this safe. With Jim, I want to be vulnerable so that he can comfort me.*

After helping her back to the chair, he kneels. In a faint voice that can only be heard by her, he says, "Baby, I am going to go check on Jada. I will be back as soon as I can."

Tianna strolls back to where her mother is sitting and notes how she is avoiding eye contact with her. She giggles inside. At first, Tianna considers teasing her mother, then decides against making jokes. Instead, she takes a more caring approach by holding her hand and refraining from commenting.

Officer Nelson arrives and spots them. Upon noticing her, Lyric sits up straight and plants her feet flat on the floor. With her hands interlocked, her muscles tense as Judith approaches. *How do I ask her for additional details even though I am not sure I want to know?*

"How is Jada doing?" Judith asks as she takes a seat next to her.

"I do not know. Jim just went back to check. He will be out soon."

"It has been a long night for us all. There are just a few more questions, and I should be able to close the case."

"What happened?" Tianna blurts out. An exasperated sigh follows. Being kept in the dark is equivalent to walking in on the end of a movie that everyone else was watching from the beginning.

"My investigation is incomplete. I cannot reveal what I have pieced together until I secure Jada's statement." Officer Nelson brushes her off and turns her attention back to Lyric. She places her arm around Lyric's neck. "This is almost over."

Just as she is about to thank her for the concern, Jim returns. With every step he makes in their direction, Lyric's eyes feast on him as she tunes out the other ladies. The closer he gets, the more she studies his eyes, his expressions, and of course, his body.

When he reaches her, he kneels again in front of her.

"Jada is doing well. She received six stitches in her hand and two in her leg. All her vital signs are normal. The attending physician thinks with plenty of rest and perhaps some counseling; she will conquer this traumatic event."

"Is it possible I can question her now?" Judith asks.

"I am not her doctor," Jim replies. "You should ask him." Before continuing, he pulls Lyric to her feet and wraps his arm around her waist. "We can all go back to visit, and you can ask him."

Officer Nelson and Tianna trail behind the couple. They marvel at his patience and care. Each, in their own way, is envious of the devotion Jim shows. Perhaps he is fulfilling something that is missing in their lives.

Until now, Judith was unaware of the depth of their attraction. After what she witnessed, it is clear that the idea of her being a couple with Jim will never happen.

As Lyric enters, Jada is alarmed as the squeaky noise made from the curtain rings clinking on the bar startles her. To offer reassurance, Jim heads to her bedside. "Do not worry—everything is fine. Look, I brought you some visitors."

A sparkle arises in her lifeless eyes and provides comfort.

Tianna shoves past Lyric and hurries to her side. Careful not to disturb her bandaged hands, she leans down and hugs her for an extended period. "Hey sister/cousin, I am happy to see you."

For the first time since her arrival, Jada speaks. "It is even better to be seen," she chuckles. "Do you know Charles and Candy are dead?" she asks through her cracking voice.

"Yes, Mom told me."

Officer Nelson interrupts. "Jada, I am so sorry to do this now, but I need to get your statement. Everyone else must leave while we talk."

After Judith's interjection, Jada turns her head and shuts down again.

Jim suggests, "What if we step out and allow Tianna to stay for support? Plus, her physician should be present in the event he does not think she is up to handling your line of questioning."

While sitting down and preparing to take notes, Judith agrees with his suggestion.

"Jada, pretend you are only explaining the sequence of events to your best friend, and no one else is around. I know this isn't easy, but I have faith you can do this. Your doctor will be here in case this is too much for you. Will that be all right with you?"

With a nod, Jada clears her throat and explains everything from the time she left visiting her mother until she discovered Candy and Charles. The version she shares fails to describe the grotesque scene, nor does she interject any emotions from the ordeal. The way she relays the facts is as though Jada is detached and is illustrating a book she read.

"Thank you, Jada, for all your help. Your assistance is appreciated. I have what I need," Officer Nelson says as she exits.

"Now that you have completed the policewoman's request, you can get dressed as I am releasing you," Dr. Phelps grunts. "Here are your discharge papers. Inside the packet is a sedative prescription to assist you with getting sleep. Upon checking out, the nurse will administer one pill. Please do not drive or operate any heavy machinery for the next day or so. The most important thing for you to do now is to make sure you get plenty of rest so your body can reset." He gathers her chart and leaves the room.

With little cooperation from Jada, Tianna slips Jada into her clothes. After Tianna ties her shoes, she guides her into the wheelchair. To engage in small talk, she asks, "Where is David?"

In her head, Jada tries to formulate her answer while battling to hide her anger. "I do not know, and I do not care."

"What do you mean? He should be here supporting you. Perhaps he could explain to you why there was a naked woman in his bed?"

"I guess they were still involved with each other. When I arrived, candles were burning, and soft music was playing. It appeared they had planned a romantic evening since David did not expect me until morning. So, I assume he was entertaining her." She blinks away the urge to cry. "I am so stupid to think he was going to propose to me. I trusted him, but he is a liar, just like every other man who has ever been in my life."

"That still does not explain why he is not here with you now. I am sure he understands how devastating this is for you." With four rapid hand claps, she shouts Tianna's question again, "Why is he not here?"

"He probably blames me for the killing of his girlfriend. How can he face the person who brought Charles into his life?"

After realizing she is upsetting Jada, Tianna calms herself. Consider, after you rest, phoning him tomorrow and listening to his side of the story. Perhaps he may have a plausible explanation. At least, he better have a good answer or his butt is mine."

Even though she believes Tianna is providing sound advice, her immediate concern is not about David but rather how her mother will respond. "No, he and I are finished. There is nothing else for us to say to one another. The thought of facing him after how I messed up his world sickens me." A pearl-shaped tear trickles down her face.

"This is not your fault," Tianna says while holding her hand. "Charles ruined everybody's life, then took the chicken way out by killing himself." Just as she is finishing her sentence, they are interrupted.

"Are you ready to leave?" the nurse asks.

"Yes," she replies while being wheeled to the waiting room.

"Mom, where is Dr. Maxey?"

"He is getting the car," Lyric responds.

Tianna runs her fingers through Jada's hair. "I will spend the day with you tomorrow. Call me when you wake up. For now, I am going to sneak back into Auntie's room before she wakes up and thinks I left her alone."

Lyric kissed her daughter. "Thank you, baby girl. Make sure you or no one else tells Nicke about the terrible events of the evening. We will tell her in the morning when she can see her daughter is fine."

"Alright, Mom."

"Oh, make sure she does not watch the news in case a reporter picks up the story," Lyric adds.

The nurse flashes a tight-lipped half smile, then rolls her eyes at Lyric as she pushes Jada past the intake station.

Watching the woman's blatant display of disapproval of her aunt, she asks, "What is that about?"

Rather than feed into her attitude, Lyric makes a joke. "I guess she is jealous because we are leaving with the finest doctor in Texas." A full, teeth grin brightens her face as she throws in an extra backside switch of confidence. "Jim is the kind of man who can make any woman envious."

Once jumping out of his parked car, Jim helps Jada into the rear seat before opening the passenger's door for Lyric. "Your chariot awaits, my dear," he comments with a sly grin on his face.

Flattered by the attention, she returns the smile while looking up through her lashes. After entering, she crosses her legs and points her toes. The designed effort of her intention she hopes will not go unnoticed by Jim.

With his hands trembling, he reaches across her and fastens the seatbelt. Incidental contact with her rear butt cheek happens from his fumbling with the latch. His reach lingers, giving rise to his imagination as he lavishes in the proximity of their bodies. *I have never seen a woman more beautiful than this;* he thinks before closing her door. Once he is inside, he steals one last glimpse at her long, shapely legs before starting the car.

Jada squirms in the rear seat. She wraps her arms around her chest. Just speaking above a whisper, she asks, "Auntie, may I spend the night at your house? I do not want to be alone."

Before Lyric can reply, Jim interrupts. "You two beautiful young ladies are going to be guests at my house. I will protect you both."

Though appreciating his proposition, Lyric contrives an excuse. "We appreciate your invitation very much, but we do not have a change of clothing. Jada can stay at my house."

With his refusal to accept 'no' as the last answer, he offers a rebuttal. "I have a guest room for each of you. Also, there is a washer and dryer, which you can throw a load in before going to bed. For something to sleep in, I have some big t-shirts that will cover all the essential parts." He looks away before expelling a short laugh of victory.

Still trying to reject his invitation, Lyric says, "We do not want to inconvenience you more than we have already." *Doesn't he understand in his house? I do not trust myself. He must not know just how vulnerable I am.*

"Auntie, knowing there is a man nearby would make me more comfortable. With your permission, can we please take him up on his offer, at least for tonight?"

"This discussion is over. I promise both you and Lyric will be safe with me." A smile graces Jim's face. He sneaks a peek, catching her wringing her hands and in deep concentration. The confident woman who walked out of the hospital now acts as timid as a child as she realizes she can no longer refuse his suggestion.

He tries to reassure her. "Do not worry. I understand you are still married, and I will act accordingly. Relax and allow me to pamper my two favorite girls. You both have had a rough day."

Without commenting, Lyric grins even though the corners of her mouth twitch. Somewhere inside her, a voice is saying she is not the one who cheated in their marriage. Johnny brought this on himself.

As they pull into a circular driveway, Jim pushes the opener to a wrought iron ten-foot fence. The gate swings open, revealing a three-car garage nestled in a blonde brick two-story house. The lawn is manicured to perfection. Spotlights are strategically placed to shine on two massive stone lions amidst the distant kidney-shaped swimming pool.

Both women stare in awe at the beauty.

After helping Jada exit, Jim rushes to assist Lyric. Next, he jumps in front of them and directs them inside.

Entering, Lyric grabs Jada's hand. With her mouth open, Lyric takes in the elegant furnishings and artwork throughout the house. Despite the home's top-of-the-line decorations, to her, there exists coldness and drabness, which shows something is missing yet unidentified.

"What can I do to make you two comfortable?" he asks.

The first to speak up is Jada. "All I need is a glass of water and directions to where I am sleeping."

The women follow him down the hall as he points out the rooms where they will sleep. Opening the closet, he hands them each a set of towels, a bar of soap, lotion, shampoo, a toothbrush, and toothpaste. "Feel free to turn on the television if you need noise." When turning, he offers words of security. "In my house, no one will hurt you. I will return with nightclothes for you ladies to slip into. Please make yourself comfortable."

Lyric plops down on the bed, rubbing her hand across the duvet, and gawks at the contemporary furniture and the well-put-together yellow, red, and orange designer accent accessories. She whispers to Jada, "Once he comes back, give me your underclothing, and I will wash them with mine."

"All right, but I do not think I am going to bathe before going to bed. The doctor gave me a sleeping pill. I can barely keep my eyes open."

Just before Jada closes her door, Jim returns with two triple-X T-shirts and hands her one.

To Lyric, he gives the other. "After you freshen up, meet me in the kitchen for a nightcap."

"That will be wonderful. A hot shower is just what I need," Lyric says, while snatching her nightwear from him and shutting him out. With her back leaning against the door, she sniffs the provided white nightshirt to get a whiff of Jim. Instead, she is forced to settle for the April fresh smell of Downy fabric softener.

Before showering, she checks her phone and sees there are fifteen missed calls from Johnny, along with several voice messages and two long texts. She chooses to ignore them all and heads to the shower. Next, she brushes her thick, curly locks into a ponytail. Before leaving the room, she prances in front of the mirror and examines her appearance. She pats and pulls everything until she is sure every hair and flaw is in place.

Greeted with soft lighting and jazz music, Lyric enters the living room in a romantic setting. The ambiance is pleasant and soothing. Headed for the laundry room, she carries a small load of clothing to the washing machine.

Struck by her fresh appearance, Jim cannot keep his eyes off her. He thinks she is even more beautiful without makeup and trendy clothes. Following her to the laundry room, he asks, "Would you like to join me and sip on some chardonnay?"

"Yes, I would love some wine," she responds.

Together, they sit on the soft Italian leather couch. Lyric tucks one leg under her body while tugging the T-shirt over her knees.

Lifting his drink, he makes a toast. "To two people meeting at a time when they both need each other." Without taking his eyes off her, he clinks her glass and takes a sip. Never can he remember a woman who has fascinated him as this one has. Their friendship requires nurturing, understanding, and time. The last thing he wants to do is interfere in her marriage. Besides, he must move slowly for fear of falling in love with her and getting hurt in the process. "Are you comfortable?" he asks.

"Of course I am," she says as she lays back. "Your home is lovely." The complete truth Lyric withholds because, although comfortable, she is nervous about planning a future until she ends her past.

While she is thinking about Johnny, Jim interrupts by standing and pulling her into his arms. He releases his heart's desire in a subtle kiss.

At first, Lyric attempts to resist. Their embrace is something she has wanted since she first laid eyes on him. She relaxes, enjoying being comforted and aroused. Their tongues intertwine while both heads bob up and down and tilt left to right, dancing to music only they can hear. Overwhelmed by their bodies touching, she withholds happy tears. Just considering the past several days, she concludes she not only wanted but needed someone to hold her.

Feeling the heat from their closeness igniting, he lowers his hands to the small of her back while his fingers rest on her buttocks. He grabs her closer to him as she melts in his grip. One, then the other. He lightly kisses her closed eyes. At that moment, they both entertain an unexplained sensation of being intertwined and resembling one body.

Her arms tighten around him. Incapable of stopping the tears, she allows them to flow freely. This wonderful man succeeded in making me fall in love with him. Help me, Lord. I need you, she confesses to herself.

He offers assurance when he whispers, "I got you, baby. I will not let go until you say Release me." While soaking in his chest, she listens to the rapid beating within. Intense, shallow breaths warmed her forehead. Slowly moving, she grinds her entire self into him. Clearly that with this hasty decision, she will be obligated to ask for forgiveness; her needs and heart overruled her brain. Every part of her seeks to release the pain and take him. The voluntary movements of their bodies touching create a desire for her to head for the bedroom. If not for the roaming exploration of her body, she would submit to him, whisking her away now.

After he makes the rounds to her breast, the realization if she does not end this groping session now, she will not be able to hold back. *Just one more thing,* she thinks as his lips surround hers.

"Lyric, it is time for both of us to go to bed before we do something. Neither of us is ready for what has happened. This make-out session is not good for us. I hope I have not offended you. Somehow, I felt if I did not kiss you tonight, I would never have another opportunity."

Inside, she suspects he may be right but chooses not to comment. With one last peck, she hurries to her room. *Lord, you said you would provide an escape route. Thank you, Father*, Lyric thinks before falling asleep.

Left standing in the living room, Jim struggles to collect his bearings. He turns the music off, places the clothes in the dryer, and puts the wine and glasses away. Then he shuts the light off and glides down the hall—every part of his being desired to enter her bedroom and bring her into his. When passing by her room, he smiles. "Not until you are single," he whispers. Upon entering the main suite, he stares at the empty bed. *One day*, he hopes. On his knees, he prays and asks for forgiveness and direction. An honest confession to God reveals he is in love with her, but will wait. After he wraps the surrounding covers, he readies himself for a beautiful and explosive dream.

CHAPTER EIGHT

THERE IS WORK TO DO

Can't stop

Gotta move

Here, there

And everywhere

Can't quit

Gotta plan

This, that

And everything

Can't rest

Gotta prepare

Now, again

And everyone

Can't leave

Gotta stay

You, me

And everybody

Can't cease

Gotta work

Harder, smarter

And everyday

The silence affords David the opportunity to think. Jumbled thoughts of both women infiltrate his mind, but for now, he chooses to concentrate on Candy. How do I tell her family it is because of me? She was murdered; he wonders. *Even though Candy did not have a good relationship with them, I am sure they loved her. Now, it is too late for them to mend their problems.* With trepidation, he turns down the street leading to her townhouse. The amount of pain he's in regarding her passing surprises him. So much so, he blames himself for her demise. Could this be a dream, and none of this is happening? He thinks.

Since pulling into her driveway, his vision has become blurry. Unable to exit the car, he grips the steering wheel with both hands and rests his forehead on it. His throat closes as tears spill over. Reflecting on his mortality, he recognizes how fragile yet how precious life is and how quickly someone may end. Paralyzed by the tragic awareness of losing someone he once cared for, he releases a gut-wrenching sound as he cries out. The tears help to cleanse his soul and provide him with the strength he needs to enter her house.

A familiar, sweet-smelling fragrance hits his nose when he opens the door. As he climbs the steps, he

dismisses the urge to holler his usual greeting, 'Candy Cane.'
Once inside, he surveys the neat home before approaching
the fireplace. A framed photograph of them draws his
attention to the expressions on their faces. They are
embracing on the beach as the Jamaican sunlight beams
down. At this point in their relationship, he was very much
in love with her.

As he shuffles his feet, he stumbles into her
bedroom. The bed is unmade, and articles of clothing cover
the floor. *Looks like she must have been in a hurry.* He sits
down and buries his face in her pillow. The lingering floral
scent he draws deep through his nose, filling his lungs to the
brim. A solemn prayer is whispered for Candy to have
fulfilled her life's purpose.

Alone in her house, he struggles to make himself
comfortable. The ticking of the clock, squeaking wood
sounds, and the absence of voices contribute to his unease.
After determining he cannot conquer the eerie fears, he
elects instead to stay at a hotel. The house holds too many
memories that remind him of their past. "I will call your
mother in the morning," he says to Candy's spirit. One last
glance pushes him out the door. Inside, his departing
signals a goodbye to what they once shared. Today is the
first time he can let her go. Even though the choice is not his

but a result of death, he is forced to accept that they can never return to yesterday. It is as though he is released from bondage and is now free from apprehension to absolutely love again. This revelation surprises him because, until now, he thought that when he first met Jada, his liberation had happened. Jada is the same woman who, some twelve hours ago, he purchased an engagement ring for and was about to ask for her hand in marriage. Now, David fully understands his lingering doubt. Yet, pieces of him are overjoyed at the prospect of loving her completely. *My prayer is that Jada will still want me when this is over.*

While pulling away from Candy's house, he develops a renewed view of his future. Now, his life makes sense. "All I need to do is make it through the funeral services, then Jada and I can start our life together. A proper burial is what I owe Candy for loving me," he says aloud.

After this revelation, he builds a mental list of the tasks he must accomplish. Most involve working with Candy's family. The other part of him is worried about his girlfriend. How is she coping? Did she tell her mother about Charles? Many questions come to his mind, but there is one plaguing him. "Why did she pull away from me? Does she blame me?" Doubts emerge about their happy-ever-after future together. "If only she would give me a chance to explain."

He enters the parking lot of The Marriott, hoping they will have an available room. After exiting, he tries to will his feet to move one in front of the other. Both the weight of life and death weigh him down. Every muscle wants to collapse from extreme exhaustion.

"Sir, do you have any vacancies?" He asks the receptionist.

"Yes, how many nights will you need?"

"One or two," he replies.

The gentleman studies him while leaning over the desk. "Do you have any luggage?"

"No," he states as he accepts the room key and walks away.

Once in the room, he collapses on the bed without bothering to remove his shoes or clothes. *All I need is some rest.* But images of both Jada and Candy take turns popping into his head. At separate times, they cried and begged him to save them. No matter how hard he tries, he cannot silence their voices. The clock reads 4:00 AM. "Please let me sleep," he whispers, though. He continues to toss and turn.

Visions of the two women who are dear to his heart appear as a slideshow presentation. The last encounter with Candy replays when she admitted to being in love with him. She apologized for her inability to convey those emotions earlier in their relationship. Her reasoning, as she explained, was because of being molested by her stepfather, Larry. She faulted herself for his transgressions, and because of this, she believed all David, or any other man, wanted from her was sex. Through the reminiscing, he understands the desperation she exhibited upon learning of his intent to marry. Afraid if he allowed himself to believe her, David would be sucked back into her web. To circumvent her trap, he runs away and puts as much distance as he can between them. *Perhaps if I'd stayed and talked to her, I could have convinced her we were over. Maybe she would have accepted this, and she would not have come to my house, and she would be alive today.* This realization helps him understand the guilt he has been carrying since being informed of Candy's death.

The scene changes to a vivid picture of Jada's face, which replaces Candy's. Though noticing differences between the two, the same pain radiates from both of their eyes. The backdrop is that Jada admitted Charles abused her. This revelation caused him to give his word that he would support her in every way. Until now, he had not recognized the similarities the women share. Why did God choose him to help these ladies overcome such horrific experiences?

I ran from Candy, but I will not run from Jada. I love her, and from this moment forward, I will protect her. Now he has identified the reason for his sense of regret. "I promised I would not allow Charles ever to hurt her again, and I failed," he confesses.

He sprawls across the king-size bed. With no further distractions, he falls asleep.

***

The late morning sun casts golden rays through the curtains on his bare body. The warmth announces the dawning of a new day filled with errands and work. The faint sounds of people rushing, horns blowing, doors closing, and birds moving from one limb to the next echo in the distance. Still, he refuses to open his eyes and begin the day. His mind is awake, but his bones and muscles seem to wallow in a bed of quicksand. Thoughts of his to-do list rush in but fail to motivate him to rise. "The sooner you tackle your tasks, the quicker you will be able to start your new life with Jada." His plan is interrupted by his cell phone ringing. To retrieve his phone, he jumps up from the bed, thinking this is the call he is waiting for. "Hello," he says out of breath.

"May I please speak with Mr. David Austin?" A professional-sounding man with a deep voice asks.

"This is he."

"Sir, this is Jake from Jake's Trauma Cleaning and Biohazard Removal Services. Your name was provided to me by Officer Judith Nelson. I am at your residence and need your permission to enter and clean up the aftermath of a shooting."

"Great, I can meet you in about forty-five minutes," he replies.

"You do not need to come now. I can fax or email you the forms. Then, I will call you just before we finish, and you can come sign off on the completed paperwork."

Something inside of David wants to see his home, but he decides it is probably better to wait. "Yes, you may send the authorization to my e-fax. I will review and return them in a bit." After providing his number and ending the conversation, he conjures up what his house would look like after the two murders. Chills run through his body from his imagination. *To see one dead body is traumatic, but discovering two, no wonder Jada was in shock. After this horrifying ordeal, I have to call her again and check on how she is coping.*

Wondering what to say and how to explain his heart's desires, he formulates the words he plans to use as her phone rings. *I am going to ask her to be patient until after Candy's funeral.* After the fourth ring, her voicemail announces she is unavailable and to leave a message. "Hi honey, I am just calling to check whether you are safe and to tell you I love you." With this said, he pushes the end button. Surprised, he bared his heart; he ponders on why. These words were not part of his planned wording and seemed to roll from his lips without consulting him. What is even more perplexing is why she did not answer his call? Instead, he mulls over whether to reach out to Lyric for a status. After consideration, he resolves to handle the business with Candy, her family, and the other more pressing things on his 'to-do' list.

First, he returns the fax. Next, he enters the bathroom. While brushing his teeth, he decides to phone Officer Nelson to thank her for the Biohazard company recommendation and to determine if she contacted Candy's next-of-kin.

Once dressed, he wipes his brow and, with his trembling hands, dials Judith. He is unsure why there is churning inside his stomach.

"This is Officer Nelson. May I help you?"

He swallows before clearing his throat as the sound seems to be locked in his vocal cords. "Uh, this is David," he stutters.

"Oh, hi, did you get some rest?"

"Not much, but I guess I did better than expected considering the circumstances."

"Good, I am happy," she responds.

They remain silent, not knowing where or how to follow up on the conversation once they have passed their greetings. To fill the space, David blurts out, "Thank you for having the service contact me. They are remediating my house now and should be through soon."

"It is my pleasure to help," she responds. "How is Jada doing?"

Not wanting to admit he has not spoken to her yet, he stutters as he offers an excuse. "I called her this morning and left a message, but I guess she is still sleeping."

"After the ordeal Jada witnessed, I am sure she is exhausted." The last thing Judith wants to do is to entrench herself in their relationship. The truth is, she understands why Jada is angry with him.

"May I ask a question?" She continues, but not before swallowing. "I am aware this is none of my business, but why was Candy unclothed and in your bed? Were you and she intimately involved?"

"Why was she in my bed naked, David repeats. I am unsure what you are asking."

"What I mean is it appears you and she were still romantic with one another," she replies in an accusatory tone.

"I did not know she was in my house or bedroom." He scratches his head and transfers the phone from one ear to the other. "Did Charles rape Candy?"

"Oh no! From what our investigation reveals, it appears she was expecting to partake in a romantic evening with you, but Charles interrupted," she states while reading from her notes. "We also found a bag in the bathroom, which contained a rather risqué negligee."

"Mmmm, which is interesting," David replies. Now starting to pace the floor, he fights to make sense of the provided revelation. Although still puzzled, David envisions the scene. Providing a timeline to Officer Nelson, he starts from the time he left the courthouse until he returned home. "You see, I do not know why she was in my house or how she got inside."

The pieces begin to fall together as Judith chews on the end of the ink pen. "How did Candy take you, saying you were going to marry someone else?"

"Of course, she was upset. Candy admitted she was still in love with me. I questioned why she would wait until now to share how she felt. Without waiting to hear her reason, I ran away and left her standing in the hospital."

"How did you feel about her?"

"Well, I must admit hearing her profess this was flattering and made me want to slow things down with Jada. However, to answer your question, no, I did not care about her in any other way than as a friend."

"Did she have a key to your house? Because there were no signs of forced entry."

"Yes, at one point, but when we broke up, she returned it to me. Unless she duplicated it before doing so."

"Well, tell me this," David says. "How did Charles know where I lived? I thought he was still in jail."

"Earlier that day, his mother posted bail. All I can think of is that he followed you or Jada. What I can't determine is how he got to your house before either of you arrived."

A sharp thump inside David's head releases pain as he tries to figure out the answer. *Did he trail Candy? Or did he follow me?* "Wait a second, Jada, and I traded vehicles. In fact, I have hers, and mine is with her. Perhaps he trailed me, thinking she was driving." At that moment, he remembers a truck at the mall that almost hit him. He also recalls just before the vehicle sped off, how he stared at the driver. Then he could not place him. Now he is sure the person in the pickup was Charles. He relays the incident to Judith.

"Did one of you come to your house earlier in the day?" Judith asks.

"After court, Jada stopped by my house. She said she forgot her phone charger and needed to retrieve the plug. I told her to use my remote to open the garage door. Is it possible Charles followed her?"

"Perhaps you may be right, but I will ask her." This update is allowing Judith to connect the dots.

"Thanks. Your help is valuable. Is there anything else you can think of that may help?"

"You are welcome, and no, there is nothing else. However, I do have a few questions for you." To make sure his racing thoughts came out succinctly, he shuffled his feet.

"I will try to answer if I can," she responds before sitting on the swivel chair and leaning back.

Clearing his throat, he asks, "Did Jada kill him?"

"No, Charles shot Candy three times, then placed the gun in his mouth and committed suicide."

While rubbing the tail of his shirt between his fingers, he gasps. "Oh my God," he whispers.

After hearing his response, Judith backpedals and tries to recall her words. She realizes she gave too much. The goal was to convey the pain and fear Jada experienced. But she failed to consider the impact on him when discussing the disturbing details.

Neither David nor Officer Nelson speaks. He is visualizing the blood and gore while Judith wishes she could erase her last statement.

"Although Charles killed Candy, I am thankful Jada is alive. He victimized that young lady for far too long. I pray she will gather the courage to put this behind her," Judith states.

"Me too," he replies, doubting they will recover. "Oh, before we hang up, did you contact Candy's mother?"

"Yes, by now she should have identified and claimed her body."

Again, there is silence on the line until Judith ends their call with a final, "Goodbye."

Although disconcerted about not being able to ascertain how Candy's mother took the news, David rests with the knowledge he will know for himself when he speaks to her. At this point, the primary concern for him is the woman he wants to carry his last name. Upon learning why Jada is upset with him, David must speak with her and explain the reason for a naked woman in his bed. So, he dials her number but receives her voicemail again. "Jada, we need to talk. Please call me so we can discuss Candy." Aargh! "I love you." After hanging up, he prays she will believe him.

Next, he calls Candy's mother. He steadies himself as the ringing starts.

"Hello," an energetic woman's voice sings out.

"Hi, Mrs. Cleo Stevens, this is David. I am a friend of your daughter."

"I have heard so much about you," Cleo says

Although he had never met her parents formally, he occasionally spoke to her mother on the phone. "I am calling to find out how you and the rest of your family are doing."

"We are fine," she answers.

Her lack of grief concerns him. He knows they had a strained relationship, but he expected she would be more compassionate. "I wanted to express my condolences to you and the family," he states.

"Thank you for being concerned. We have made no arrangements yet because we are trying to determine if Candy has a life insurance policy. We cannot come up with the cash for a burial. Do you know if she has any money?"

This question takes David back to a conversation he and Candy once shared. She told him her mother did not care about her; she only cared about how she could support her financially. Gasping, he answers, "I am not sure if there is any insurance or not, but I do possess the key to her condo. If you would like, you can go to her house and search through her papers."

"Honey, I do not plan to ravage through her house looking for a policy. She should have given me a copy. I told that girl to make sure she had her business straight."

After pounding his fist on the bed, he wonders, "Did she love her daughter at all? I will let you know what I can find out."

"If you locate any money, I will need it for her funeral. Otherwise, I will arrange for cremation," Cleo states.

A volcano bubbling inside of David threatens to implode as he struggles to keep his mouth from expressing anger. Finally, he understands why Candy spent so little time with them. *How could anyone be this cold?* "I will call you later," he shouts before pushing the disconnect button. He considers throwing the phone, but logic overrules. Instead, he pitches an ink pen which bounces off the mirror and lands on the floor. "What a piece of work," he thinks.

Glancing at the clock, he notes 10:00 AM. I need to either check out or extend my stay by *another night.* As he collects his belongings, he elects to leave the hotel. There is too much to do.

While scrolling to see if he missed a text message, his phone rang. "I hope this is not that crazy lady calling me back." The screen reads 'no caller ID available.' Maybe it is her. "Hello–Hello, Jada?"

A male voice answers, "No, sir. This is Jake again. I am the gentleman cleaning your house."

Dejected, he states, "Oh, I am sorry. I was expecting another call."

"The job of cleaning your house is complete. Are you available to sign off on the contract if you are satisfied with our work?"

"Sure, I can be there in ten minutes."

"Great, I will see you there."

As David drives, he prepares for what awaits him while anticipating that his emotions will scramble like eggs. Beads of sweat form on his forehead as his heart rate stampedes inside his chest. When he pulls up, there are no police cars, ambulances, and the bright yellow tape is removed; he is relieved. Other than a dump truck and Jake's Trauma Cleaning and Biohazard Removal Services van, his neighborhood has returned to how it looked for the last three years. Before getting out of the car, he says a prayer. With all the drama he had been going through, he neglected to consult his father. "Lord help me, please," he whispers.

He enters the open garage door and is met by Jake.

"May I call you David?" he asks.

Nodding yes, he responds.

"In the primary bedroom, I disposed of the mattress as well as the bedding, carpeting, and some drywall. Everything else, I cleaned."

A chill causes David to tremble at hearing that. Following him inside, he swallows his nerves. Upon entering, he freezes when stepping on the wood subfloor. The trail of carpet tacks around the base of the room. He follows until his eyes rest on the section of eight-by-ten missing drywall and insulation. There is a transparent plastic sheet covering the hole. In his mind, he imagines where the bodies lie. He figured Candy was either on or in bed when she was shot, and Charles must have been near the now-damaged wall. An urge to run overpowers him, but he turns quickly and walks back into the front room, plopping down onto the couch.

Jake opts to give him a few minutes to soak in what he has just witnessed. "There was glass in the hallway from a picture that may have fallen. I could save the print, but you will need to have it reframed. I placed the artwork on your kitchen table," he says.

While sitting with his legs open, arms resting on his knees, and his head down, David mumbles, "Thank you."

"Are you ready to review the list of things we completed?" Jake asks.

Without lifting his head, he responds, "Just leave me the invoice and I will check it later. How much do I owe you?"

He hands him the bill and tells David to call his office with his credit card number. "If there is anything else, please do not hesitate to reach out to me," he says while letting himself out of the house.

Once alone, David lays his head back before breaking out in a cold sweat. The room is spinning. He fights nausea, which threatens to bring up his last meal that he digested long ago. All he can manage is to pray for mercy.

After about fifteen minutes, he regains some of his strength before realizing he has eaten nothing since lunch the day before. He wonders if he feeds his body, if that will settle his mind down. Whatever he eats, he is confident it must be light. So, he decides to head around the corner to IHOP. At least I can get a cup of coffee before going back to Candy's home, he thinks. As he is backing out of his driveway, one of his nosy neighbors passes by while walking her dog. She glares at him with a look of disgust. He is sure that by the way she is staring, she witnessed the commotion of last night. To avoid making eye contact, he turns his head and speeds down the street. Watching his neighbor through his rearview mirror, he can tell she is gawking at his house. I am so embarrassed.

CHAPTER NINE

A RESTFUL NIGHT'S SLEEP

When you close your eyes,

And prepare to go to sleep

If your thoughts are clear

There is no need to count sheep

When your body is relaxed

And your pain has disappeared

If your troubles are put aside

There is no reason to fear

When you've been properly kissed

And held tight by your lover's arms

If you can forget your troubles

There's a peaceful sleep for you've gotten

just what you wished

The smell of hickory bacon and freshly brewed coffee permeates through Lyric's room as she lies on the bed. She stretches and inhales the aroma. A smile of joy and desire lights up her face as she remembers the kiss she and Jim shared. With her finger, she rubs her lips, striving to savor the flavor. For sure, she enjoyed it, but there is no comparison to the way he held her. The security and the strength of his arms provided shelter for her from the pain caused by Johnny. She struggles to ascertain why Johnny is delaying signing and returning the document, especially since he is the one cheating and has an illegitimate child.

A review of her phone shows her husband blowing it up with many calls and messages. "Do not call me. I think you should talk to Donna," she mumbles. *It is time to start this day, and I will not waste a moment on Johnny*, she thinks. She peeks into the adjacent room and is surprised by Jada having made up her bed and that she is gone.

On the dresser lay Lyric's clean undergarments folded neatly. She showers and dresses.

Once completed, she follows the alluring smells of breakfast and coffee to the kitchen, where they have an in-depth discussion.

"Good morning, everyone," she announces as she interrupts their conversation.

At the sight of her, Jim jumps up, pulls her chair out, and motions for her to sit. Without breaking eye contact, he leers at her. The sides of his eyes crinkle. "May I fix a plate and a cup of coffee for you?"

Delighted by Jim's attention, she fidgets in her seat. "Yes, I am starving, but if you do not mind, I can pour my drink."

With his hand, he gestures toward the pot. "Please, I told you to make yourself comfortable."

While observing the love-smitten couple, Jada laughs aloud.

They blush as they are aware she finds their flirting entertaining.

By mistake, Lyric bumps into him while fixing her coffee. Cognizant, his eyes are following her every move; she shivers, trying to ignore the incidental contact. Once returning to the table, he leans down and whispers in her ear. "Why must you be so beautiful?"

Playfully, she pinches his arm. "You are truly charismatic," she jokes while continuing to sip her drink. "So, what were you two talking about?" she asks Jada.

Jada replies, "I was telling him about my evening. We decided he will take me to the hospital so I can tell Mom about Charles."

Still stirring her coffee, Lyric tries to decide if she wants to join them. Convinced that if Nicke can see her daughter not seriously injured, she thinks she will be supportive. Despite everything, she is aware of how much her friend loved Charles.

Jada clears the plates from the table, washes, and stacks them in the dish strainer. "Well, I think I am going to take a short walk so I can clear my head. I need to prepare myself for this conversation."

"No problem," Jim replies. "We will be here when you return."

After she leaves the room, he stands behind Lyric and massages her neck and back. Neither of them speaks for several minutes. Once done, he pulls her to her feet and engulfs her in his arms.

"How did you sleep last night?" he asks.

With a slight chuckle, she replies.

"Like a bear hibernating. How about you?"

"After tossing and turning, I finally fell asleep. The hardest part was walking past your bedroom and not stopping." A hearty laugh follows.

"I am glad you did not stop. For if you had not made me go to bed when you did, I am not sure what the outcome would have been."

With complete sincerity, he leans her back and stares into her eyes. "Look, Lyric, I am falling in love with a married woman. Adultery goes against all my principles. The last thing I want is for you or me to become a casualty of love's ugly side."

"Jim, I do not want that either. I, too, am in love, but with a single man with nothing to lose. I never want to hurt you. For the first time in years, I can embrace being a sensual woman, and it is all because of you."

They search deep into each other's eyes, trying to glimpse their souls. Both are aware that the truth lives there and does not always come from the mouth.

He said he loves me. No man ever aroused me the way he does. "I need my divorce now," she mumbles under her breath.

"Perhaps you should try to work things out with your husband. It is not until we men get threatened with losing our women do we realize what we have."

It is too late for that, though. The mere fact that I allowed Jim to kiss me means my marriage is over. From experience, she understands Johnny will not give her up easily. The last thing she wants to do is to drag Jim into the kind of drama Jada and Nicke are going through. "You do make a good point. There is a saying that goes, I first must finish what is on my plate before I ask for more."

"Ouch, those words sting and have me trying to decipher their meaning. Are you saying you are going back to Johnny and trying again? Never mind Lyric, do not answer that question. Can I steal one more kiss? This one may need to last me a lifetime."

He hovers before she has an opportunity to respond. With his tongue, he outlines her lips. Failure to close his eyes enables a chance for him to marvel at her reactions. He notes how her eyes flutter under their lids. He sees the rapid speed of her chest moving up and down, hears the increased heart rate, and her shallow breaths. Again and again, he presses the tip of his tongue just inside the opening of her mouth. The tension in her body dissipates, and she becomes limp. Unable to keep his eyes open any longer, he closes them, and together they escape to the home of their souls.

Neither of them ever wants to leave, but the sound of the door opening shocks them back to reality. He retracts his tongue, but not before one last peck as Jada enters.

Almost knocking her over, Lyric announces, "Let me grab my purse, then we can leave to go to the hospital."

"Is there something wrong?" Jada asks Jim.

"Yes, there is. I just pray that wrong will become right soon."

"What is that supposed to mean? I am sure it does not concern me. My aunt is a survivor and can handle herself."

With a shrug of his shoulders as his response, Jim gazes out the window.

Ready to leave, Lyric returns with her purse. One day, she thinks she may want to describe this setting. She stops, spins around, and inspects the details of the house. Next, she walks to the fireplace and picks up a framed picture of Jim in his scrubs. A fabulous sketch of the photograph is etched in her mind for safekeeping. She says what she hopes is not her last farewell.

After locating his phone, Jim records the moment by snapping an unsuspecting photo of Lyric, capturing the transparency illuminating her face.

Through the silence, Lyric's phone rings, interrupting everyone.

After answering, Lyric responds, "Hi, baby, is everything all right?"

"Yes, where are you?" Tianna asks.

"We are on our way to the hospital."

To prevent Nicke from being alarmed, Tianna speaks in code: "Oh, great. I overheard a discussion about the Candy you bought from the store last night. This hospital is buzzing."

"Oh boy, is Nicke awake?" Lyric asks, indicating she understands her daughter's attempt to let her know Nicke suspects something is going on with Jada.

"Yes, Auntie is wide awake. She had a nightmare about Jada and is demanding to see her daughter, but so far, all is good," she replies. "Is Jada with you?"

Aware of her daughter's diversion, she responds, "Yes, she is. We should be there in about ten minutes," she continues while glancing at Jim.

***

The room door opens as Tianna is about to hang up. In walks her stepdad. Unable to address his unexpected appearance, her mouth flies open, though she fights to appear calm. "Great, I will see you soon." To avoid revealing with whom is on the other line, she smashes down the end call button.

After the initial shock, she demands, "Johnny, what are you doing here?"

"Hey, Nicke. How are you?" He turns to Tianna before getting an answer. "Can you greet your dad with a proper hello, glad to see you, a kiss or something?" he asks as he faces Tianna. With his arms open, he awaits her embrace.

She ignores his request. "When did you arrive home?"

"Last night. Where is your mother? She did not come home. I thought she might be here."

A smirk graces Tianna's face. Earlier, she told him her mother went on a date. "Mom will be here soon." Not willing to hide her satisfaction at being questioned about her mother's whereabouts, she cannot hold her laughter inside.

When Tianna does not hug him, Johnny's limbs drop to his side, and he turns his attention back to Nicke. "I am so glad Jada survived. I saw the news this morning."

"Dad," Tianna shouts, as she jumps from her seat.

Covering his mouth with his hand, he stammers, "On the TV they said..."

"Said what, Johnny?" Nicke asks while trying to throw her legs out of bed.

With both hands, Tianna pushes him out of her way, runs to Nicke, and grabs her hand. "Auntie, please calm down. I promise you, your daughter is doing better. Just wait until she gets here." To comfort herself and keep her from getting upset, she rubs her hand. Unable to suppress her anger, Tianna glares at him and then rolls her eyes. *You are a big dummy. Go back with your girlfriend. How dare you come in here and start running your mouth about something you are unfamiliar with?*

The tension in the room is thick, most of it from Tianna. The rest is from her father upsetting Nicke.

Tianna can tell by Nicke's facial expressions that she has questions popping in and out of her mind. She is sure Nicke wants to know why Johnny is here, why they are hovering over her, and what they are keeping.

Addressing them both, she asks, "Where is Lyric, and why did she not go home last night?"

Angry with her dad for alarming her, Tianna chimes in first. "Mom stayed with Jada," she rushed out.

Nicke flicks her wrist at her niece and turns her head. Tianna knows she is not buying her explanation, but she is relieved. She hopes Nicke is thinking that Lyric spent the night with her doctor and stops prying. "They will be here soon. Do not worry," Tianna states as she speaks to her, but scowls toward Johnny as she fights to control her emotions. Patience is now necessary as she focuses on the door awaiting their arrival.

Glaring at Johnny, Tianna watches his feet pat the floor while he picks invisible lint from his pants. She wants to yell, "Will you stop fidgeting and sit still?"

No one says anything until the trio arrives.

***

Once they come, they rush in with their sights directed at the patient.

From the corner of her eye, when Lyric spots her estranged husband she skids to an abrupt stop. The look in her eyes reveals sheer panic as she swings around and stares into Jim's face then turns back to Johnny. Unsure of what to do next, she drops her head and tries to figure out why he is in town.

As Lyric studies Johnny's reactions, he is looking Jim up and down. Hopefully, he will consider the gentleman that is accompanying them is the attending physician and not the man she would love to be his replacement.

Next, she looks into Jim's eyes. The sparkle when they first walked in seems to deflate like a tire with a nail. The exchange between the men holds her attention, as she is sure Jim realizes the stranger is Johnny.

A burned red shade replaces the vibrant pecan color of Lyric's face. To snap her out of the visible shock, she greets Tianna, running to her. With her arms around her daughter, Tianna spins her around, so she faces Jim instead of Johnny. "Hi, Mom," she shouts. "I am so glad you are here."

Although bothered by the rising testosterone in the room, Lyric shares a quick reply to her daughter then quickly turns her attention to Nicke and Jada's bandaged hands and leg. These are the things that must take precedence over everyone in the room. "Nicke, Jada has some news she needs to share with you."

"What happened to you?" The blood pressure machine shrills, indicating a drastic change is taking place.

After the alarm sounded, all eyes direct on Nicke. Dr. Maxey pushes past them and makes his way to the bedside. "Hey you," he says as he grabs her hand. "Please, calm down. I told you I would protect these ladies," he stutters as he glances at Johnny, then back. "Nicke, last night was rough on Jada, and now the support of her mother is the medicine she requires. Will you promise me not to get upset, for her sake?"

Nicke looks at her daughter and detects the tears in her eyes. She nods in agreement and reaches for Jada's hand.

To allow her access, Jim steps back in front of Johnny and acts as though he does not notice him.

With her head lowered, Jada relays Charles killed David's ex-girlfriend and then committed suicide. The explanation includes how she discovered the deaths and how she cut herself on a glass picture which fell off the wall. After conveying the details, she seeks assurance from her mother that she will not allow this to cause a setback. "Mom, if something happens to you, I am not sure what I will do." Jada lays her head on her chest, and she proclaims, "I love you so much."

With closed eyes, Nicke caresses her baby girl. "I am sorry Charles took his own life, but I thank God you are alive. For now, we need to be sure you receive all the help and support we can manage to give."

The room is quiet except for the monitoring equipment. The doctor listens to Nicke's heart. He then speaks as he gazes into Lyric's eyes. "May I ask everyone but Jada to leave the room?"

Hollow darkness shows when looking through the windows of his soul. Lyric detects the mourning of his despair. Though he works to disguise his disappointment behind a fake smile, his eyes drooped eyelids shout of pain.

With an effort to hide her tear-filled eyes, Lyric lowers her head but does not prevent the droplets from landing on her trembling hands. Unable to forget, her thoughts drifted when Jim licked her tears away. This time, they freely roll down her cheek and fall unobstructed.

Tianna witnesses her mother crying and releases a conjoining effort of agony. To aid her out the door, she wraps her arm around her waist. As they exit, Johnny follows while massaging Lyric's neck.

The sight of his hands touching Lyric makes Jim want to holler, take your hands off my woman but he understands this would be out of line. Even if Johnny is the one who hurt her, she is his wife, and he has every right to touch her. As they egress, his stomach is queasy, but he recognizes the necessity to concentrate on his patient.

After they are gone, Nicke turns her head toward Jim. "You love her, don't you?" she asks.

"Yes, I also care for you, Jada, and Tianna." He relaxes, considering his reply may dissuade her from asking any additional questions.

Jada signals her to be quiet.

But Nicke is unwilling to stop. "That woman and I have been friends for a long time, and I do not remember ever seeing Lyric this happy. Give her some time." Then she directs Jada, "Please go get your aunt. I want to tell her something."

Once alone with him, Nicke ask for her prognosis and if she will have a full recovery.

Taking her hand, he states. "You are not out of the woods yet. The most important thing you can do is to stay calm. Your fluctuating blood pressure causes me grave concern. I will do everything in my power to help you return home, but it is in God's hands."

"Doc, just keep me around long enough to see my daughter and grandson happy again."

"I will do my part, but you must do yours. Now, let me complete your vitals."

There is a clanking sound from Jim bumping into the food tray. He hustles, trying to collect Nicke's chart and finish up before Lyric returns. "I am going to make rounds now. Should you need anything, the nurses know how to reach me." Opening the door to leave, he finds Lyric standing at the entrance. Their eyes meet for a few seconds. Their bodies make incidental contact as Jim passes. "If you have a chance, call me later," he whispers.

Their impact causes a wisp of air to expel from Lyric's lungs while the door is closing. Every part of her wishes she can stop him and explain Johnny's presence is as much a surprise to her as it is to him.

After deciding to dismiss thoughts of both men, Lyric approaches her confidant. "Hey, friend, I am sorry about what happened to your husband. I know you are also hurting."

As Nicke reaches for Lyric's hand, Nicke whispers, "Thou will be done."

The eyebrows on Lyric's face join, resembling a unibrow as her head tilts. "This is not God's will but rather a choice Charles made when he took his own life. Suicide is a sin," Lyric declares.

"You are right, but since I regained consciousness, I send constant prayers up to protect my baby. Even though I am hurting for Charles, I am thankful God answered my prayer." Looking out the window before continuing, she states. "He was mentally ill. Charles planned to kill Jada because he knew she would never commit to him. Tell me, who was the other girl who lost her life?"

"Her name is Candy, the ex-girlfriend of David and an internist here at the hospital."

Nicke's head pivots. Her chocolate eyes widen as she throws up her hands. "Now wait a minute. Are you talking about the guy who asked me if he can marry my daughter?"

"Yes, he is the same one." Placing her hand over her mouth, Lyric stifles any other words from releasing them because of Nicke's demeanor.

"Do not stop now. I want the details."

Just as Lyric finishes updating Nicke, Jada opens the door. The two ladies hush to avoid upsetting her. Each tries to imagine the hell Jada must be going through.

"Jada, I want you to go with Lyric and try to rest," Nicke commands.

"Mom, I have already spoken to Tianna, and I am going to stay with her. Besides, with Uncle Johnny just getting in, I figure they will want their privacy." After which, she searches Lyric's face for her reaction.

Without changing her expression, Lyric states, "I am going to spend the night at the hospital with you."

"No, I am going to be fine. I do not need anyone here. You go home and help your husband pack," Nicke smirks.

With her eyes narrowing and her lips puckered, Lyric snarls, "You got jokes."

"Well, you can be a fool and leave my doctor. If I do not take him from you, there are a line of other women waiting their turn."

Lyric laughs but her laughter trails off into a deep sigh.

"Besides, there is no way Johnny will let you be alone at this hospital knowing Dr. Maxey is lurking around. I know you saw his face when Jim said he promised to protect Jada and you," Nicke taunts.

Unable to respond right away, Lyric nods. "I have some heavy decisions to make. Understanding is what I need from you. The last thing I want to do is to hurt anyone."

"You are right. But on another note, when you contact your legal counsel, have him draw up a power-of-attorney for me. Since I am Charles' widow, I would like you to work on my behalf. All my paperwork is in my file cabinet.

Do you think you can collect everything and bring them to me tomorrow?" Glancing out the window, Nicke continues. "I guess we need to plan a service for him."

Jada and Lyric look at each other in disbelief. They did not give any thought about who would make the arrangements for Charles or for that matter, if they were necessary.

"I know Charles's mother will have a lot to say, but technically she does not have any rights. I am the wife."

"With this being the weekend, we cannot accomplish much, but at least we can start. We can meet at your mother's house tomorrow morning at about 11:00," Lyric relays to Jada.

"Mom, I will help collect the paperwork, but I do not think I can handle much more," Jada pleads.

"I understand," Nicke replies. "I want you to relax."

The tension in the room rises. Lyric senses Jada needs time to process everything. She attempts to lighten the mood. "You are right. I should find out why my husband came home. I know he received the divorce papers. Beyond that, we have nothing else to discuss." Standing, she continues. "Nicke, promise me you will call if you want anything."

"I will, and I swear."

Lyric kisses Nicke on the cheek and prepares to leave. "By the way, you may want to refrain from flirting with your doctor. I heard his female friend is the jealous type." With a wink, Lyric closes the door and returns to the waiting area where her daughter and husband sit. Neither of them is speaking. Aware that since his arrival, Lyric has not spoken to Johnny. They act as if they are complete strangers instead of a married couple. "Tianna, I am going to go home and get some rest. Am I correct Jada will stay with you tonight," Lyric asks.

"Yes, and I will take wonderful care of her." Then Tianna cuts her eyes toward her stepdad. "Have a nice evening. Call me, Mom, if you need me."

As Lyric starts to walk away, Johnny rushes to catch up with her. "Are you even going to say hello to me?" he asks.

"What do you want? You are the one with a mistress and a child. Now you want me to fall all over you because you came home?"

"No, I just want you to hear me out."

"This is neither the place nor the time."

"Why? Is it because of your new boyfriend?"

Lyric stops. With her hands around her waist, she bristles up and speaks through clenched teeth. "Look! You cannot have both of us. Did you receive the divorce papers?" she asks while banging on the elevator button.

The door opens as he is about to respond. Dr. Maxey steps back to allow the feuding couple to enter. He nods, then lowers his head and pretends to be engrossed in a patient's chart.

Lyric returns the greeting, then turns her back to Jim and prays the ride will end soon.

However, Johnny is unwilling to avoid a confrontation. He extends his hand out to Jim. "Hi, I am Johnny, Lyric's husband. And you are?"

Jim glances up but ignores the attempted handshake. "I am late for surgery. Enjoy your evening Lyric," he states before high stepping out of the door.

Covering her mouth, Lyric does all she can to withhold her laughter, but a smile manages to escape. *Wow, Jim is a cocky man. That serves Johnny right.* "Thank you, I wish I could," she replies to Jim as she rushes out behind him.

"Are you going home?" Johnny yells at her.

Ignoring him, she speeds to her car to make a phone call to Jim. Sure, that meeting him on the elevator was not an accident but a calculated move on his part. But why, she wonders as she phones him. He answers on the first ring. "Hello, Mr. 'I am late for surgery'–."

"Hi Lyric, I have been waiting for your call. Did you know Johnny was coming home?"

"No, Jim, I did not. I am just as surprised as you are."

"Good, because I was concerned you may have known and did not tell me."

"I would not do that."

"I hope you understand why he is here," Jim states.

"No, I do not."

"He is here to win his wife back. I am sure he realizes what he stands to lose and now wants you." After a slight pause, he says, "I cannot blame the man."

Stopping at the red light, Lyric glances in her rearview mirror. Behind her vehicle, Johnny is following in his car. However, she returns her attention to the conversation with Jim. "He is the one with another lady and a baby."

"Look, Lyric; it is obvious he wants his wife back." Rhetorically, he asks, "Why do you think he wanted me to know his relationship with you? I'll tell you why—he was marking his territory."

"I do not belong to him," she fires back.

"Yes, you do. I just want you to realize why I am backing out. I cannot come between you and Johnny. I'm sorry for interfering in your marriage. I assume your husband had made his decision, but it seems he has changed his mind. It's obvious he still wants you. I have to end this before it starts."

Sometimes the truth is a hard pill to swallow. Unable to provide a rebuttal, though, Lyric understands and chokes while trying. "I agree," she sniffs before ending their call. Regardless of what her heart wants, she agrees he is correct to limit their contact. She and Johnny are still legally married, and no matter how much she wishes things could be different, she must face reality. *To continue having a relationship with Jim means the two of us are being hypocritical in our beliefs about Christianity.* "I have to trust God that what is meant to be, will be," she says out loud.

CHAPTER TEN

WHY ME

When I entered this world

I did not have a clue

Of all the things

I'd have to go through

As a baby, your little one to hold

The one you were to love

And protect from anyone

Who would seek to control

My mind, my body and even my dreams

It was your responsibility to

Mold and develop them

Giving me self-esteem

Instead, in my life you did not see

The abuse that occurred

And left me today questioning

And wondering

Why me?

Returning to Candy's house, David says a silent prayer then climbs the stairs. Today the home appears cold and dreary, as though aware the owner is gone—never to return.

He locates the file cabinet. Struck by how organized the folders are, he fingers until he lands on the 'Life Insurance' policy. While scanning the page, he determines there is a one hundred-thousand-dollar term policy, but Candy's beneficiary shocks him into silence. He drops the paper on the floor, and with a gasp, his knees knock when reading his name listed as being the sole beneficiary. *Of all people, why would she list me?* He tries to understand her reasoning as he slips down into the chair. An additional examination reveals a sealed envelope addressed to him. His fingers tremble as he flips the enclosed message over, then back again. *This is not my responsibility. You should have appointed someone in your family.* Fear changes to anger while he attempts to determine her rationale. *I do not want to handle any of this. Damn you, Candy and damn you, Cleo Stevens.* A renewed strength gives him the courage to continue reading the details. He is to arrange an estate sale, use the insurance proceeds for the burial, pay Candy's bills, and donate any remaining money to C.A.P.S (Children Are Protected Against Sexual Abuse). Also mentioned, the will names him as the executor of her estate, and that she does not want her stepfather or mother to receive so much as a dime of her money.

After completing the necessary calls, he heads to the master bedroom closet and rifles through the rows of elegant and stylish clothing. He must pick out something worthy of displaying her beauty as she lay in her coffin. Through the rack, he searches until he settles on a light blue crew neck and sheath gown, sporting chiffon keyhole long sleeves.

He remembers how he felt when he saw her wearing this outfit. They were attending a Charity Ball fundraiser to benefit a sexual abuse organization. The moment she stepped out of her room with the dress hugging her curves while cleverly concealing her cleavage, he was smitten. How innocent she appeared in this dress and yet how difficult he found it to contain his lust. On the evening they returned home, they'd made love for the first time.

Just thinking about Candy and how she led him to Jada reminds him Jada hasn't yet gotten back to him. Once again, he calls and receives her voicemail. "Jada, this is David. Can we meet so we can talk and exchange our cars to each other? I miss you, and there are things I need to tell you. I love you."

After disconnecting, he sits on the couch and lays his head back. He visualizes his life going around and around like a merry-go-round as he studies the motion of the ceiling fan. *I am no good at this relationship thing. It may be better to be by myself.* The ringing of his cell disrupts his thoughts. Jada! "Hello, I am so glad you called me. How are you? Are your hands and leg healing? Can I see you?"

After he finishes bombarding her, a low, smoky voice that doesn't belong to Jada answers.

"Hello, David, this is Tianna. I am using Jada's phone because she asked me to make arrangements to exchange vehicles with you." There appears to be a tinge of anger in her tone.

"How is she doing?" he asks with trepidation.

"She is fine. Where and when can we meet?" she demands.

"Look, I understand you were asked to contact me, but this is between Jada and me. Please put her on the telephone so that we may discuss this."

In a raised voice, she lashes out. "She has nothing to say to you. All she wants is her car. I told you she asked me to call you. What part of 'she doesn't want to talk to you,' do you not understand?"

His muscles tense up as he pulls the receiver from his ear and leers at it. Just let me speak to Jada, and everything will be fine, he thinks. Unable to control his emotions, he yells back. "Well, since you are her manager, please tell her I said she could have her vehicle when she makes time to speak to me." Now shouting from raw nerves, he fails to temper his words. "When she needed me, I was there for her. Where is she now when I need her? I thought Jada knew me better. I refuse to babysit her. A murder happened, and I must arrange the funeral because Candy walked into Jada's mess."

After spewing his venom, he slams the phone down. The sudden end to their conversation leaves him perplexed and guilty about his rant.

"Just like a man, to blame the woman for his indiscretions," Tianna mumbles to the dial tone.

Snatching open the closet door, David returns to packing up the clothing for Candy to wear. After retrieving all the necessary paperwork, he locks up and roars out of the driveway. For whatever reason, the loud sound and fast speed offer a few seconds of relief. The sun is blazing, and the heat is sweltering, but he resists the urge to roll up the windows. Instead, he turns the air conditioning on the highest setting. In his mind, he likens these sensations to his relationship with Jada, a combination of hot and cold.

Once he arrives at the bank parking lot to handle Candy's finances, he strides inside. A young woman greets him with long golden blonde hair who is checking him out from head to toe. She flips her hair and straightens her clothing. "How may I help you, sir?" she asks in a sultry voice.

"I would like to open an estate account."

The two of them step into her office and take their respective seats. After introducing themselves, they get down to business.

Left by himself to handle this unfamiliar complexity and battle the butterflies dancing in his stomach, he ignores the woman's intentional 'come-on'. Once the account is set up, he thanks her for her assistance and exits as quickly as he entered. Now to move on to the hard part—planning Candy's burial.

After entering the funeral home, he is taken downstairs to a basement office. While waiting, he spots several empty caskets on display and an abundance of catalogs stacked on the desk. The room is chilly and dimly lit. He swivels the chair back and forth, a little spooked.

Finally, Mr. Doug Reeder comes to join him and expresses his condolences. He then asks if the deceased is David's significant other.

"No sir, she is a close friend."

"Why is her family not present?"

Without being specific, he answers, "Candy left a power of attorney, a will, and instructions for me to handle her affairs." He hands a copy of the documents to him.

After having him sign an assignment of benefits, Doug takes him to pick out a casket.

They complete the planning and agree on Wednesday the wake and funeral will be held. On the way to his car, David strikes off the completed things from his mental to-do list. *Now I must contact Jada and exchange cars, advise Candy's mother about the arrangements, notify my attorney to have the will probated, and then call a moving company to pack up her house.* Exhaustion sets in as he reviews the remaining items. "How will I ever get all this done? I am scheduled to return to work next week."

Again, he dials Jada's number.

"Hello, David. This is Tianna."

I guess Jada still does not want to speak with me; her silence feels heavy and cold. He asks in a dejected tone.

"Sure, I will come to you."

Without stopping to think, he gives her Candy's address. "I will be there in about fifteen minutes."

"All right, I will see you soon," she replies.

"Why is she not giving me an opportunity to explain? I could use her assistance. Dealing with all of this is the hardest thing I ever had to do." He pushes the end button and throws his phone on the passenger seat before smashing down on the accelerator and speeding away.

Once he arrives at Candy's home, he gathers his paperwork and calls his attorney to schedule an appointment for Monday morning at 9:00 AM. Next is the daunting task of phoning Candy's mother. Before doing so, he inhales as he dials the number. "Mrs. Stevens, this is David."

Without saying hello, Cleo questions him. "Did you find my daughter's life insurance information?"

"I did, as well as her will and a power of attorney."

"How much did she leave me?"

Is this woman serious? "Candy named me as the administrator of her affairs."

"Sure, sure, but how much money do I receive?"

He stands up and walks to the window as he struggles to remain polite and calm. "There is a one hundred-thousand-dollar policy."

Before he can finish explaining, Cleo cuts him off. "Oh great, this will be enough for me to bury her, and I will have some cash left over."

After clearing his throat, he continues, "I am sorry Mrs. Stevens. Per her direction, I'm to pay for her funeral, debts, and the remaining is to be donated to a specific charity for sexual abuse."

Cleo screams into the receiver, "I do not believe you! She told me she broke up with you months ago. So why would she leave you, her money?"

Just as David is about to respond, the doorbell rings. He welcomes the distraction because it prevents him from yelling back at her. He opens the door while Mrs. Stevens continues ranting.

"You are trying to rob me," she shouts.

With a finger motion, David directs Tianna in before they turn and head up the stairs and she sits on the couch crossing her legs.

As David listens to Mrs. Stevens, he is aware that Tianna can overhear her loud and obnoxious voice coming from his receiver. He studies her as she surveys the room and attempts to appear uninterested in his conversation. Following her eyes, he notices as she stares at the picture on the mantle of him and a woman in a heart-shaped frame. Her nostrils widen, and her breath appears to stick in her throat as she studies the photograph.

"Mrs. Stevens, I am not sure why Candy left me to handle her affairs, but I am going to honor her wishes."

Cleo continues shouting. "I am going to sue you. You are nothing but a gigolo."

Unable to hold his temper any longer, he fires back. "Please have your attorney contact mine, Mr. Josh Greene. Do not blame me. Candy specified she did not want you or your husband to receive one dime of her money or possessions. What did you expect when, as a child, she told you she was molested by your husband, and you did not believe her?"

"She is a liar. I know the man I am married to, and he did not touch her fast ass."

To remain calm, he inhales several times before observing Tianna hanging on to his every word. Rather than allowing her to witness his loss of control, he decides to rush off the phone. "Candy's services are on Wednesday. The wake is from 10:00 AM to 11:00 AM. The funeral will follow. Everything will take place at Restland Funeral Home. The announcement will be in tomorrow's newspaper." Once finished, he exhales and awaits her response.

"My husband and I will see you there, but we are not through with this situation."

After pausing, David whispers, "Candy requested he not attend."

"If he cannot come, then I will not attend either. Who do you think you are to ban him?" Cleo snarls.

"My attorney will provide you with the documentation that I have in my possession. Now I must hang up because I have other business to handle." With that, David ends the call.

With his head hanging, his eyes pool with water. Resentment toward Candy creeps through his spirit. *Why would you put me in this predicament?* For him to regroup, he allows time to pass before speaking.

"From the conversation I just overheard, it appears that Jada and I were wrong about you." To offer comfort, she softens her voice. "I can see you are upset. If you give me Jada's keys, I will excuse myself so you can finish making the arrangements." As he turns toward her, there is a mist in his eyes.

In his posture, he transmits that the heavy load he is carrying is becoming lighter. His shoulders droop, and the anger melts as though butter in the sun. "Please do not leave yet. Before I lose my mind, I need to talk to someone."

Though hesitant, she agrees. "What would you like to discuss?" She asks.

He stretches his arms open and lays back on the couch, relieved he can finally tell someone his version of the story. With all the sincerity he can exude, he confesses his love for her friend.

"Why don't you explain this to Jada? I am sure she will understand."

He sits up as his eyes widen. "I am trying to tell her, but Jada will not take my calls. I would never hurt her. I thought she understood that about me. But now I need her by my side helping me, the way I helped her."

"Give her some time to work through everything. This situation is a very horrifying experience." Pausing, Tianna offers her assistance.

To show his appreciation, he hugs her. For some unknown reason, he does not want to let her go. The scent of her body is intoxicating. Enjoying the comfort of a woman's arms, he prolongs their hug but, she is not Jada. The strength of her clutch provides the assurance things will work out.

So as not to regret his actions later, the sparks escaping from and through him need harnessing. With his head lowered, he wonders what Tianna is thinking. A replacement or a substitute will not work, as there is only one woman for him.

"What can I do," Tianna asks.

"I will get everything handled. Just knowing you gave me the opportunity to explain is enough."

Throwing a soft punch at his arm, Tianna attempts to change the mood. "Do not be silly. As a friend," emphasizing the word, "I can assist you with whatever needs to be done." Looking around, she asks, "Do you want me to help with packing up Candy's belongings?"

"No, I am going to contact a moving service."

"Well then, I will call a company and make arrangements." Tianna pulls her phone out and searches the internet for a list of movers. "What are you going to do with her things?" She asks.

"She left instructions to give everything to The Purple Heart organization."

Before David can refuse her assistance, she speaks for him. "I think we should pack her items, papers, and all the things which you do not want the movers to take."

"This is a good idea. But I will first need to get some boxes. Can we pack later? That is, if you will be available."

"Tomorrow is great," she says with a smile. *Maybe once I explain to Jada that David was not involved with Candy, she may also come over to help.*

With a grin on his face, he pivots towards her. "I know what you can do for me today. Will you please join me for dinner? I am hungry and do not wish to eat alone."

Looking into his pleading eyes, Tianna agrees. "Sure, but you are paying."

To avoid her stare, he grins as he turns. "Come on, let's go before I change my mind and decide you should pay," he says, as he skips down the steps.

CHAPTER ELEVEN

LAYING IN THE BED YOU MADE

Be careful what you do
For it will boomerang right back to you
The bed that you make could end up in heartbreak
And if it should
Suck it up and take it
Welcome to adulthood

L yric pulls into her garage with her mind on the pain radiating from Jim's voice. She swallows her sadness along with the urge to cry. While glancing in the rearview mirror, Johnny is exiting his car. At the sight of him, she slams her hands down on top of the dashboard. She snatches her purse and rushes inside the house, with him lagging behind. *Why did he come back? I am through with him and our marriage.*

"Darling, I am glad to be home. I missed you." Johnny says as he enters.

The words sink in as she spins around, and a fire ignites inside her eyes while he is scanning the house as though he never lived there and was visiting for the first time. She swallows the impulse to hurl out a four-letter curse word while locking the door to her bedroom. Through the wood barrier, she ignores his comment and hollers, "I am tired, and I am going to sleep."

With Lyric's quick exit, Johnny pounces down on the couch. The room is clean, but there is no life other than a green budding plant sitting in the corner. The only sounds are the ticking of the grandfather clock. With each second, the minutes rush. Johnny jumps to his feet and runs to the bedroom. He bangs on the door yelling, "Lyric, I need to speak with you now."

The loud noise that sounds like the police trying to serve a warrant causes her to jump. She lifts her head from the tear-stained pillow. "Please leave me alone. I have nothing to say to you," she quivers. "Our marriage is over through no fault of mine."

"Give me a chance to explain," he pleas.

The usual calm demeanor she normally exhibits changes faster than a lightning bolt. Her legs swing to the floor as she stumps to the door. One snatch on the door handle and the door swings open. With closed fists and sheer rage emanating from every cell in her body, she shouts. "What, do you think I do not know how babies are conceived? Did you forget I had two children myself?" Without waiting for a response, she continues. "You screwed around while we were still married and now, she has your child."

To sit on the bed, he brushes past her. "Yes, you are correct. All I know is I want us together." With his head down, he speaks. "I feel horrible for bringing this into our lives."

Determined and unwilling to entertain his apology or spare his feelings, she screams. "Are you as sorry as the last time you brought another woman into our relationship or because you got caught?" Her eyes are red and bloodshot as she plants her hands on her hips and awaits his rebuttal.

He walks toward her and gathers her into his arms. With his head leaning to the side, he uses his hand to lift her head. "Please look at me. I am certain you still love me. We can work through this."

Out of his grip, she squirms and pushes him away. "No—Johnny, not this time. We will not have sex and pretend as though nothing happened. You are a father, and your child needs you. My children are adults, and I refuse to start over with another one."

Still not willing to accept her rejection, he snatches her back in his grip and kisses her.

With all her strength, she releases herself. From a place of childhood fear, she yells. "Step away from me!" To avoid collapsing on the floor, she stumbles to her bed and plops her shaken body down. Out of breath, her trembling hands wipe the pool of sweat from her forehead. Visions of her childhood sexual abuse encounters flash to the forefront of her memory. She cannot catch her breath. In and out she heaves while managing to whisper, "Leave my room, my house, and my life."

Jumping back, Johnny threw his hands up. "Hey Lyric, calm down. I would never hurt you."

"That is a lie, and you are a liar. You already did, but this will never happen again." Lyric sits on the bed. Hypnotized by her loss of control, she glares at Johnny, leaning against the door. She can tell he is trying to make sense of her reactions. Still, she does not feel the need to explain. After all, this response was triggered by him. The woman before him differs from the quiet, gentle, and loving one he left months ago. This Lyric is heartless and unforgiving, she thinks.

I thought she loved me. What would make her change into this angry black woman? "It's that doctor friend of yours. Have you been having sex with him? Is he the reason you do not want me anymore?" He scowls as his eyes narrow.

Without looking at him, she responds. "Unlike you, I did not break our wedding vows." Inside of Lyric, she wants to stretch the truth and say Jim, and she was intimate. Would he hurt as much as she is from knowing of his indiscretions? Instead, she is cautious when explaining her relationship. "Jim is my friend. He comforted me and helped me through the stress of the last several days. I needed you, but you were too busy with your other family to be there for me."

"So, because I was not there for you, you went to another man?"

"Is that not what you did to me?" Lyric asks.

"So now we are even. Can we please fight to save this marriage?" He swallows before continuing. "I will forgive you if you forgive me?"

She smirks. "No, Johnny, this is not about forgiving but rather forgetting. The first time was a mistake, but the second time is a pattern. I want out. I can never trust you again. Like a bird taking flight, the fight flies out of her body. Now please close my door behind you. I am tired. Our attorneys can figure out the details."

"You are my wife, and I will never let you go," he declares before slamming the door.

Not sure of any hidden meanings behind his parting words, she rushes and turns the lock. Mentally and physically drained, the need to lower her stress level is paramount. A hot bubble bath coupled with candles and soft music is the answer.

While soaking in the steaming water, visions of Jim creep through the cluttered thoughts. Never can she recall a time when she allowed anyone to pierce through her self-protected heart—not even Johnny. With Jim, a sense of freedom emerged. The safety of his arms is reassuring and offers her the one place no man ever penetrated through before—the core of her trust.

The overhead fan cools her down. She draws her knees to her chest and grips them close as the bubbles and dirty water rush down the drain. This life she shared with Johnny vanishes counterclockwise into the waiting piping. After drying, she lays down with the goal of forgetting both men, at least until morning.

**

Forced to acquaint himself with the guest bedroom in his house, Johnny struggles to make himself comfortable. For the first time, he is sleeping in this room. Inside, Johnny hopes this is only temporary and he will soon return to their marital bed. With his hands propping his head on the pillow, he pictures Lyric walking into Nicke's hospital room. It has been three months since he last saw his wife. Into her glamor, she drew him in at first sight. Perfect arched eyebrows hover over her fluttery, full, and long lashes while protecting her sparkling, amber-colored eyes. Her small ears frame the thin tapered nose resting on her face. The hue of her caramel brown complexion shimmered while accenting her oval face. Lips adorned with deep red lipstick and outlined with a darker shade seemed to invite kissing until the removal of all the color. From his reflections on their earlier meeting, he shivers while visualizing her body. Breasts, full and erect, overflow from the white and black V-neck blouse she wore. For him, though, the most enticing part of her appearance was the way the pencil skirt hugged her compact protruding bottom. While reliving this time, he realizes he did not always notice her assets. In the past, he compared her physical attributes to those of Donna's. Until now, he preferred Donna because her sex appeal was like a drug he craved. Once blinded by lust, now he recognizes his feelings for Donna have nothing to do with love. It took receiving divorce papers to understand it is Lyric he loves. Today his eyes and heart can now appreciate her beauty. He is not sure, however, if it is the threat of losing her or the thought of her being with another man. Before drifting off to sleep, he prays he is not too late.

    ***

The next morning, Lyric awakens to silence. There is no smell of coffee brewing or the aroma of sizzling bacon as it had been the day before. A downtrodden Lyric rolls out of the bed and dresses. While brushing her teeth, she plans her schedule for the day. The first item on her agenda is to meet Tianna and Jada at Nicke's home. Because of Nicke being in the hospital, they must arrange Charles' cremation. How could he kill Candy, an innocent person and add her to his drama-filled life? What if rather than her, it had been Jada? Unable to wrap her mind around the senselessness of his actions, she says a silent prayer for strength. Also, she asks God to give her a forgiving spirit toward him.

She ties her hair back in a ponytail, then calls her niece.

"Good morning. Did you get some rest?"

"Yes," Jada replies while yawning, "I took the pill they gave me and did not wake up until about ten minutes ago."

"Great, after the stress you are going through, you need to sleep."

"Where is Tianna?" She asks.

"I think she is in the bathroom—last night when she came in, I was asleep."

"Well, get her up. I am about to leave the house so I can meet you two at your mom's house. We need to find the paperwork to plan his memorial service." She is careful not to use Charles's name because she is not sure of how she will respond.

"I will help you look, but I do not think I can assist with planning anything. I am on my way to Tasha's house to tell my son his grandfather, or should I say, father, is deceased," she stammers.

Unsure of how to reply, Lyric decides it will be better to ignore the comment. While opening her bedroom door, she states, "I will see you soon," and ends their conversation.

From the dining room table, Lyric snatches her purse and traipses through the kitchen before being interrupted by Johnny.

"Where are you off to this morning?" he asks, cutting his eyes in her direction.

Abashed by the intrusion, she mumbles, "Going out to handle some business."

"Business," he repeats. "What kind of business do you have on a Sunday?"

With the rolling of her eyes, she decides not to turn the conversation into an argument. "I am meeting Tianna and Jada. Nicke asked us to collect some information." After explaining, she continues walking out the door leading to the garage.

"Are you sure you will not be with your doctor friend?"

"What?" she yells as she spins to face him, revealing her reddened face. Her eyes squint closed, and lips tighten as though she bit into a sour lemon. After gaining control, she softens to say, "Enjoy your day," before closing the door.

Taking a second to exhale, she extends her chest with pride as she was able to fend off his blatant attempt to upset her. Truthfully, she wishes she was going to meet Jim. However, the temptation is far too high for both her and him.

In front of Nicke's home, she parks and takes a few seconds to gather her thoughts. Tasked with planning a memorial service, she is now forced to deal with Mrs. Smith, Charles's mother. *This lady will start some trouble. I will say some things to her I should've said years ago.* While she sits outside, she hopes the girls will arrive soon. Pulling down the rearview mirror, she studies her appearance. A couple of strands of hair are misplaced and in need of fixing. With her tongue, she wets her index finger and rubs her eyebrows, forcing every hair back in place. Once satisfied, she returns the mirror to the correct position and wonders if she will see Jim. Half of her hopes he will be working, but the other understands it will be best if he is nowhere around. Either way, she is assured she is presentable and may even cause his head to turn. She giggles to herself while tucking her top into her jeans. "Finally," she mutters as Jada and Tianna pull into the driveway. She greets them both with kisses and tight bear hugs. "Hello, my beautiful ones," she exclaims grinning.

"Hey, Mom, are you okay?" Tianna asks while still holding on.

"I am fine. Why wouldn't I be?" Lyric asks as she steps back to study Tianna's face.

"I was worried about you since Johnny came home unexpectedly. The thought of him saying or doing something stupid had me on edge."

"Johnny," she repeats. "He is still your stepdad. Address him at least for now."

"Mom, I am not a little girl anymore. I know about his affair and his child. From now on, I cannot call him dad. His name to me is Johnny. Plus, you must be careful because some men do not know how to let go."

The exchange between them causes Jada to lighten the mood. "Good morning, Auntie—by the way, you look beautiful. I am sure my uncle is beating himself up for even considering another woman over you. That is his loss because Dr. Maxey is waiting to capitalize on his mistake," she declares as she twirls Lyric around like a ballerina dancing in a music box.

"Thank you, Jada," she replies with her cheeks flushing to a scarlet color as a nervous giggle escapes. "I am going to get a switch and beat both of you ladies if you do not stay out of my business." She motions them to the front door. "Now, come on. We have work to do." Though she is aware of being judged by the way she blushes at the mention of Jim; she receives pleasure from having him as a distraction.

Jada grabs Tianna's hand. The tension from Tianna's muscles lessens as Jada forces her hand to swing back and forth as if they were children. "Auntie, we are too old for a spanking—besides in today's world we will have you arrested for child abuse," Jada says as they both break into loud laughter.

Lyric shakes her fist at them, then joins in the hearty laugh. "Get your grown butts in here and find these papers," she says. As they pass, she plants another kiss on their cheeks.

Tianna and Lyric sit on the couch while Jada runs up the steps. "I am going to rifle through Mom's file cabinet. I will be right back."

Snuggling close to her mother, Tianna lays her head on her shoulder. In a soft whisper, she confides, "I met David yesterday to exchange his car for Jada's."

"How is he doing?" she asks.

"He is upset because he must plan Candy's funeral. She left him as the executor of her estate."

"I wonder why she would not leave her kin to handle such a task. It sounds to me like maybe there was more going on between them than we first thought."

"No Mom, he loves Jada. Candy had a lot of family problems, so it appears she relied on him because she trusts him."

"What did Jada say about this?"

"She does not know yet. David swore me to secrecy because he wants to be the one to tell her what happened that night." Raising her head, she continues, "I told him I would help him pack up Candy's things."

"Do not forget your loyalty is to your friend. You cannot allow him to put a wedge between the two of you."

"That will never happen," she emphatically replies.

Staring into her eyes, Lyric sits on the couch and lifts her daughter's chin. "Young lady, be careful. They need to work this situation out."

"I know, Mom, but she refuses to give him an opportunity to explain. He says if she insists on believing he was unfaithful to her, then she is not the woman he thought she was."

Thinking about his statements, Lyric tries to find a way in which Tianna can keep her promise to David and yet respect her friendship with Jada. She ponders several alternatives before; she is interrupted by the galloping sounds of Jada descending the hardwood steps.

"Why are you guys so quiet?" she asks.

"Ugh, we are resting our minds," Lyric replies. "Did you find everything?"

"Yes, I located two wills, the power of attorney and insurance policies. Mom is very organized. All you need is in this envelope," Jada says while handing Lyric the manila folder.

"Good, I will handle things from here." After standing, she wraps her arms around Jada's neck. Even though Jada is trying to be cheerful, Lyric can see through her pretense. "Jada, it is time for you to call David."

Jada tries to pull out of Lyric's clutches, but she will not allow her to wiggle free. "I do not have anything to say to him."

"This is the time the two of you should come together. The situation may not be the way things look. You owe it to him."

Through her tears, she manages to speak. "It is because of me Candy is dead. I know he can never forgive me. I am the one who brought him and her into my life."

Wiping her face, Lyric tries to comfort her. "You are not the one to blame for this. Charles pulled the trigger. When are you going to stop holding yourself responsible for the bad things Charles has done?"

"I can never face David again. I need professional counseling and the time to heal."

Lyric considers her plan and decides to respect her decision. I wonder if she knows men like David come along once in a lifetime. If only she could see he needs her as much as she does him. Sure, do hope she does not lose him. Perhaps she should not impose her thoughts or beliefs. "All right baby, I just do not want you to work on healing alone. Please reach out for help."

"I will. I promise," Jada declares. "Now I am going to Tasha's house so I can spend time with my son. I have missed him so much."

Tianna remains silent while her mother and friend talk. Standing, she walks out the door.

Lyric follows. As she enters her car, she waves goodbye to the ladies. From her window, she yells, "I am on my way to the hospital. I will call you two later." With a toot from her horn, she drives away.

CHAPTER TWELVE

HONOREE SEEKS A GUEST

Will you be my guest
My life is such a mess
I need to decide
Who will be my bride?
Can you attend?
As my friend
Because,
The one I love
I must be careful
of

Chewing on the end of a pencil, Jim leans back in the aniline leather chair and studies his office wall adorned with a diploma and awards. He spies the ideal spot to hang his latest, 'Doctor of the Year' addition. What an honor to receive this designation for the second time in three years, but it doesn't quiet the events of the previous days. To slough off the negative thoughts which insist on creeping into his head, he staggers to the window and stares out. "I am supposed to be happy and shouting for joy to have received such recognition. Instead, because I cannot ask Lyric to accompany me to the dinner, I wish I was never selected." His eyes dart from the cars to the people hurrying about until he focuses on an old man sitting on an egg crate with his cup extended. What strikes his attention is how he appears invisible to the many passersby. There were many times he recalls he also passed the man and avoided making eye contact. Somehow, being on the fifth floor and looking down gives him a different perspective. He makes a mental note the next time he encounters him he is going to speak and place some money in his container. "Why am I sorry for myself when I have so much to thank God for? Lord, please forgive me for being so ungrateful." After repenting, he strides back and plops down. From his middle drawer, he locates a business card and repeatedly taps it on his desk. Should he use the contact information he considers while staring at the telephone? He rests his elbow on top of the table and rehearses a speech. After gathering the nerves, he snatches the receiver and dials.

"Officer Nelson," Judith says.

"Hello. This is Jim Maxey."

Pulling the handset away from her ear, she looks at the name. Visible, however, is only the phone number. "Dr. Maxey, is everything all right?"

"Yes—and please call me Jim. I am calling to find out if you can stop by the hospital sometime today."

"I hope nothing has happened to Nicke or Jada."

"No, they are doing well. In fact, I am about to check on Nicke to determine how she tolerated her physical therapy. In a week or two, if she keeps improving, she will be released."

"Oh, Dr. Maxey—I mean Jim—that is wonderful."

There is an awkward silence on the line. Neither is sure of what to say next.

Finally, Jim speaks. "May I call you, Judith?"

"Why sure?" she squeaks out.

"Well, Judith, what time do you think you can stop by?"

Does he want to discuss Charles's suicide or perhaps Candy's murder? Rubbing her forehead, she asks, "It depends. Is this visit about personal or business stuff?"

After a chuckle, he answers. "It is personal."

What do we have to talk about? "In that case, since I am just leaving work, I can be at the hospital in a half hour. Should I meet you in Nicke's room?"

"No, let's make it my office on the fourth floor."

"Sure thing," she states and ends their call.

After completing his invitation, he reclines in his chair a little baffled and conflicted. A part of him wants to call Judith back and rescind his offer. Somersaults from his intestines churning causes severe cramping in his stomach. His thoughts continue to wander while combing his fingers through his hair. A sudden urge to punch the wall takes over him, but sound judgment prevails. He steadies his hands as he glimpses his reflection in the mirror. All he can recognize are hollow, sunken eyes that lack sparkle. Unable to shake his disappointment or his desire for Lyric, he glances at his watch and decides he should get back to work. After closing the door, he walks toward the elevator. Each step he takes feels like he is dragging an extra person. He reconciles he will save Nicke for his last stop. Two quick stops are necessary before going to see her.

Once Jim reaches the room, he hesitates before pushing on the door, afraid he'll see Lyric. He straightens his lab coat and combs his beard with two fingers. With a forced smile, he bops inside. Quickly, his eyes dart around the room, checking to see if Nicke has any visitors. Once he determines she is alone, his stride slows. "Good afternoon, Nicke. How are you today?" he says as he startles her awake.

It takes her several seconds to become alert. "Hi, Doctor Maxey. Your favorite patient is exhausted. Physical therapy was brutal, but I survived."

The monotone sound of her voice leads him to approach her bedside while staring deep into her eyes. He recognizes a similar emptiness he observed in his own eyes before making rounds. He sits on the stool and rolls closer to her. "Are you in pain?" he asks while tilting his head.

"Physically I am healing, but my heart hurts for Jada."

Careful not to disturb the IV needle, he clasps the dorsal surface of her hand between his extra-large fingers.

Again, she states, "I am concerned about my daughter. All night, all I could think about was Charles could have killed her instead of the other young lady. I imagine the way her family and Charles's mother must be feeling is the same way I could be today. She turns away from him and glances out the window. "I am sorry for everybody involved." Again, she stops, then mumbles. "I am responsible for this tragedy. I am the one who married him."

Jim fights the urge to interrupt and offer a sense of reassurance. There will be plenty of time to provide consolation, he figures. For now, it is best to allow her to lament. "Did you know I once loved him?" she asks.

Without letting go of her hand, Jim nods affirmatively.

Nicke continues. "I thought we were forever. Never in a million years did I ever think Charles would molest Jada, kill himself, and leave me hating his memory." She squirms in the bed and closes her eyes. In slow motion, her head rolls from one side to the other. The monitor beeps as her resting heart rate rushes to 100 beats per minute.

"None of this is your fault. I know it is hard for you to comprehend but there is always purpose in your pain. I need for you to remain calm, get healthy, and be thankful to your creator."

A frown adorns Nicke's face while turning back to face him.

Noting her confusion, he anticipates the questions she may have about grasping the reason for their enduring circumstances. Aware he is not qualified to address them, he leads her to the one who does have the answer. He prays with and for her. After he has completed his prayer, he pats her hand and leaves.

On the walk down the hallway, he considers the way he will invite Judith to accompany him to his appreciation dinner. Will she accept? He wonders? After turning the corner, he looks straight into the face of Lyric. Shocked at seeing her, he fights the desire to run. He rubs his hands together, searching for the appropriate greeting. Without breaking eye contact, she stops in front of him. His lips quiver, and his eyelids feel hot as his vision blurs.

"Hello, Lyric. How are you doing today?"

Jim wonders why she does not respond. Her body shifts from one foot to the other as she stares at the carpet, seeming to search for words.

I cannot allow him to witness me crying. I should be happy to see him.

The pain she is fighting to conceal is obvious and easy for Jim to detect. Unable to control his impulse to change into her black knight in shining armor, he grabs her hand and pulls her close to his side. The familiar aroma of her essence infiltrates his being. Deep inside his lungs, he holds the scent until his body cries out for him to breathe.

Stuck are the sounds in her throat. An awkward silence leaves Jim concerned about what he should do next.

Say hello, Lyric. That is easy. Her head instead nods a greeting while the words stay buried.

Upon noting the time, he pushes the elevator button and ushers her inside. Neither of them speaks. Like robots, they head to his office.

After unlocking the door, he leads her to a chair. Even though her head lowered, he can tell there are remnants of her hurt by a dried white trail down her cheeks. He kneels in front of her and gently lifts her chin. Without stopping to think or censor his words, he releases his heart's thoughts. "Please, baby, tell me what is wrong. I cannot stand to see you in this pain."

Lifting her head, she looks him in his eyes. "I am spiritually conflicted because I am with Johnny, but I want to be with you. I know better as a Christian and a wife. So, Doctor, is there a prescription that can cure my condition?" she pleads.

He considers her question as he stands and walks toward the window. Searching for his arsenal of quick-wit and usual responses, he digs to come up with something which will brighten the atmosphere. No matter how hard he thinks, he cannot conjure up a humorous reply. To hide his heart, he gives her some spiritual advice. "Lyric, follow your heart. For me, you are a married woman, and I must keep his commandments. It is who I am. I cannot covet my neighbor's wife."

The comment, although true, appears to lack empathy. His delivery is so cold and seems uncaring. It is as though they never shared any intimate moments. Peering into his face, she expects to find the man who once kissed her and made her legs buckle. To calm her nervous energy, she walks over to his desk, picks up an invitation and reads out loud the congratulatory paper. "Doctor of the Year, I am proud of you. The ceremony should be a nice affair for you and your date."

"Thank you, yes, it is quite an honor. I wish I could take you" but, He is interrupted by a knock on his door — The clock on the wall answers who is on the other side of the door. Several times he rubs the back of his neck while scrutinizing her and the rapping sound. Unable to delay the inevitable any longer, he shuffles to answer the door.

"Hello, Jim. I had a hard time finding your office," a deep female voice ring.

Fumbling with the door before addressing his guest, he steps aside. "Please, come on in Judith."

"I believe you both know each other," he stutters, while motioning her to sit down.

"Hello, Judith, thank you for the help you provided Jada last night."

"No problem. I was just doing my job. Is Jada better?"

Lyric twists a curl in her hair before speaking, "She is working to deal with the shock of the aftermath, but Jada is resilient."

As the ladies exchange small talk, Jim watches with anticipation. First, he crosses his arms then uncrosses them while shifting from one foot to the other. An effort is placed to appear engaged in their conversation even though Jim struggles to prevent his mind from drifting. For him, this encounter is as though his current girlfriend caught him with another woman. Inside, he searches for an explanation for both women.

"Lyric, Jim did not tell me you were going to be here. He just said he had something to ask me," Judith says while turning her attention to him.

"Well, I—I—Lyric just stopped by and I, I, I mean, we are catching up with one another."

While Jim stutters explaining, his body language resembles a nervous kitten in the room with a large dog. He is aware both women are studying his bizarre behavior. The blood rushes to his face. With each word he speaks, dry mouth occurs, causing him to swallow continuously.

As if an epiphany occurred, Lyric spins around. *He is going to take Judith to the recognition dinner.* After which, she trips on the leg of the furniture while rushing to the door. "Well, Officer Nelson and Dr. Maxey, I will let the two of you talk. I need to check on Nicke. My husband will expect me soon." Without making eye contact, she flounces out of the room.

As the door shuts, Jim turns to Judith with a perplexed stare. What the hell just happened? He wonders. Lyric is very upset.

Not sure if she or Jim are the culprits, Judith asks, "Did I interrupt something?"

"No, you did not. I ran into Lyric on the way to my office and invited her to talk about what is bothering her. I think she will be fine," he replies while focusing out the window. *Why did she remind me of Johnny? She is savvy enough to comprehend how much I care about her.*

Judith awaits Jim's mental return. *Am I the only one who notices the sparks which exist between those two when they are together?* "What did you want to speak to me about?"

Though he forces a smile, he avoids making eye contact with her before handing her a card. After reading, she glares at him with a questioning stare. "Congratulations on being named 'Doctor of the Year' but what does this have to do with me?"

Clearing his throat, he asks, "Will you do me the honor and accompany me to the function?" As he awaits her response, he bites his lower lip.

Smirking, she asks, "Are you asking me to be your date?"

"Yes," he responds, then wonders if her laugh is because of being nervous or if there is a hidden meaning represented. Still waiting, he shifts in his chair.

"Thank you for inviting me to attend the function. May I ask why you did not invite Lyric to be your guest?"

"Umm, she is a married woman," he says with confidence. "I am a single man, and you are an unmarried woman."

She slides to the edge of her chair, folds her hands and places them on his desk. "Can we be honest with each other?"

"Of course."

"There is a spark between you and Lyric. Everyone can see it. I like her, and I like you, but I do not want to be caught up in a triangle."

At first, he denies their attraction but decides there is no use pretending. Instead, his macho nature takes control. "I did not ask you to marry me. I asked if you would accompany me."

"True, but as I said, I like you both. I am not interested in causing any tension between us. I need to protect myself."

"Who are you protecting yourself from?"

She gulps before answering. "I am safeguarding me from you. Let's face it; you are an attractive man with a good job," she chuckles. "The only reason I have not been more forward before now is that I can discern the magnetic attraction that exists between you two. Why would I want a man who wants someone else?"

With his head down, he replies, "You are right, and I am sorry. I am attracted to her, but we decided as long as she is married, I will respect both her and her marriage. In the meantime, I need a beautiful and understanding date to take to this affair."

"In that case, I would love to attend but only as your friend and until you, and she settles whatever is going on." She pulls out a piece of paper and writes her address. As she hands him the information, she jokes, "You can cancel anytime up to two hours before the event." A big smile lightens her face as he watches her walk on her way to the door.

He grins, charmed by her 'get to the point personality.' "Thank you for understanding my dilemma."

She bats her eyes before turning. Her head is held high, and her shoulders erect as she prances out the door.

As he wipes his forehead and reclines in his chair, his eyes shut, signaling his brain to clear all thoughts of both Judith and Lyric.

CHAPTER THIRTEEN

PACKING DAY

When you leave this earth

Your possessions are packed away

You take nothing with you

Naked you enter

Naked you return

When you leave this earth

Your wealth remains to be divided

Broke you enter

Broke you return

When you leave this earth

Your education level is meaningless

Mindless you enter

Mindless you return

When you leave this earth

Earth to Earth

Ashes to Ashes

Dust to dust

You return

David pulls into the Home Depot parking lot while considering the items he needs to pickup. There are boxes, wrapping paper, tape, and bubble wrap required to pack Candy's home. Once David realizes he has about an hour and a half before he must meet Tianna who agreed to help him today, he slows his pace. He smiles as he reminisces about last night. The evening was light and full of jokes. He had no clue Tianna was such a comedian. Their exchange helped him to relax and changed his somber mood. As he completes his shopping, he cannot help but wonder if she shared anything with Jada. Oh, how he hopes she will also come over, but he believes this is doubtful.

After loading the supplies, he heads to Starbucks. The open sunroof grants the warm air a chance to rush through. His need for speed acts as a catalyst to transform his out-of-control life into manageable chaos until he whips into the drive-through window lane.

Soon he hears the cheerful voice of the clerk say, "May I take your order?"

For a moment, he hesitates while reading the menu before blurting out, "Three Grande, Cafe Mochas, please." Curious as to why he would buy one for Jada knowing the chances she will show up is very slim, he ponders while he waits. *I would rather pay for an extra drink and not need it than not to have one and need it. The power of positive thinking might change things.*

Once he secures their coffee, he punches the accelerator. To dismiss his thoughts, he blasts the radio. His speakers rattle from the bass line of Bruno Mars' fast thumping '24K Magic'. Though off-key, he sings, "I am a dangerous man with some money in my pocket, keep up. Why you mad? Fix your face." With one hand on the steering wheel, he uses the other to fist-pump in time with the music. The song ends as he parks in front of Candy's house. Even though he climbs two steps at a time, he manages to balance the tray without spilling a drop. While singing, he continues to unpack the automobile. The last of the items left to carry inside corresponds with the arrival of his car skidding into the driveway. Without stopping to think, he drops the boxes back in the trunk and dashes in that direction. Somber replaces the once jovial mood when he reaches the driver's door. Not wanting to show his dismay, his gait slows, and he plasters a fake smile on his face. "Hey, Tianna, thanks for coming over to help pack and to bring my car back."

"No, I am not Jada. You are stuck with me, so suck it up buttercup," she laughs.

The blood from his body rushes to his head, leaving a reddish hue to his face and ears. He labors to think of a smart comeback, but the emptiness inside blocks his wit. "A man can wish, can't he?"

"Aww, poor baby. He needs a hug," she states as she commandeers him with an unsuspecting tight wrap around his neck. Her breasts engulf his chest.

David's body stiffens, and his muscles become rigid. By gingerly pressing her arms down, he frees himself from Tianna's grip. Turning his head away, he attempts to disguise his shock. Not that he didn't enjoy her holding him, but her touch provided an unanticipated electrical current. The type which two friends should avoid unless they are heading to the bedroom. A constant struggle to dismiss the prickling sensations traveling down his spine occurs. Using his hands as a shield, he tries to hide his engorged genital.

She giggles while observing his maneuvers. "I see it has been a while since you and Jada had sex," she comments as she stares at his rather enormous erection.

"We are not intimate," he stutters while continuing to avoid her eyes.

"Man, you better call that girl and tell her if she does not hurry and give you some, you are going to end up with blue balls." After offering this unwanted advice, she covers her mouth and howls, so hard fat tears roll from her eyes. "Tianna, that is enough. What do you expect? I am a man, and yes, I can admit I am also a horny one. We are practicing celibacy," he proclaims as he gradually returns to a non-aroused state.

She wipes her face and lets out one last chuckle. "I will make sure she is aware you have an oversized package," she jokes.

His head shakes back and forth, but he does not bother to respond. From the trunk, he grabs the last load of boxes and heads for the house. This time, he moves at a slower pace, climbing each step one at a time.

She follows behind him. A diversion from the electricity they shared, she also found necessary. *Why did I not meet him before Candy or Jada? Neither of them realizes he is a great catch.*

They reach the living room, and she flops on the couch. "Look, David, I am sorry I got carried away. I apologize if I annoyed you."

The boxes slam to the floor before he turns to face her. "No need. I love your humor and your honesty. With you, I never worry about what you are thinking."

"On the subject of what I think, if you belonged to anyone else other than Jada, I would help you out with that little, I mean big, problem," Tianna snickers. "However, since you are her man, you are off limits. Now, go take a cold shower, and I will start packing."

Unable to control the urge to pay her back for embarrassing him, he retaliates. "Oh, don't worry. Within days of our meeting, you would buy me a ring and ask me to marry you."

"Yeah right, boy, you better stop smoking those drugs. They kill brain cells."

"No, for real—once I tell you I am remaining celibate until marriage, you would beg to become my wife. I can see you now on our second date wearing your bridal gown and veil to Red Lobster." This vision leaves him repeating her previous laughter spell.

"Ha, ha, hilarious." She throws a box at him. "Stop dreaming and start wrapping," she growls while also taking one for herself and taping the ends together. "Tell me what you want me to do because I do not plan to be over here all night," she demands.

"You are right. It is time to go to work. You can wrap up all the figurines, and I will begin in the bedroom." Still smiling, he looks to her for her agreement.

"I will but, only if you turn on the radio to inspire me."

"Yes ma'am, do you have a preference for the type of music you would like to hear?"

"Anything but slow love songs. I cannot take seeing a grown man cry."

Sure, this is an inference to his situation; he ignores her comment. He continues searching for an appropriate channel while his thoughts drift. "Tianna, does Jada know you are helping me pack?"

She sets the box she was putting together on the floor. "I thought you asked me not to tell her."

"I did say that, but knowing you, I figured you would tell her, anyway. In fact, I expected her to show up with you to help."

"You did, did you? Is that why you brought three cups of coffee?"

"Right, I forgot I picked up a latte for us," he states as he hands one to her and disregards her comment.

"You did not answer my question."

After taking a sip, he replies, "I just got an extra one"--

She interrupts. "In case Jada showed up. Admit it. Look, you two are getting on my nerves. I wish you would talk to each other."

"I tried, but she will not return my calls. One time she even had her henchman, or should I say woman, screening and speaking for her," he chuckles.

"Well, turn up the music and let's make it happen, Captain. I got places to go and people to see," she touts as she torpedoes another box at him.

He ducks and avoids the collision. "Yes, I will start right away," he smirks while sticking his tongue out at Tianna.

Once he leaves the room, she shouts, "I will be right back. I need something out of my car." *These two are going to talk. I am going to see to that*, she thinks as she dials Jada's number. "Hey girl, what are you doing?"

"I am just leaving your sister's house. Micah and I are going out to eat. You are welcome to join us."

"I would love to spend some time with my nephew, but I need a ride."

"Where are you?" she asks.

"I am helping a friend. The address is 1268 Michigan Avenue in Lewisville. It is about ten minutes from Tasha."

"All right, I am on my way. Please be ready."

"Okay," Tianna says and ends the call. Pacing, she awaits Jada's arrival. All the while, she practices what she is going to say once she arrives. Something inside her believes Jada is going to be upset. Time seems to creep until she spots her driving down the street.

After parking, Jada hollers from the window. "Let's go." A cursory review of the neighborhood reveals David's car parked in the driveway. Jada's eyes bulged as she flashed a quick glare toward Tianna, then back to the vehicle.

"Hey Micah, how is my favorite nephew?" Tianna asks, trying to avoid his mother's scowl. The two embrace after Micah opens his door.

"Hi," he replies, looking at the floor. "Auntie, did you know my Grand-pap died?"

The ladies' eyes meet and they lock on them like two bulls' horns. It is as though time stops and everyone freezes in place.

"Yes, I know, and I am so sorry you have to experience death," she says.

"Is that David's car?" Jada asks while pointing.

An instant sunlight beam emerges across the boy's face. "Our David," he asks of his mother.

"Yes, it is. Why don't you run upstairs and speak to David?" Tianna replies while stepping out of his way.

Despite Jada's hollering for him to stop, he jumps out and trots off.

Jada exits and slams her door but not before rolling her eyes at her friend.

"Aww Mom, please. I just want to say hi. I will come right back. I promise."

Waving him Micah permission, he speeds up to the house. After he is gone, she whips around to face Tianna. With her hands propped on her hips, Jada raises her voice. "Why did you not tell me you were with David?" she demands.

"Calm down. That man has been calling you, and you refuse to return his calls. I think you owe him a chance to explain. Things may not be what you think." Tianna walks over and reaches to put her arm around Jada.

Unable to control herself, Jada slaps it away. "Why would you do this to me? Whose house is this, anyway?"

"This is Candy's house. He asked me to help him pack up her things."

Once revealed to Jada, the owner, she sprints back to her vehicle and snatches the door open. "Are you serious? You had me come to *her* house." With her mouth curved and her eyebrows touching, her eyes seem to emanate flames. "How could you?" she screams. "Go get my son."

"You are overreacting," Tianna says while strolling to the driver's side. "I know you have been through a lot, and I am sorry, but other people are also suffering. Stop thinking about yourself long enough to see you are not the only one in pain."

Jada grips the steering wheel with both hands. Still struggling to resist the anger that threatens to erupt, her breathing speeds up as tears roll from her eyes. "This is just like you to fix my life. You need to concentrate on your world and stay out of mine. Get your own man."

These words ring in Tianna's ears as though someone pulled the fire alarm. Her mouth drops open. By Tianna being rendered temporarily speechless, a wave of guilt engulfs Jada for throwing such a low blow.

"I am sorry T. I had no right to say that." The tension in Jada's face melts, and her voice lowers.

While gripping her stomach, Tianna whispers, "I will send Micah out. I was only trying to help." Unable to say anything else, she scuffles to the house with her head lowered, oblivious to the apology.

Jada opens the door and tries to catch up to Tianna. If only she could push the delete button and erase her last statements. "Come on T, wait up."

Just as Tianna is about to enter the door, Micah and David meet her. Tianna stops to look into David's eyes for him to rescue her.

Holding Micah's hand, he looks straight past her and spots Jada skidding to a complete stop. The look on her face is as though she is looking at a ghost.

David passes the child's hand to Tianna and steps around them. At that moment, his only thought is to comfort and hold his woman. His arms encircle her. Surprised but yet unfazed by the stiff tension her body emanates, he pulls her closer and squeezes a fraction tighter until she relaxes. "We need to talk."

"I am not going inside that woman's house," she rattles as she wiggles free from his grip.

"Micah and I are going to McDonald's," Tianna announces.

"Yea, mommy, is it okay? Please, please," he begs.

"Sure, you can go."

David turns from Jada and winks. Through his excitement, he makes sure Tianna realizes he recognizes her intervention.

"Perhaps we can go around the corner to the diner," he requests of the woman he was so eager to see.

With her head lowered, she nods her agreement.

In a low whispered voice, Tianna announces, "I need to gather my purse and keys from the house."

"Sure, please pull the door closed," he relays while interlocking his arm in Jada's and leading her to his car. As he opens the door for Jada, he studies her face, trying to ascertain her mood. Replacing the gleam he once admired is a dull emptiness. She appears lost in her thoughts. Although her body is here with him, her mind is distant and detached. After helping her inside, he enters, searching for the words to say to restore the confident and strong woman from the shell occupying the seat beside him. He gulps before speaking in a deep but deliberate tone. A tinge of helplessness tries to raise its ugly head, but he forces the negative voice to remain silent. "Jada, I am sorry for the distressing and disturbing experiences you are forced to deal with."

"Me too," she responds while staring out the window. The reply lacks voice inflection as well as conveys her acceptance of remaining cold and numb. She wiggles in her seat with her arms folded across her chest.

There was hope before. Now he is unsure if he will reach her. His eyes drift off the road and shift toward her. About five minutes passed without them speaking. Both are inside their heads, visiting with their thoughts. David wants to bring their issues out, but searches for the best approach to address the oversized elephant separating the two of them.

Now pulling into the diner's parking lot, he parks and turns the engine off. Turning to face her, he decides instead of going into the restaurant; their conversation should take place out here. "Jada, I did not know Candy was coming to my house. Without my knowledge or consent, she showed up."

Instantly, he can see the anger ignite in her system that she no longer can contain. Her head snaps around. "Then why was she naked and in your bed?" she asks in an accusatory tone.

"Earlier that day, after visiting with your mother, I ran into Candy on the elevator. I told her I was proposing to you. She also knew I was on my way to the mall to pick up your ring."

What? Her eyes buck, and her head bounces back. With her hand, she covers her mouth, hoping to conceal the dichotomy of shock and poise. *Lord, please help me believe him.*

"My assumption is, she had plans of trying to seduce me." He swallows as he continues. "While I was shopping, I assume she used a duplicate key to enter my house. On the way, I stopped by the grocery store for some things to make breakfast for you. At some point, Charles showed up. I do not know if he thought she was you or why he killed her." David drops his head. The grief he suspends crashes on top of him. "So, you see, it was not your fault. It was mine. I knew she would do whatever she had to do to prevent us from being a couple. Especially since she confessed to me she was still in love with me." The place in his mind storing his worries is full to the brim like a glass of water. An additional drop will cause it to overflow. He stops talking and rubs his hands across his knees. The lump that forms in his throat, he swallows in search of relief.

"No David, you cannot blame yourself. I brought you into my life. It is because of me; Candy died. Now you are left to assemble the pieces." *Tianna was right. So consumed with myself, I neglected even to consider the hell anyone else is going through.* Unlike David, she cannot stop the tears from rolling. She digs into her purse looking for a tissue. After blowing her nose, she turns and takes a long, hard stare at him. "In the hospital, I found a box gift-wrapped. We, I mean, I thought it might be an—an—an-an-an engagement ring," she stutters. After collecting herself, she continues. "So, I rushed to your house. When I arrived, I walked into a loud blast, and both Candy and Charles were dead. The next thing I can remember is flashing lights everywhere and all kinds of uproar." She closes her eyes and sucks in the air-conditioner's blustery chill. After expelling it from her lungs, she prepares to ask what she believes will be a life-altering question. "What if you had found her naked in your bed? Would you have been able to resist her?"

Deep into her eyes, he gazes. Truth is his gateway to building her trust. "I am not sure. Once she told me she loved me, I was uncertain if I should propose to you or not. I needed to make sure that what I felt for you was real."

Upon hearing him confess his doubt, her heart shatters into pieces. The words burn as though someone threw gasoline on her and lit a match. Powerless to think of an appropriate response, she engages the door handle. "Perhaps we should go inside and grab a bite to eat. Tianna will return with Micah soon."

As the couple walks inside, Jada detects a distance between them, which is wide enough for a tractor-trailer to fit through, both figuratively and bodily. Only going through the motions, he stands stiff and erect and waits for service. To her, his body appears lifeless and lacks any resemblance to happiness and enjoyment. The energy he emits reeks of physical suffering and discomfort. "Do you prefer a booth or a table?" the hostess asked.

"We would like that section in the corner," David says, pointing.

Jada slides inside. Her emotional seesaw lies still on the ground; the silence amplifies the weight of her unspoken feelings. She struggles with the desire to kick and push herself up to at least the midpoint, where she could teeter, but she finds herself unable to do so.

The server hands Jada a menu, then places the other one on the table. "May I get you something to drink?" she asks.

Instead of taking his rightful seat, David slides next to Jada and returns the other menu. "Thanks, but we can share."

The invasion, though she craves it, causes her to scoot over and lean forward. "I would just like a cup of coffee with cream, please."

"And I will have a glass of ice water with a lemon."

"I got it. I'll be back with your drinks and will leave this menu in case you wish to order some food later," says the server.

Aware of the distance between them, he places his arm around her waist and gently pulls her closer to him. The overflow from his heart spills from his mouth. "I have missed you, young lady. Please never shut me out again. We can talk about anything, even if that something hurts," he tells her.

Crossing her arms and resting them on p of the table, she swallows before responding. "I am sorry I did not return your calls. I needed time to process everything that was happening."

"Do you mean you were trying to determine if Candy and I were physically involved?" he asks, but in a way that is more telling her that this is what she did instead of asking.

"Okay, I will admit my first thoughts were negative." At the urging of her mind, she continues their conversation. "After all, what would you think if a naked man was in my bed?"

"I suppose I would have drawn the same conclusion. But I would have, at the very least, given you a chance to explain."

She faces him with the corner of her mouth raised. "Right, sure you would've."

"May I get you anything else?" the server asks, peering over her spectacles?

Without looking away from Jada, David says, "No that will be all for now." Once they are alone again, he addresses her skepticism. "I just gave you an example of how I am willing to bare my heart out to you—even when doing so could jeopardize our relationship."

Agreeing, Jada's head shakes as she cannot address with words. The illustration she views as his way of saying he is still in love with Candy. She stirs her coffee, searching through the seeping steam circulating above for a place to hide. *Well, at least he is man enough to acknowledge he is not ready to marry me.*

"When I got back to my house and saw the police, I did not know what to think. It was not until I heard killed was a man and a woman that I feared someone took you from me." Tears well up in his eyes, but he blinks and contains them. "Once I found out Candy was dead and not you, I thanked God. Although I am ashamed to admit this, she lost her life for trying to manipulate me. The mere thought of this could have been you woke me up." Facing her, he cups both her hands inside his. No longer able to keep his tears contained, large droplets roll down his cheeks and on their hands. Biting his lip, he says, "When I thought he killed you, I realized the depth of the love I have for you. Today, I understood what I felt for Candy had no substance and it was a genuine pity. I did not want to be another man to abuse her again."

Touched by his moving speech, she buries her face in his chest. Her shoulders tremble and move uncontrollably up and down. Unable to stifle her desolate sobs, her wounds broadcast the sound of an ocean wave crashing into a boulder. *He really does love me. Even after everything he has endured, he still loves me.*

The overweight server returns to the table sporting a chrisom red face. "Is everything all right? May I help in any way?"

While consoling Jada, David lifts his head, revealing his puffy eyes. "Yes, you can pray for us."

"Father God," she began. "You said in your word when two or three are gathered in your name; there you will also be. Please help this couple with whatever their needs are. You and only you can fix what they are battling. I ask for their strength to accept your will, in Jesus' name. Amen." After concluding, she pats him on his arm and struts away.

Thrilled, he threw his head back and stared up as though peering through the roof into the sky. "Thank you, Lord."

Although Jada's face remains hidden, she did participate. Instead of bringing relief as it had for David, the invocation makes her weepier. The dam inside her breaks for Candy, Charles, David, her mother, and herself. Ashamed because people in the restaurant are witnessing her emotional breakdown, she buries her face deeper to hide her pain and identity. The fear of her stepfather ever hurting her again spills, then soaks through his shirt. What did help, though, was that this time provided her with a chance to relieve her pinned-up frustration and torment. On the other hand, what sparked joy is that they reconciled. Having him hold her restores the security and safety she first felt when he promised to protect her. His unconditional love is cleansing her soul.

At a snail's pace, her head raises. After securing a napkin, she wipes her face, then blows her nose. Her hands tremble as she sips the lukewarm coffee. Still unwilling to look up or around, she stays focused on the contents of her cup.

With a huge smile, the server bops back to their table. She hands David the check marked paid-in-full. There is a smiley face, then the words, 'God Bless.' With her voice rising to a higher octave, she relays, "Sir, the couple sitting across from you paid your bill and left me twenty bucks. They asked me to tell you two that God can do anything, but fail." A bright smile adorns her face. "Shall I refill your coffee? This one is on me. I can take it from my generous tip," she jokes.

Without looking up, Jada nods and slides her cup nearer. *Everyone must have seen or heard me. Get it together, Jada. You are in public.* "How embarrassing," she mumbles, "for strangers to see me so out of control."

David shields her face with his hand. Also, he drops another twenty onto the top of the table. "Thank you, and this payment is from us to you. For your kindness and compassion, you earned this and more."

Still grinning, the server tells him, "There is no charge for prayer. God knows what we need before we ask. This morning, my son asked me for twenty dollars to buy books from his book fair. I did not have anything extra, so I told him to try me tomorrow." She stretches open the money and proudly displays it in his face. "But God, won't he, do it?" she exclaims! After winking, she spins on her heels as if her heart is beating in time to a joyous song and dances to the booth behind them. Displaying a Cheshire grin exposing almost all her white teeth, she boisterously states to a gentleman. "Good evening, sir. May I get something for you to drink?"

Jada's phone rings. She rummages through her purse until she locates the distraction needed. "Hello, Tianna. We are just finishing and can meet you back at the house in about five minutes," she stutters.

Reaching for the cell, David interrupts. "Is it alright if I speak with her?" he asks.

She hands the phone to him, sits up straight and stares into his mouth while wondering why.

"Hey, thank you for agreeing to help pack Candy's things, but I am going to let the moving company handle the rest." He chuckles at her response. "That is a wonderful idea, but Jada will have to approve." Again, he finds humor in something she says. Only this time, he laughs louder and longer. "Thanks. You have a pleasant night as well." He laughs as he hands her back the phone.

Perplexed by the one-sided conversation she overheard, she seeks clarity. "T, what is it I have to give my approval for?"

"So, you are saying Micah wants to go to the movies? Are you sure it is him and not you, Miss Cupid?" Jada asks with sarcasm.

More alone time, David rejoices in his head. The same thrill of riding a roller coaster consumes him. Then, as quickly as his excitement came, it diminished. *We cannot go to my house. The memories of what happened are too fresh for both of us. I guess we will have to spend the night in a hotel.*

Now Jada chuckles. "I will pick him up in the morning. Thank you, I shall. You also have a good night." After hanging up, she shakes her head. "I see our matchmaker is at work again."

He stands and reaches for her hand. "Hold on for a second," he says as he takes his wallet out. He thumbs through his money, then pulls out a crisp one-hundred-dollar bill. He lays it on the table. On the clean napkin, he writes a note. 'Acts of kindness are to be shared. May God Bless you and your son'.

David suggests they stay at her apartment.

A sense of relief followed by a massive smile spans Jada's face. "Brilliant suggestion," she exclaims.

Slightly speeding, David enters the highway, heading away from Candy's house. A split moment decision leads him to want to take advantage of the weather, music and their time of being together again. He turns towards DFW airport to the lookout point where he can park, and they can gaze at the planes leaving and landing. *I know I love this woman. No other woman has ever made me feel like a kid again, exploring the world for the first time. It also does not hurt that her beauty either inside and out hypnotizes me so all I want to do is be with her. I wonder if women know the power they possess when a man is in love with them.*

CHAPTER FOURTEEN

SEARCHING FOR SOMETHING LOST

Please don't leave me
I know I did you wrong
I'm searching for you
Please ... you can't be gone

Please don't let our love be lost
I was stupid to hurt you
I can't pay this cost
But I guess it's too late
No need to negotiate
I'm searching for
Something lost

The elevator rocks as it stops on the floor to Nicke's room, and Lyric steps off. From her mind, she attempts to erase the thoughts of Jim and Judith. The scene she witnessed in Jim's office she tucks away for a later time. One time when she is alone and will not have to explain her hurt to anyone. On to visit Nicke, she tells herself while gently opening the door.

Even though she is engrossed in her thoughts, Lyric greets Nicke with a grin.

Nicke threw a hand up and says, "I knew I would see you soon."

"How did you know that, Miss Thing?" Lyric taunts in jest.

"Your boyfriend just left. Whenever he is near, you are not far behind."

Not possessing the strength to discuss Jim, Lyric changes the subject. "How are you today?"

"I went to physical therapy, and they say my right side is getting stronger. Dr. Maxey thinks I may go home in a few weeks."

"That is great news. Keep working hard so you can leave this place," Lyric replies. Her words are upbeat even though Lyric's inner self-fails to agree with the positive attitude.

Nicke easily spots the ambiguous way Lyric speaks as compared to her face and body language. The lack of luster in her eyes and her stiff posture are signals.

Afraid that Nicke's inspection may evoke unwanted questions, Lyric offers a distraction. "Would you like a glass of cold water?" Without getting an answer, Lyric pours some into the cup. What she did not count on is the way her hands shake, causing her to overfill and spill water on the tray. In the bathroom, she snatches a handful of paper towels and returns to sop up the spill. While cleaning up the mess, Lyric knocks the television remote to the floor. "Why am I so clumsy?" she rattles. "I suppose I am just tired. I got up early this morning and met Jada and Tianna at your house. I brought the paperwork with me." Fast-talking, she works to control the conversation to prevent any interjection about Jim. "Are you ready to talk about making the burial arrangements for Charles?" While reaching under the chair near her purse, her hand swings back and forth as she tries to locate her shoulder satchel containing Charles's will and life insurance policy. Not able to touch what she searches for, she turns her head and looks down, trying to locate the bag. Once she scanned the entire room, she sat back. There is sweat forming on her nose and forehead. Upon retracing her steps, she remembers having it in Jim's office. The mystery of where the documents are hiding is now solved, though she would rather not tell Nicke. After pausing, she made up an excuse. "I guess I left the information in my car."

"No problem. My attorney will not be here until tomorrow afternoon. However, today we must allow a mortician to pick up his body."

Learning there is additional time, Lyric is relieved. *I will call Jim after I leave and ask him to drop my bag in her room.* "Is there a preference for which company you want to use?"

With her head tilted, Nicke replies. "No, but I need to telephone his mother and advise her that, according per Charles' instructions, he requested to be cremated. If she wants a service, she can work with the undertaker."

"I do not think it is a good idea for you to speak with her because she is sure to say something stupid. Maybe I can call her for you."

"No Lyric, this is something I should handle. All I need you to do is dial Viola's number."

Upon completing her request, Lyric hands her the phone with the speaker feature engaged.

"Mrs. Williams, this is Nicke." Taking a deep breath, she continues. "I would like to express my condolences to you and your family for the death of your son."

With vigor, Mrs. Williams shouts, "I do not need or want your sympathy! You and that no-good daughter of yours is the reason he is dead. Your lies killed him just as though you two pulled the trigger."

"Listen," Nicke begins. "I am only calling to advise you Charles requested a cremation. If you are interested in setting up a memorial service, please let me know. Otherwise, I will grant his request."

"Don't you dare burn him like he is a hog! I will sue you and then tell the police to throw your ass in jail. A long time ago, I told him not to marry you. I wished he had listened to me. I knew you were trouble."

Unfazed by her threats, Nicke continues. "I guess I will take your response to mean you are not inclined to arrange any burial service. So, I will tell the funeral home to send you his ashes. Again, I am sorry for your loss." Nicke ends the call, disconnecting before she can hurl any additional insults. After powering down the phone, she hands it to Lyric. "Please put this back in the drawer."

Amazed by the restraint she showed, Lyric watches in disbelief. How in the world did Nicke not show any emotions? Perhaps earlier she took a sedative, she resolved. The graceful way she handled his mother still baffles her. To allow Mrs. Williams to ridicule both her and Jada and not retaliate assures Lyric that Nicke accepts her husband's death. Still, she must ask. "Wow, how are you capable of being so composed?"

"Girl, the worst thing you can do is fight ignorance with ignorance. I feel bad for her because she loves her son. There is no sense in me being upset with her. She has always felt he should not have married me. The truth is, she is correct. I wish I never met him." Nicke turns her head away.

"I guess you are right, but I must take my hat off to you. I almost responded with some choice words."

"I'm so glad you restrained yourself. Now, will you please call a mortuary? Ask them if they can come here as soon as possible."

After securing a number for Brown's Funeral Home, Lyric calls and explains the situation. They confirm a representative will be by the hospital within the next hour to secure her signature, an assignment of benefits, and to pick up the body. "Well, that is done. Is there anything else I can do for you?" Lyric asks.

Through the window, Nicke stares at the clouds while answering by shaking her head no. "I will need a nap before they arrive."

"Okay, you rest, and I will be back shortly." She kisses her before leaving.

Walking down the hall, Lyric prays for her friend. Each step is as though she is sinking into quicksand. Rather than inviting Jim, she elects to eat alone. The fresh image of him and Judith is a poignant reminder he is a single man and able to date any woman he chooses. *Why did Johnny have to come home? He should have stayed in New York with Donna and his son. While Johnny was away, Jim was willing to wait for me to get divorced. Now, he is moving on with his life.* She pushes the elevator button and leans with her back pressed against the wall. With her eyes closed, Lyric listens to the pulley system, motor, and the hang ropes rushing to answer her summons. As the door squeaks open, she pulls herself up and prepares to step inside. From the corner of her eye, she glimpses a familiar face. She jumps back. "Johnny, what are you doing here?" she stutters.

"I was missing my wife, so I came to be with you," he says as he grabs her hand.

Her eyes roll to the back of her head as she yanks out of his grip. "You know, and I know that is a bunch of bull. You had months to miss me. Why now?"

"What floor do you want?"

"Push one. I am on my way to the cafeteria. I am unsure where you are going. 'Lobby' is marked as the exit. If you head there, you can find your way to the airport and back to Donna." Awaiting his comeback, Lyric stares into his eyes as her nose flares.

Unable to penetrate her anger, he becomes frustrated. *Until now, she has never been this upset with me. Everything I say or do seems to irritate her. I think she hates me.* "If you do not mind, I would like to accompany you, unless you are expecting someone else to join you."

The innuendo Johnny spouts scratches her nerves like chalk on a board. Lyric's head whips around revealing her face contoured in an all-consuming fury. Her mouth quivers and drools as she slurs her words. "Look, please stop playing with me. I am not meeting anyone. I am going to eat while Nicke takes a nap. This jealous act of yours is getting old. You created a bastard child outside of our marriage." Once she hears herself, she wishes she could take back her last sentence. It is unfair of her to refer to his son in those terms. He is an innocent victim. Her eyebrows begin to lower back in place, and her shoulders droop. Lyric steps off the elevator, making her way to the eating area.

Without responding, Johnny walks beside her, careful not to get too close. What can he do or say to win his wife back? he wonders?

The light flowery smell emanating from her body penetrates his nostrils. The seductive scent reminds him of when they made love. He silently inhales as a half-smile appears on his face. To steal a quick glance, he slows and admires her apple-shaped butt, which bounces as she walks. The tight jeans she wears gathers around her small waist and accenting her bowed legs. The clicking of her heels adds a rhythm to the flouncing movement of her steps. An unknown man passes by, captive by her beauty. Johnny is amused as he observes the gentleman walking backward and staring at her behind. Their eyes locked. The stranger shakes his head and whispers "whew." They nod to each other using the universal male sign language, which says she is not only a showstopper but is also sexy.

No wonder the doctor wants my wife. She is breathtaking both inside and out.

They step up to the grill, and Lyric orders a club sandwich, securing a tray, and slides it down the rack. A lift of the spout allows the diluted espresso to fill her cup.

After pouring his coffee, Johnny steps in front of her and pays.

In the back of the room, she locates a table. On route, she remembers this is the same place she and Jim would usually sit. She smiles at herself.

"Here you are ma'am," Johnny states while pulling her chair out.

"Thank you," she mumbled. After a quick prayer, she starts to eat her sandwich.

He fumbles with the sugar package as he pours it into the mug. Not sure what to say to Lyric, Johnny fidgets while considering several starting points. Left with no other choice, he decides to accept responsibility for his actions. "Lyric, I just want you to realize how much I love you and how I did not mean to hurt you. She means nothing to me. I am just trying to do right by my son. He is innocent in the mess I created." Not looking up, he stirs his additional cream in his cup to avoid making eye contact. "I do not want a divorce. I want my wife."

There is a real pain in his voice, but Lyric continues eating. A part of her feels sorry for him, but she refuses to drop her guard. Her mouth wants to say what her mind is thinking, *what's love got to do with it*. However, she decides it is best to allow him to share his feelings without interruption.

"If you consider giving me another chance, I will seek the counseling I need. Perhaps they can tell me why I keep making the same mistakes. I have done some serious soul-searching and realize I am doing to you what my father did to my mother." With tears in his eyes, he finds the strength to investigate her face. "My cheating was never about you but had to do with my insecurities."

"What are you insecure about?"

"I never felt like you required me in your life. You are so independent and capable of caring for yourself. Why would you want me?"

"Did it ever occur to you that all I wanted was love and respect from you?"

Repositioning himself in the chair, he continues. "I could not tell because I was so selfishly considering only my needs. I wanted to be special to you, but it seemed like Nicke, Tianna, Tasha, and everyone else got your energy and time."

"So, are you telling me your affair is my fault?"

"No, honey, this is all on me. I am just trying to share my thoughts. I am not justifying them or claiming they are right. When I met Donna, she financially needed me and wanted my companionship. She made it clear I mattered to her."

"Then sign the divorce papers and go back to where you are valued," Lyric snaps.

"She cares for me, but you are the woman who loves me. I mistook her need for love. I completely understand now. Yes, I did matter to you. The problem is, I wanted you to make me whole. Now I know I must be important to myself. There are things in my past I buried." After surveying the room, he leans in closer. Whispering he confesses to Lyric, "I was both sexually and physically abused as a child. I have told no one."

Lyric swallows and then chokes on her coffee. The sound of her spitting and coughing alerts other guests. They are staring as she struggles to exercise a more polished behavior. *Did he say he was molested?* After processing his admission and regrouping, she responds. "I am very sorry this happened to you. I wish you had told me this before now."

"Why? What difference would it have made for you to know?"

Looking around and searching for an answer, her eyes land on Jim's as he enters the cafeteria.

Without breaking contact, he heads toward her. The moment he spots Johnny; he halts and starts walking backwards away from them but maintains his connection.

No longer is Lyric engrossed in her husband's conversation. Although she tries to stay engaged, she follows Jim's every move. Lyric stutters, "Because I would have suggested for you to seek professional help earlier."

"What is important is that I get the help I need. Will you please stand by me," Johnny begs of Lyric?

"You are right," she responds to the first part but does not answer his question.

The immediate notice of her inattention causes him to investigate. He turns to follow her eyes. Five feet in front of him is Nicke's doctor, Jim Maxey. The blood rushes to his head as his heart thumps at speeds capable of ejecting it from his chest. There is a sheen of sweat on his forehead.

In tune with his awareness of her friend's presence, Lyric returns her attention to her husband. To regain her composure, she sips from her cup.

In a jealous rant, he shouts. "Do you love him?"

The disregard he shows for their privacy causes her to flip her head around to see if anyone else heard his outburst. "Calm down; we are in public."

In a much lower voice, he repeats his question. "Do you love him?"

Without stopping to consider, her heart responds, "I think I do."

Inside his head, her answer replays several times over. *How could she love a man she just met?* From a place of defeat, he stands and pushes the table. His eyes blaze with a fury capable of shooting daggers at both of them as he stomps away.

Uncertain of whether she should run behind him, Lyric decides to let him go. After all, he cheated twice. "What does he expect from me? Am I supposed to allow him to disrespect me continually and each time take him back? "

Lyric is aware that Jim observed the heated exchange. She looks up in time to see him staring at her. Though she wants to invite him to join her, she is unsure if Johnny left the hospital or not. Perhaps Johnny will return and take his anger out on the man he views as his competition. Especially, armed with the knowledge of the role the doctor has in her life. Based on this, her necessary decision is made. She twists her hair around her finger. Somehow inside, she must swallow down the nagging sense of spiritual conviction. *I am still somebody's wife, and I should honor my vows until and when this changes.* This self-revelation gives her the strength and courage to leave without approaching him. While sashaying away, she hopes he is watching. To be sure, she adds an extra twisting motion to her hips as she glides out the door.

Jim is captivated and drawn to her beauty and grace. Reminiscent of the night she spent at his house, his thoughts are sexual and passionate. A daydream of being with her forever consumes him until his conscience reminds him, she is a married woman. He subdues the temptation that threatens to make him jump from his seat, run after her, and beg her to make love to him. *This woman is driving me out of my mind. I have never wanted someone as much as I want her.* "Lord, please help me," he mumbles before biting into his hamburger.

Like him, Lyric is also sorting through her aspirations. On route to Nicke's room, she wishes Jim had followed. Although she rationalizes it is best, he did not.

Quietly, Lyric enters as Nicke is speaking with an unknown older gentleman that reminds Lyric of her grandfather. From their conversation, she gathers he is from the Funeral Home.

As Lyric sits down, she spots her briefcase. Her eyes rush up towards Nicke. With shaky hands, she opens the case. Jim must have brought this from his office. *I am sure Nicke is going to have something smart to say.* While Nicke signs the final paperwork, Lyric locates the will, insurance policy, and the other pertinent forms.

"Lyric, this is Simon Kirkpatrick. Would you mind asking the nurse if she will please make a copy of Charles' power of attorney? I need to provide him with one."

"Sure, I will be right back."

Propped up by his walking cane, Nicke turns back in time to catch Simon with his mouth open, gawking, as Lyric leaves the room. "Is she a relative?" he asks using a somber tone.

"Lyric? No, she is my best friend and like a sister to me."

"Wow! She is quite attractive. I am surprised her husband would allow her to go anywhere without him," Simon says while wearing a grin befitting of a devil in disguise.

Not amused by his attempt to extort information, Nicke shares a side-eyed glance while twisting her mouth to show her disapproval.

Simon fumbles with the paperwork then stammers, as his false teeth snap in and out. "When Lyric returns, I will secure your husband's remains from the morgue. Are you sure you want the cremation without any memorial service?"

"Yes, I am certain," Nicke says as her voice starts to crack. How insensitive this must seem to Mr. Kirkpatrick, but she brushes off what Simon may think. *If he knew Charles had molested my child and killed an innocent woman, he would understand why I cannot celebrate his life. I do not care how Simon perceives my actions. He probably would react the same way if he were in my shoes.* The door opens, and Lyric returns with the requested document. "Here you are Mr. Kirkpatrick, a copy of the POA."

"Thank you, Ms. Lyric," he states while licking his lips and drooling.

Repulsed by his apparent advances, Lyric steps back as her forehead wrinkles and portrays her disdain. *Please tell me this fool is not trying to flirt with me, looking like he is six months pregnant.* Without acknowledging his gestures, she performs an abrupt spin around and sits on the opposite side of the room. She pretends to be preoccupied with reading a magazine.

Simon chuckles as he stuffs all the necessary papers in a folder, then jams it into his disheveled briefcase. "Thank you for your business, and again, I am sorry for your loss," he reiterates before rushing out.

Once the door shuts, both the ladies laugh. Neither can believe how obnoxious his behavior was toward Lyric.

"Oh well, if things do not work out between you and Johnny or you and Dr. Maxey, Simon is definitely interested," Nicke jokes.

"Thanks, but I will pass. Simon is old enough to be my grandfather," she says.

The comment provides the opening for Nicke. "My doctor dropped your case off, adding you left it in his office on your way to visit me earlier," she taunts.

"Oh, I thought it was in my car. I forgot I had it with me when I, I," she stutters searching for a plausible explanation. "I bumped into him in the hallway." She waits before continuing. "I wanted to see how much longer you were going to be in the hospital." To avoid Nicke's piercing eyes, Lyric returns to thumbing through her reading material.

"Look, Lyric, you do not owe me any explanations. What you do is none of my business. I understand you do not want or need my opinion," she says.

"Stop trying to make me feel guilty. I just do not want to saddle you with my problems."

"Oh, I see."

"You see what?"

"I see. You are all involved in my world but want me to stay out of yours."

"All right, Nicke you win. What do you want to know?" She asks as she moves and sits on the bed. In the crevices of her heart, she wished for this opportunity as it provides a chance to share with the one person which knows her inside and out.

"Just tell me all the juicy stuff," she jeers. "That way, I do not have to think about my problems. Let me vicariously live my life through yours."

"Guess who came by the hospital today?" Lyric asks.

Nicke concedes to asking. "Who?"

At first, Lyric is going to tell her about Johnny. Instead, she answers, "Judith."

The pressed button moves the head of Nicke's bed to an upright position. From her eyes, the gleam disappears. "Is Jada, okay?"

Visibly noticing how shaken Nicke is, she rushes to assure Nicke that her daughter is okay. Quickly, she explains Jim asked Officer Nelson to attend his recognition ceremony as his guest.

"Are you saying he asked her out on a date? No wonder you went to his office. What kind of player is he? I thought he wanted you."

"He does. I mean, I guess he asked her because he did not want to interfere in my marriage. I think because Johnny came home, he does not believe I am going to divorce him."

"Well, are you?"

"Yes, I am, and after today I am sure he will sign the documents to make it official."

Raising the bed higher, Nicke scoots up. "What happened?"

"Johnny showed up here."

"When? I did not see him."

"On my way to the cafeteria, my husband met me at the elevator. He claimed he missed his wife." Further, she also relays the encounter between the two men. At last, sharing his question and how her reply caused him to explode.

With her cupped hand, Nicke covers her lips. "No girl, how did you answer?"

Lyric hangs her head while speaking. "I told him I think I am in love with your doctor. After he heard this, he shoved the table and stormed out."

"What did Jim say?"

"Nothing. He could tell from a distance that we were arguing, but what we said, he could not hear."

"Oh well, I guess Simon does not warrant a chance. I am sure this will crush him." A loud laugh tickles Nicke to the point she doubles over. "Whoop! Whoop!"

Falling across Nicke's body, Lyric also partakes in the laughing fit. The rapid exercising of her diaphragm makes Lyric's stomach hurt.

Laughter is the stress reliever Lyric needed as she struggles to catch her breath. This session is a reminder of all the fun they once shared before Nicke's hospitalization and Lyric finding out about Johnny's infidelity. If for only a few minutes, she can forget and enjoy the sisterhood bond, which continues to remain in both good and bad times. This shared moment is a signal that Lyric's heart is on the move to a speedy recovery.

CHAPTER FIFTEEN

YOU DID NOT SAY GOODBYE

Why did you leave without a word

Didn't you care what I preferred

Couldn't you have stopped long enough to say

That you were leaving me today

Did you even care what I would feel

Or

Was this a selfish move and no big deal

You did not even bother to say goodbye

You just decided what the hell

It was your time to die

Tianna and Micah ride in silence. Over dinner, neither of them had much to say. All they are clear on is that they are together while Jada and David try to rekindle their relationship.

"Since we did not eat dessert, would you like to go buy an ice cream cone?"

Chin wobbling, Micah shakes his head no.

"Aww honey, what is the matter?"

The tears burst through like water from a dam break, spilling down his innocent face. His shoulders move up and down. The only sound is him sniffling as he buries his face in his hands.

Once Tianna can stop in a shopping center and park her car, she rushes to the passenger side. A couple of quick tugs opens the door and loosens his seatbelt. Her arms pull him to her chest, and she rubs his back to soothe him. "Little man, everything is going to be fine. You shouldn't worry about anything."

Like most children, the bear hug she provides is comforting to him. He wipes the tears from his eyes, showing he is settling down.

"Now, will you tell me why you are crying?" Tianna asks as she continues to rub his back.

After a few minutes, he says in a breathy, child-like voice, "my grandfather died, and I did not say goodbye."

Her first thought is to say good riddance, but because she does not want to taint Charles's memory for him, she is quiet until she finds the correct words to use. She starts by telling him how sorry she is that he was unable to speak to him before he passed. "If he could have said goodbye, you would have been the first one he told. Unfortunately, many people leave a lot of things unsaid and undone. Now that he is no longer here, always remember he loved you very much, and he would want you to look after your mother."

"My mom does not need me. She has David. The doctors are taking care of my grandmother. I think she is going to go away forever, too." He examines Tianna's eyes before asking, "So, who is going to care for me?"

This question causes a hitch in her breath as she gets choked up. The more she tries to talk the more choked up she becomes. Tears roll down her face.

With eyes the size of golf balls, he says, "Tianna, are you okay?" he asks with sheer panic written across his face.

She manages to whisper, "I swallowed, and something went down the wrong pipe. I am better now that things are moving around. Give me a second." After a few times of clearing her throat, she can speak. "Now Micah, you do not have to ever worry about who will care for you. Jada will always be there for you. Your mommy is upset, too. To help make her feel better, David took her out to dinner just like I did for you."

"I understand and thank you for taking me out. The food was yummy, but I am still just a bit sad. Maybe after we stop for ice cream, I will be happy again."

She laughs out loud, then tickles him. "All right, we will try, but please tell me if it helps or not. There is another idea that for sure will help."

"Okay," he states with a tad more excitement in his voice while he fastens his seatbelt.

Micah's worries run through Tianna's mind. Did she answer them in the way a six-year-old boy can understand? The comment nagging the most is his fear Nicke is also going to die. She surmises he must miss his grandmother but decides after they secure their dessert to visit her. Once he spends some time with her, Tianna hopes his fears will be alleviated. About to order from the drive-through lane of Dairy Queen, she turns to him. "What would you like, sir?"

"May I please have a vanilla and chocolate swirl on a waffle cone?" With his hands folded on his lap, he sits straight.

"Yes, sounds tasty and I think I will have the same." After paying for their order, she passes him his treat.

Eagerly, he snatches the ice cream and manages a muffled thank you with the first swallow. "This is perfect," he states as remnants of the brown and white frozen liquid roll out of the corner of his mouth.

Just before attacking with a series of licks, Tianna hands him a napkin. "You are right, Micah. This ice cream is delicious. Hurry, because we need to make another stop."

With a squeal, he bops around. "Oh great, where are we going now?"

"It is a surprise, but I can tell you we are going to make someone happy."

Unable to respond, he shakes his head in a quick back-and-forth motion.

"Do not eat so fast. I bet you gave yourself a brain freeze." While watching him struggling to cure a stabbing headache, she laughs. "Press your tongue against the roof of your mouth to warm the area."

"The trick worked," he replies with relief. "I know where we are going," he exclaims while stretching his head and neck to peek out the passenger's window.

Once in the hospital parking lot, she faces him. "I thought you needed to visit your grandmother. By the way, you are jumping in your seat; I can tell you are excited."

After stuffing the last of his cone, he speaks with a full mouth. "I miss my granny. Now I can say goodbye before she dies."

"Why do you think she is going to die?" she asks as she opens his door.

He searches the ground before answering. "I am smart, and I can tell these things. Just like I knew my Paw-Paw was going to go away."

Unsure whether to reassure him, she stares at him until deciding it may be best not to comment. After all, who is she to dispute his thoughts? "Wait until you see how much progress she has made since you saw her last. I am certain she will be overjoyed seeing your face." With his hand, she swings his arm back and forth as high as she can.

Amused by the game, he giggles each time their swing reaches the top peak.

They near Nicke's room when he glances up at her as though asking for permission. Able to detect his desire before he can even articulate his wishes, she nods in agreement.

Off he runs, then shoves the door before coming to an abrupt stop in the doorway.

Both Lyric and Nicke jump from the sound of the intrusion.

He takes off again and jumps on her bed. "Granny, Granny," he shouts. "All those tubes are not tied to you anymore. I missed you."

A beam of light brightens Nicke's face. With her arms wrapped around Micah's neck, "I missed you too little man," she exclaims.

The two embrace each other for several seconds.

"What are you doing here this time of night?"

"Tianna gave me a surprise, but I figured out Aunt Tianna was taking me to visit you."

When mentioning Tianna's name, she walks through the door yelling, "guess who? We went out to dinner and then for some ice cream. Micah said he was sad, so I brought him to the one person I was certain would make him smile. Hey Mom, I did not expect you would still be here. I assumed you went home long ago."

"That is what you get for thinking," Lyric jokes. "I stayed to help Nicke work on some business." Standing up, she turns her attention to Micah. "Can your auntie steal some love?" she asks with her arms outstretched.

He jumps off the bed and runs into her grip. "Hi, Aunt Lyric," he says before running back to his granny.

"I guess I should've passed on anything with sugar. Micah is so full of energy that he cannot be still."

Nicke lifts his head using his chin. "So why was Granny's baby sad?"

"I don't know." Micah turns to Tianna for help.

On cue, she rushes to his rescue. "He did not have time to say goodbye to his Paw-Paw. Also, he is worried you are going to leave him, too." A wink at Nicke is her way of indicating she handled his concern.

"I am sorry you did not speak with your grandfather before his demise. God took him before he had a chance to tell you. I am certain, though; he wanted one of those big hugs like the one you gave me." Her eyes drop, and the light surrounding her dims as she pulls him closer.

"Mom, can you walk with me to grab a cup of coffee? I am sure Micah needs some time alone with Aunt Nicke."

"I am glad you brought him to the hospital. I think both need this visit," Lyric says.

"Yes, you are right. I was concerned when Micah expressed his fears. I am going to call Jada and suggest he spend some time with her. With all these changes, he is apt to be uncertain of his future," says Tianna.

"I must agree with you. There needs to be some semblance of normality in this child's life. She will understand and will also want him nearby. By the way, where is she?" Lyric asks while frowning?

"Thanks to my match-making skills, she is with David," Tianna boasts.

"Wow, how did you pull off this feat?"

"To be honest, I tricked her into coming by Candy's house. I told her if she did not want him, I would take him. So, to keep me from getting him, she agreed to talk to him. Surely, after he explains how Candy showed up unexpectedly trying to entice him, she will forgive him."

"I hope they work it out because I like David for Jada," Lyric says.

With her head tilted and her eyes closed, Tianna responds, "I think you are right. I hope I can find a man who will treat me the way he does her."

While patting Tianna's thigh, Lyric too prays for her daughter's desire. There is nothing she would like more than for her to settle down and raise a family, just as her sister is doing.

"How about you, mom? How is your love triangle going?" Tianna teases.

A slap to Tianna's knee by Lyric ricochets off the wall.

"Ouch, Mom, that hurts," Tianna states, while rubbing and wrenching in pain. "Even though you broke my leg, I still want details on which man you are going to be with, Johnny or Jim?" To avoid another hit, she pulled away.

On the one hand, Lyric is afraid to share her real thoughts that, on the other, she is longing to discuss her dilemma. A voice inside reminds her of how objective and direct her daughter can be. "I told Johnny I thought I was in love with Jim."

This confession causes Tianna to spit out a mouthful of coffee all over the floor. "What did you say?" she asks.

Lyric rolls her eyes and waits for a follow-up comment. Inside, she laughs at her reaction but dares not address it.

"How are you able to be so placid after dropping such a bomb on him and now on me?" To capture her undivided attention, Tianna grabs her mother's hand. "Mom, please tell me more. What did Johnny say?" Several additional questions get fired, hoping she will address or answer any one of them. "Are you going to be with Dr. Maxey? Are you sure?"

"First off, calm down. I did not just blurt out how I felt about Jim. Johnny asked if I was in love with Jim. Unable to lie, I told him I thought I might be. He is the one who started this avalanche. I did not intend to fall for Jim. It just happened. If he had not done what he did, I would not give the handsome doctor a second of my time."

"What happened?" she repeats. Capable of reading the real meaning of Tianna's question, she responds right away. "No, young lady, there is not anything physical between us. In fact, for as long as I am married Jim or no man will send me to hell."

"Well, if I were you, I would not leave this eligible bachelor out there for too long. Someone else is sure to snatch him up."

Although Lyric agrees with Jim's upcoming date with Officer Nelson, it may be too late. *Divorces take time, and I am not sure he will wait.*

The once confident and cocky mood of her mother dissipates, and an uncertainty replaces it. Tianna notices all. "Mom, are you okay?"

"I am trying to be but, I do not mind telling you this is hard. What I did not tell you is Jim asked Judith on a date to a hospital recognition affair."

"You, my amazing mother have been through so much. I am going to say what I think you would tell me if I were in your situation, five simple words. 'Let go and let God.' If he is meant to be with you, then no other woman will have him. Handle your business first, and God will do the rest." With this said, Tianna places her arms around her mother's neck.

They embrace while the advice resonates in both of their spirits.

"How did you become so smart? I needed to hear sound Christian counsel. You are right. What God has for me is for me," Lyric proclaims after taking Tianna's hand. "I guess we should walk back to the room and check on them."

When they return, Micah is sitting on Nicke's bed giggling and enjoying their visit.

Upon their arrival, Nicke asks, "Will you please call my daughter? There is something we would like to share with her."

Without answering, Tianna obeys the request. "Hey sis, I am at the hospital with your mother and son. They would like to speak with you."

"What do you guys want?" Jada asks as the door swings open, and she walks into the room with her phone held to her ear.

"Wow, that was quick," Tianna declares while ending their call.

Surprised and pleased, Micah jumps from the bed and runs into her arms. "Hi Mommy and David, how did you know we wanted to see you?"

"Because we missed you too," Jada replies as she hugs Micah.

Oh, how I'm thankful for this little boy. My life is perfect now. Everything I will ever need is right here—my mom, Micah, David, and family. With this thought, she moves to her mother and plants a kiss on her forehead. "You appear to be better. It seems like you are getting much stronger. I bet you will be coming home soon."

"I do not look as well as you. You are flashing a smile that runs across your face and is so wide I can hardly detect your nose. I wonder if it is because of the handsome man over there," Nicke says as she extends her arm and motions, David, to come closer.

Everyone laughs at her comment.

"Hello, Mrs. Williams. I am glad you are feeling better." Holding her hand, he uses his other to pull Micah against his side. "Hey little man, I missed you."

In a quiet voice, he replies, "Me too."

"Okay, okay, it is getting too mushy in here. I am just happy to see everyone smiling." Tianna turns to her mother and winks. "See what happens when we all let go and let God?"

"On that note, I am going home," Lyric says.

With her hand extended as a human stop sign, Tianna prevents her mother from leaving. "Jada, shall I take Micah with me?"

Before she can answer, David chimes in with, "He is going to go with us. I have a gift for him."

"A present," Micah repeats as he jumps up and down. "Tell me, what is it?"

On one knee, David kneels to look into his eyes. "It is a surprise. I am going to give it to you in the morning."

With this news, Jada places her hand across her heart. This man cannot be real. He loves my son. He is going to make an excellent dad.

"Well, I am going home. I need to be certain this beautiful lady gets to her car safe," Tianna says as she loops her arm inside Lyric's and repeats, "Goodnight to everyone."

In unison, they reply.

***

After they leave, Nicke turns her attention back to her remaining family. She marvels at how attentive David is to them. The love between them is visible.

"Micah, what did you and Mom want to ask me?"

Instead, his grandmother responds. "He wanted to know if you were still sad. He said you were crying."

While answering his concern, Jada looks up at David. "No, honey, I am not upset anymore. I had a lot of things on my mind."

"Micah also thought I was going to die and not say goodbye to him like his Paw-Paw did," Nicke adds.

Jada's eyes widen as she tries to dissect Micah's concerns. What would make him think such a thing? Several answers surface before Jada settles on Micah missed seeing his grandmother. Now that he can tell how well she is progressing, she supposes he is relieved. "Micah, your granny is getting better every day. Soon she will come home."

"It is okay Mommy. Granny had a chance to tell me goodbye. Granny said she could not promise she will not die, but Granny did tell me no matter what she will always be here for me." With this, he lays his head on Nicke's chest. "Paw-Paw did not know he was going to pass. If he had, he would have said goodbye."

Everyone is astonished by his conversation. This revelation suggests he is growing up. Though, it also sounds as though he has prepared himself for Nicke's demise. The room is quiet. The only noise is the beep from the medical equipment. Jada stares at David. Not sure, he peers back as he shrugs his shoulders as his way of admitting he too is puzzled.

Nicke caresses Micah's back with her eyes closed. She seems to accept his prediction.

"Mom, we are going to say goodnight and allow you to get some rest. I will call you in the morning. Micah, why don't you kiss your granny?"

After complying, he jumps off the bed and runs to grab David's hand. Micah remains quiet as he looks into David's eyes and offers a huge grin.

"Everyone, before we leave, I think we should have a moment of prayer," David says.

Without hesitating, Micah reaches for his mother with the opposite hand.

They connect the circle by grasping Nicke's hand.

A request that Nicke continue to improve includes her doctors, nurses, and all medical professionals. He ends by asking God's will be done for them all.

They release their hands. Jada embraces her mother. "I love you, Mom, with everything in me. Please do not leave me," she whispers.

"Honey, that is out of my control," she quietly replies. "Just know that no matter what, your mother loves you with every beat of my heart." To add some humor, she adds, "As long as my ticker ticks."

David places Micah's hand in Jada's. "I will see you two in the hallway. I need to speak with Nicke in private."

Taking her cue, Jada leads Micah out the door.

"I just want you to know I still intend to support them."

She nods.

"Tomorrow, I plan to ask them to marry me. I already have the ring and a gift for Micah. If and when they say yes, we are going to wait until you are well enough to attend the ceremony."

"Honey, do not worry about me. Just please, make sure they are happy."

This time he returns the nod, kisses her hand and says goodnight.

After stepping out, he takes Micah's hand and wraps his other arm around Jada. With a smile on his face and joy in his heart, he struts down the hall. *The world, this is my family. I am the luckiest man alive.*

CHAPTER SIXTEEN

FACE TO FACE WITH THE OTHER WOMAN

It takes nerve to come to my home
Looking for my husband
With no regard for me
You broke the woman's code
Entering my house
Without thinking about it
Now I'm face to face
Forced to wear a shoe that
Doesn't fit

As the sun begins to hide behind the clouds, Lyric and her daughter walk toward their cars.

"I am exhausted," Lyric admits. "I cannot wait to go home and soak in the tub."

"Sounds like a splendid plan for both of us. Call me if you need anything."

"My body wants to sleep. Bye Tianna," Lyric shouts when entering her car.

On the drive home, Lyric gives her mind permission to think about Jim and wonders what he is doing. Perhaps he and Judith are having coffee. Comparisons between herself and Judith arise. This woman works a job that others admire, including him. Her body is firm, toned, and the kind men classify as a coke bottle shape. She is smart and caring. More importantly, she is single and available for a man like him. She recalls the devouring look Judith gave him when they first met. At the time, Lyric was amused because it was the same lionization stare, she also enjoyed on her original encounter. As Lyric reminisces about his six-foot lean muscular body, a mental picture reveals how his thick eyebrows arch over his deep brown almond-shaped eyes. The softness of their kiss she remembers as she licks her lips. Goosebumps pop up on her skin while she relives their shared evening. As she approaches her street, the familiar surroundings snap her back to the issues she must face with Johnny. A parked car in her garage answers whether or not he is home. To prepare, she takes a deep breath and walks inside. The television is blaring from the family room. A stop at the kitchen table to thumb through the mail adds the necessary time to brace for his presence. To herself, she whispers, "Bills, bills, and more bills." After kicking off her heels, Johnny enters the kitchen with squinting bloodshot eyes.

"I was not expecting you to come home. I thought you were spending the night with your new boyfriend," Johnny says, sitting and glaring at her.

On the back of a nearby chair, she rests her hands. "Johnny, I am tired and beat down. Today has been a full and exhausting day. Can we please not talk about anything heavy?" She turns to walk out of the room.

To prevent her from leaving, he jumps up and blocks her exit. "I need to discuss our future together."

"Why is everything always about what you want? Therein lies our problem. There is more to life than your wants and needs."

He drops his hand. "Please, can we take thirty minutes to review what might be the rest of our life?"

Unable to put him off, she relinquishes and sits. Upward, her mouth twitches as she folds her hands. "Go ahead, Johnny, say what you must say."

Pulling his chair out, he hops into his seat. "I know I hurt you, but I want you to know I never stopped loving you. I made a mistake."

Without looking up, she interrupts and replies, "Three times."

He tilts his head as his eyebrows touch.

Reading the confusion on his face, she explains in a short but succinct way. "Two affairs and one baby."

After her explanation, he lowers his head. "I did not intend to create life, but I will not deny my son. It is what it is."

She pounds her fist on top of the table. "Your child is created. I am not asking you to pretend. I am freeing you so both you and his mother can raise him together."

His voice raises. "Lyric, this is not about them or me. Why won't you admit this gives you the reason you need to be with your doctor friend?"

She smirks. "You taught me an excuse is not necessary. I can be with whoever I choose, just because I have the desire, opportunity, and a willing partner." Her arms swing to a straight, stiff position at her sides as she pushes her chest forward.

Defeated, he states, "I just did not think my wife would have an affair."

Unwilling to feel sorry for him, Lyric continues. "The problem is you did not think through the consequences of your decisions. You screwed up the life we had together, and now you want me to forget it and just move on as though nothing happened? I cannot and I will not. What I will do, however, is forgive you and release you in love."

"May I make one last request of you?"

"What is it?" she responds.

"Can we speak with a counselor before we end our marriage? Once we complete the sessions, if you still want a divorce, I will walk out of your life."

She lowers her head as though considering his suggestion. The opportunity to respond is interrupted by the doorbell. As Lyric looks up, she is entranced by Johnny frantically pacing back and forth. He is repeatedly glancing at his watch and then back at her. Perspiration forms on his forehead as he hyperventilates.

The bell chimes again. This time, he grabs his face with both hands.

She sits staring at him. *What is wrong?* She wonders. Calmly, Lyric speaks, "Are you expecting someone?"

"I thought you were not coming home, and our marriage was over, and you were in love with that doctor, and—and—and," he rambles.

"So, you invited someone to our house," she says while heading to the door. Just as she is about to answer, the button is engaged again. Only this time, the person on the other side holds it without being released. She flings the door open. A young woman with breast the size of two basketballs and a little boy appearing to be about 3- or 4-years old stand before her. "May I help you?"

The woman steps back and places her hands on her hips. "Lyric, I am here to pick up Johnny."

With no need to be introduced, Lyric knows the strangers at her door are Donna and Johnny's son. Unable to speak, she stares down into the big brown eyes of the toddler. His facial features bear an uncanny resemblance to those of her husband. Plagued with the feelings of a pressure cooker singing as steam escapes from its whistle, she fights to keep from blowing up. *No, this bitch did not find the nerve to come to my home. If it were not for her having that child with her, I would punch her in the face. She does not look as old as my baby daughter. This man went out of my house and got with a girl half his age.* Still wrestling with her temper, she releases a gut-wrenching sigh. "I assume your name is Donna unless my spouse has another woman of whom I am unaware."

"Yes, you are correct, and this is our son, JJ, short for Johnny Junior," she conveys with a smirk.

"Well, Miss, please do me a favor and wait in your car for my husband. He will be out shortly," she retorts with a scowl before slamming the door. Just as soon as the lock engages, the bell sounds again. Lyric snatches the door open once again with such force as it rattles on the hinges before swinging back and hitting the door stopper. Every part of her wants to smack Donna in the face, but the eagerness with which the child stares at her is everyone's saving grace. As Lyric steps aside, she addresses him, "Your father is in the house. Will you please go in and tell him your mother is here to pick him up?"

JJ squeezes past her and runs inside yelling, "Daddy, Daddy, where are you?"

After he enters, Lyric walks outside and closes her door. "Donna, I am going to assume it is because of your youth you do not know better. No woman should ever come to the home of the man she is having an affair with. First off, it is disrespectful to both you and her. Second, it is uncouth, and finally, it is dangerous."

The fire coming from her eyes seems to penetrate through Donna with a supernatural force that propels Donna back a few steps. In the frozen seconds between restraint and mercy, the magnitude of the possible consequences of Donna's actions starts to sink in. "I, I am sorry. I did not expect you to be here. Johnny asked me to come get him," she stutters while back peddling to her car.

"The next time a man requests this of you, tell him to call Uber, Lyft, or a damn cab," Lyric snaps before turning and reentering her house. After shutting the door, she leans against it, counting to ten to control the angry ball threatening to propel her into an anxiety attack. Her body quivers. *Lord, please help me remain calm. I am so mad I could hurt someone.*

Seeing JJ and Johnny struggling with two large suitcases and two strapped bags incites the negative energy she is attempting to bury.

"Lyric, I will be back for the rest of my things," Johnny says as he stands to wait for her to move.

She stares at his offspring with a forced smile on her face. "No problem, I will make sure to pack everything of yours, and you can follow up with my attorney for the best time to secure them." After patting JJ on the head, she replies, "There is no need for us to attend counseling. This visit is the ultimate betrayal. Now, I wish you a wonderful life," she proclaims as she closes the door behind them. Helpless to hold back her tears any longer, she charges to her bedroom, jumps on the bed, and curls her body into a tight ball. The sobs echo throughout the house. *How could he hurt me and then stick a knife in an already bleeding wound by inviting his girlfriend to the house we share?* She tries to pray but is unable to gather her thoughts to start a prayer. The urge to phone Jim to hear something that can erase her pain pops into her head. To quiet this impulse, she remembers he made it clear he does not want to be drawn into her life until she is divorced. Another voice suggests she should call her daughters for consoling. This one she overrules for fear of damaging their relationship with Johnny anymore. Finally, she determines this is a burden she must carry alone. At a previous marriage counseling session, she recalls, the counselor advised her sometimes you need to allow the pain to flow and just let it run a natural course. Accepting this is one of those times, she releases screams that fill the entire house until she becomes nauseated. Quickly she jumps up, and dashes for the bathroom as her last meal is entering her throat. She heaves until nothing remains. After cleaning her face and rinsing out her mouth, she walks back to her bed with the assistance of walls and furniture. Just as she is about to lie down, her doorbell rings. The thought that her husband could be returning causes her to dry-heave. She makes her way to the front door. With a weakened voice, she asks, "Who is it?"

"Lyric, it is Officer Judith Nelson."

The few seconds' pause gives Lyric the needed time to figure out why she is at her home. Fearful that something happened, she pushes herself to fling the door open. With bloodshot eyes that widen as she shouts, "What is wrong?

Are Jada and Nicke all right?" Fear and anxiety are in her voice and face.

Judith rushes to assure her everyone is doing well. "I hope you do not mind, but I stopped by to check on you."

"Thank you for your concern." *How could she know my world is crashing?* She wonders.

"May I come inside?" she asks.

Without speaking, Lyric motions for her to enter the kitchen. Judith steps inside and sits at the table. The house is clean and neat but, glancing around the room Judith notes what others may not see. There is a silence that reeks of pain.

Lyric trails behind her but turns toward the cabinets. She tries to fluff her hair and straighten up her clothing. "May I offer you something: coffee, water, Pepsi, or wine?"

"If you are having a drink, I will take a glass of wine. Otherwise, water will be fine."

Thought about her stomach being upset reminds Lyric to stick with ginger ale instead. She hands Judith the Moscato and places the Vernor soda on the placemat by her seat. After preparing their refreshments, she sits down still wondering the reason for her visit.

Once taking a sip, she looks up at Lyric. The traces of tears and distress remain on her face. Speaking softly, she asks, "Is something wrong? You look as though you are not well."

Once again, Lyric wipes her face. "My stomach is queasy. I think it is something I ate."

"I am sorry. I just stopped by because when we were in Jim's office, I could see you were upset. I thought you might need a friend."

Just knowing Judith is offering to listen to her problems causes tears to fall from Lyric's eyes. The pain refuses to stay locked inside or to wait until she is alone. With her head lowered, she tries to prevent Judith from witnessing her despair, but it is too late.

"Why are you crying? I hope it is not because of me. Jim asked me to accompany him to his dinner, but I can decline."

Not expecting her to bring up his name or the impending date, the tears halt in their tracks. She cannot bear to think about that now. She likes Judith, but she is unsure if she can trust her with the real reason for her tears. What if she genuinely wants Jim and uses what Lyric says to become close to him? As Lyric takes another sip, the bubbles pop on her nose. "Judith, both you and Jim are single. If you two want to go out together, it is none of my business."

Judith sits back in her seat. "The attraction between you and him is obvious. In fact, he and I discussed his feelings for you."

This information piques Lyric's curiosity. She slides her chair closer to the table and leans toward Judith.

"Listen, I came by because I like you. At first, I refused to go with Jim. I asked him why he asked me instead of you."

"Oh, really?" Lyric questions as she waits for her to continue.

"He replied because you are married."

Dropping her head, Lyric speaks under her breath, "Not for long."

"Jim wants to take you but is waiting until you are divorced. I told him I would go with him but only as his friend."

Hearing Judith causes her face to relax with a beatific smile. Perhaps she is trustworthy. With nothing to lose, she decides to share her innermost thoughts. "I think I love him."

"Well, I know he is in love with you. This spiritual man wants to ensure he gives you a chance to make it work with your husband."

Lyric chuckles as she shares, "my marriage is over. My husband recently left with his child and his baby's momma."

"What?" Judith ask in disbelief while leaning back in her chair.

"Yes, girl, this is why I was crying. He allowed his woman to come to our house. For me, being able to put a face to the other woman and seeing their son did it for me. I am DONE! If I was ever considering giving him another chance, that stunt changed my mind for good."

"I am so sorry you had to go through this ordeal. Your husband is crazy to let a woman like you go."

"I can tell his girlfriend is either young or stupid to subject herself to this type of predicament."

"She is both of those, and I told her so. Girl, I prayed God would keep me from putting my hands on her. With a little less religion in me, you would come to lock me up with handcuffs and all."

The two women share a laugh. Their laughter lessens the tension and helps them relax.

"I probably would have helped you kick her ass," Judith declares as she balls her fist up and pretends she is throwing punches in the air.

"I would be in jail, and you would be without a job," Lyric jokes.

"Well, I am glad you kept your cool. You are one classy woman, which is the reason Jim loves you."

"Thank you, I try hard to stay in control of my feelings, but I do not mind telling you, I almost came out of my character."

"Now, what are you going to do about Jim?" Judith asks.

"There is nothing I can do until my divorce is final. We both know when we are around each other, we struggle to remain Christians. Since God already knows my thoughts, the truth is I want to take that man to bed." To stop her laughter, she covers her mouth with her hand. For the first time, Lyric admits she is sexually attracted to him, showing she is comfortable enough to confide in Judith.

"When you and Jim become a couple, you will have to find me a man. Is there a brother?"

"I am not sure. There are, however, some single doctor friends."

"Well, set me up. In the meantime, how would you like me to handle this date with Jim? I figured you and he would get together, so I told him if he changed his mind, he had to cancel forty-eight hours in advance. The dance is next Friday."

"I think you should attend," Lyric replies. "There is no way my divorce will be final by next week. Perhaps I could be a widow by then."

"Stop it. What if when Jim comes to my house to pick me up, and you are there waiting?" Judith asks.

"Yeah, right," Lyric sarcastically states.

"No, I am serious. Jim wants to take you, and you want to go. What if both of us go? He can have two dates. With me tagging along, I will be there to keep you from attacking him. Then I can survey his colleagues for a decent prospect."

With a wave of her hand, Lyric dismisses her comment. "Didn't you just say how classy I am? Your plan does not make me sound like I am sophisticated, but portraits me as desperate."

"No, you are not desperate. I am," Judith laughs. "Well, if you reconsider, let me know." After pausing, she adds, "You have forty-eight hours before the event to decide."

A burst of uncontrollable laughter fills the room. Both women enjoy a bend over, side busting and tension-relieving laugh.

"It is getting late. I guess I will leave so you can go to sleep."

"Judith, I hate for you to go. I am enjoying your visit. You are welcome to stay in my guest room tonight. We can knock this bottle of wine out, pop some popcorn, and catch a movie. Besides, I do not want to be alone. With the way I am feeling, I might strip, put on a trench coat, and show up at Jim's door."

"I am sure he would love that."

"Yeah, but when the morning comes"–Lyric stops in mid-sentence and tilts her head. Even though Lyric is laughing, she understands her own confusion. There is a need to have a distraction to avoid dealing with the pain.

"A single woman always keeps a bag of clothing and personal items in her car. I will be right back. In the meantime, fill my glass up and empty that soda out of yours. If I am drinking, so are you."

Happy because Judith is taking her up on her offer, Lyric jumps up, takes the popcorn from the pantry and places the kernels in the popper. Per her instructions, she empties the ginger ale and replaces it with wine.

Once Judith returns, Lyric leads her to the guest bedroom. "Just leave your stuff in here. Follow me to my room because I have something for you." She opens her dresser and takes out a packet. She throws the package at her. "In your overnight case, I am sure you carry sexy negligees. This is not that kind of party so here; you can wear these. I bought them for Nicke. We have a lot of sleepovers, especially since Johnny is often out of town."

After opening the bag, Judith pulls out a knit onesie-pajama with the feet attached. They are a bright plaid. She giggles. "Well, thank you, I will go and change."

Lyric closes her door behind her and puts on her matching pair—except they are zebra print.

After changing, Lyric strolls to the front room and turns the music on. She is grateful for the healthy distraction.

While Judith is dressing, she breaks out into a grin. This invitation from Lyric, not wanting to be alone, is serving a dual purpose. *It's been a long time since I had a date with a girlfriend. Sisterhood is the best medicine for loneliness and a betrayed heart.*

When they are both in the kitchen, Lyric announces, "It is turn-up time," as she pours more wine. Judith offers a toast. "Here is to a new life of joy and happiness from this day forth."

Raising her glass, Lyric responds, "Likewise, my new friend."

The glasses kiss as the sound rings in an upcoming change for both ladies.

CHAPTER SEVENTEEN

THE PROPOSAL

I found love in you
No other one will do
Someone to safeguard my heart
Even though I knew from the start
That you were afraid to love
Yet, someone I felt so deserving of
For all the things you went through
Most would run and not pursue
A future of forever for the rest of my life
Would you do me the honor of becoming my wife

A full moon peaks below the clouds as the sun disappears to provide the darkness of night, the light to shine through. David cannot help but marvel at the calming sight. He, Jada, and Micah rode silently in route to her residence. David glances in the rearview mirror just as Micah's eyes close and his head bobbles back and forth. *Wow, this little boy is going to be my son, beaming,* he thinks. *I am going to assist him to become the kind of man any woman will be proud to call her husband.* A quick glance toward Jada reveals her head is turned to the side as she is engulfed in the scenery whizzing past her passenger window. *I love her and will protect her from anyone who would dare cause her harm. To survive being deflowered as a child, an alcoholic mother, and now the guilt of Charles committing suicide is a testament to her strength. Do not worry about anything baby. I will replace your pain with love. How do I propose?* He wonders. *Should I be traditional and fall on one knee or perhaps try something unique?* He rehearses several options in his head but cannot land on what he believes will be the most memorable for her. Upon entering the parking area, he pushes the other thoughts out of his mind and concentrate on getting them safely into her apartment. After shutting off the engine, he remembers both Jada's ring and Micah's gift are in his glove box. Not wanting to arouse her suspicions, he considers how to take them inside with him. He asks Jada to retrieve his overnight bag. Without commenting, she complied, giving him time to secure the packages. From the rear seat, he lifts Micah and hides two small boxes between their bodies. Together, they head for the apartment. "I am going to lay him in his bed. Why don't you pour us a nightcap?"

"Sure," she agrees as she kicks off her heels. She secures two wine glasses, a bottle of Chardonnay, and the electric corkscrew. After opening, she pours their drinks and walks into the living room. She dims the lights as she places the glasses on the coffee table. One leg securely tucked under her buttocks, she sits on the couch and awaits her man.

In front of her, he drops to his knees and lays his head on her lap. "Thank you, baby, for believing in me. I was scared I lost you."

She rubs her fingers through his curly hair. "I am sorry I doubted your love for me. It is because my insecurities took over."

"Do not blame yourself. Given the same circumstances, I might also suspect something was going on between you and your ex-boyfriend. My only point is once I explained my version, you believed me. After everything that you have been through, I cannot fault you for thinking I betrayed you. You were traumatized by the discovery."

Even though he is understanding, he is struggling with accepting the reason for Candy's death. A young woman with a promising future had her life cut short because of loving a man.

"There are still things I must resolve, Jada admits. So, I plan on speaking with a therapist. I have a lot to work out."

"I understand, and I support your decision." The strength that it took to confess she will seek help causes him to question if the time is right to ask her to marry him. The last thing he wants to do is to add more pressure. He hopes to become her answer and not another problem. Moving to the couch, he lifts his glass and makes a toast. "To us," they both take a sip.

After placing the glasses down, he frees their hands and pulls her close to him. Deep in her eyes, he stares, trying to reach her soul. With a tilt of his head, their mouths locked. Her soft lips provide a barrier and refuse to allow an escape. The sweet zest of her strawberry lip gloss spreads. While thrusting his tongue into her mouth, his hands slip up her blouse. Gently, he massages her back while gliding up and down her silky skin.

Her fingernails drift down his face and pull him closer. After freeing her leg from its tucked position, he pulls his body on top of hers. Wrapping her arms around him, he flinches as she grabs the cheeks of his butt and slips between his groins. Against his enlarged and rock-hard nature, she rocks her hips. There are grinds, moans, and racing heartbeats. A cinnamon smell is exuding from her pores.

His breathing changes to rapid panting. "Owoo Jada, please," he groans.

Aware if he does not stop his vow of celibacy soon will inevitably be broken, but he can't because his body is overruling his thoughts. Unable to pass by her breasts, which are perky and much too large for him to grab with one hand, he cups them with both. Abruptly ending their kiss, David throws up his arms. "I surrender," he shouts. Perspiration is running down the sides of his face. "Forgive me. I tried to hold off." His mouth works its way into her blouse as he touches the cleft between her breast while she nibbles on his ear.

"Aww," he groans. The warmth of Jada's tongue produces a chill on and through him. Gradually, self-awareness wins over his flesh. "We must stop now before I reach the point of no return. Our promise to remain celibate is because we wanted God to bless our union."

He sighs as he slides off her and drops to his knees. "Well, you need to say goodnight and make sure to lock your bedroom door. I am going to sleep in the guest room. I cannot stay in the same bed with you and be expected not to continue what we started. This is our second time starting something we cannot finish."

On the couch, she sits running her fingers through his disheveled hair. "I am sorry. In the worst kind of way, I want to make love to you, but I am honoring our commitment, even if it kills me."

He grabs his chest and falls on the floor pretending to die. "I am already dead. I suffered a heart attack while rounding the home base."

The couple partakes in a much-needed laugh. Their last hug shows they agree to postpone making love until they are married.

She whispers in his ear. "The way you kissed me is off limits. The next time you do, I promise I am going to take what I want."

He chuckles. "Yes, but I only said I was going to remain celibate. There was nothing mentioned about kissing and touching. Can a guy have something to hold on to until he can enjoy the consummation of our nuptials?"

Punching his arm, she replies, "As I said, you better save those actions for our wedding night, or you are going to be in major trouble. Until then, please limit your kisses to pecks." A demonstration ends with a smacking sound. "Just like this," she states.

"Naw, girl, that will not work. I need something I can feel." He crushes his lips against her, showing her just what he means but careful not to entice her further with his tongue. After finishing, he licks his lips. "Yes, that tastes g-o-o-d, good."

"That was just all right. On a scale of one to ten, it was about a six." Jada laughs while standing. "It is time for me to go to bed." Even from that mediocre kiss, my body is once again tingling.

"Oh yeah," he says as he too stands and pulls her into him. "I love you. Soon, very soon," he promises, while holding her tighter. The loving thoughts of his heart flood his mind. *How did I be lucky enough to catch this woman? She makes me laugh and is sexy as hell. Not only does she want me, but she needs me. To top it off, I gain a son. No other woman compels me to be a better man. Now, I want to rush to the altar.* "Goodnight, my love. We have a busy week ahead of us." One last pat on her butt and he bounces away.

After closing her door, she yells, "I left the door unlocked just in case you get scared sleeping alone."

"Remember, I told you to lock yourself inside. Do not blame me if you wake up naked," David jokes.

"Should the house burn down, with me being as exhausted as I am, I will probably sleep through everything."

Smiling, he plans how he will ask her to marry him. It is going to involve some work and time. Almost ready to implement his strategy, he enters Micah's bedroom and secures the three boxes stashed in the dresser drawer. Once he returns to the living room, he flips open the one containing his promise. Initially, he thought he would hand her the box as a gift. But now, he develops a unique method. From the container, an expensive 2.5 carat Asher cut pink diamond is displayed. He admires the brilliant stone nestled in the platinum setting, which crisscrosses like a perfectly tied bow. Mesmerized by the sparkle, he is certain she will especially be fond of his selection. She is going to appreciate this almost as much as I love her. The other two boxes, for Micah and Jada, are wrapped and tied with a red ribbon, and he takes them to the kitchen. After locating a fancy blue salad plate, he places one of them in the center to make sure his soon-to-be son sees it first thing in the morning. Once complete, he glances at the clock. It is time. She should be in a deep sleep. After grabbing the ring off the coffee table, he tiptoes into her bedroom. Thrilled by her left hand being exposed, he slowly slips the diamond on her finger. A jam of his fist to his mouth prevents his excitement from spilling out at seeing it resting on her finger. Tears form in his eyes as he thinks soon this beautiful and caring woman will become his wife. After sliding out of his pants and shirt, he cuddles next to her and places her hand on his chest. There is a part of him that wants to shout 'wake-up Jada and look at what is on your finger.' He whispers a prayer of thanks while stroking her face with feather-like fingers. He gazes at her motionless body while his eyelids start to droop and flutter before finally closing tight.

***

A thick cloud of smoke fills the dark basement. David struggles to see through the fog by rubbing his eyes several times to focus in the haze. Through the thin fold of skin protecting his eyes, a room full of metal caskets appear one at a time. There are silver, blue, and bronze with their lids open and lining the wall. Barbed wire fencing prevents him from getting too close. The dressed corpses are familiar to him. Although he stretches on his tiptoes, he is unsure who the bodies are inside the boxes. He walks past the area hoping to identify at least one person but to no avail. The fear of being pierced by the sharp edges and pointed steel arranged at different intervals along the strand, he dares not touch. In the background, he hears a pipe organ playing a familiar tune. He hums. By the time he reaches the second stanza, he recognizes it as, 'Here Comes the Bride'. The sound leads him to a set of steps and into the sanctuary. The church is packed with strangers, friends, and family. A preacher is motioning for him to join him at the altar. As he complies, he notices he is dressed in a white tuxedo.

The congregation stands as the bride marches down the aisle. A short white male accompanies her. A twenty-two-inch train is attached to a fitted white and mermaid style gown. Cameras flash as the crowd's oohs and awe ring out.

Unable to make out the face under the long veil, he squints thinking it is Jada. As she approaches, the preacher asks, "Who gives this woman away?"

Her escort replies, "I do," while placing her hand on his and taking his seat.

They turn to face the raised platform, and in front of them is a casket. Before hiding behind David, Jada lifts her veil and shouts, "Oh my God, David, please help me!"

Shocked David hollers, "Candy, what are you doing at my wedding?"

His nightmare is interrupted by another shout.

"Oh David, I love it. Thank you," Jada exclaims.

Jumping out of the bed as though someone hollered fire, he awakes to shrills of joy. He shakes his head back and forth while his heart races as he bounces from a dream state into reality.

In front of his eyes, Jada's left hand is dangling. "I am sorry. I did not mean to scare you. It's just that I, I, I love my ring. I have seen nothing more beautiful than this." An attack of kisses bombards his face only stopping when she is admiring the pink-colored stone.

After the fright subsides, David relaxes and enjoys the happiness beaming from her face. He holds Jada in his arms. "I am overjoyed you are pleased. I slipped it on your finger while you slept. Now I have something to ask you."

"Yes, yes, I will marry you," she yells.

"No, wait a second before you say yes. You do not know what I am about to say."

She moves to the edge with her head slightly tilted to the right and stares into his mouth. "This is an engagement ring, right?"

Instead of answering, he drops on one knee while holding her hand and removes the jewelry. While placing it back, he swallows.

Before he speaks again, he is interrupted by a tapping on the door.

To his feet, he leaps and rushes to answer.

With her hand still extended, she remains in the same position.

"Hey little man," he greets his future son.

"Good morning," Micah responds while extending his body to peep around him. "Mommy, you woke me up screaming. Are you okay?"

"Yes baby, I am great," she answers and slaps the bed beside her for him to join.

"I will be back," David says as he rushes into the kitchen.

When he returns, he asks, "Now, where was I?" Once again, taking a knee, he continues. This time, he holds both of their hands. "Jada and Micah, will you marry me on Friday and become my family?"

Micah's head snaps around to face his mother. His eyes resemble two oversized chocolate cookies.

Jada's mouth falls open as she looks from her ring to Micah then back to David.

Sensing her hesitation, David is prepared to address the items he believes Jada is struggling to accept. He is sure she did not expect his proposal to include her son or the date to be so soon thinking the timing means her mother cannot attend. As most women and mothers, they may have hoped for a formal wedding with all the frills.

"Can we become a family today, Micah shouts while jumping up and down. Why do we have to wait until Friday?"

"Well, first we must get a marriage license. Friday is the first available day that will allow us enough time to prepare."

Back to Jada, his attention returns as he realizes she has yet to agree. "I do not want to postpone this any longer than is necessary. When I almost lost you, I realized you are the woman for me. I understand you want your mother's attendance, and you probably would like to have a ceremony. So, what I am thinking is we go to the Justice of the Peace and then plan a big wedding for our friends and family when your mother is better and can help."

A wide grin replaces her solemn mood as tears roll from her eyes. She dances around the room. "Yes, we will marry you," she yells.

Micah joins in the excitement. There is jumping, yelling and together they repeat their consent.

As quickly as it started, Micah stops in mid-sentence and plops down. His joy seems to fly out the window.

Both notice his abrupt change. They look at each other to figure out what could have switched his mood.

Jada humps her shoulders at David.

Unsure of what to think, David takes him into his arms. Perhaps he is afraid of losing his mother's love.

The mystery ends when he pushes back to look into David's eyes and asks, "Are you going to be my daddy?"

Surprised by his question, he turns to his fiancé as though pleading for her to answer.

"Would you like him to be your father?"

Micah places his hand on his chin and looks up. "Hmmm," he mumbles as though he is trying to determine whether he does or does not.

They await his reply.

After a few minutes, he speaks, "Only if I can call him Daddy."

A sigh of relief is released. "You bet, buddy," David says. "Now, I have a gift for you," he says while pitching him on the bed.

Still jumping up and down, he yells, "For me!"

From under the bed, he pulls two boxes wrapped with red bows on top. He hands one to him and the other to Jada.

The paper is ripped off with the speed of lightning as only a child can accomplish. Inside is a silver necklace with an engraved pendant. Squinting, he reads, "God Made Me Out of Love." He then repeats it a second time while sticking out his chest. "Thank you Dav—I mean Daddy. May I wear it now," he pleads. "Mommy, what did you get?"

"It is the same, but mine says, God made you for me," she sobs. What have I done to deserve this man?

As David fights back his tears, he hugs Micah. "Time for you to take a shower and get dressed, son. We have a lot to do today."

Without hesitating, Micah leaps off the bed and runs out of the room slamming the door.

After his quick exit, David lifts her. "In four days, you will be my wife."

"I love you," she whispers, before stealing another glance at her ring.

"I am going to start breakfast while you are dressing. We must go to the courthouse. Then I will have to drop you off because I need to verify Candy's house is packed up and also make sure everything is ready for her services on Wednesday."

"I have been so caught up in my happiness; I neglected to consider others are grieving their family or friends. Is there anything I can do to help you?" Jada ask.

"Get moving," he says as he heads for the kitchen.

While cooking, snippets of his dream pop in and out of his mind. He can dismiss everything but the scene of him and Jada getting married in front of Candy laying in the casket. He does not understand this picture but concludes he would instead think about the family he will gain on Friday. *She has no idea I am planning a surprise wedding.* As he fries the bacon, he outlines the details and notes to be sure and involve Dr. Maxey as he needs his approval for Nicke to attend. Besides, he will also ask him to secure the hospital chapel. A quick call to Jim handles the items on his list. Once David gets Jim's agreement, he texts Tianna, "She said yes. I need your help to plan a secret wedding. I will phone with additional information."

Next, he speaks with his parents. Still whispering, he invites them to the ceremony. At first, his mom objects to the haste because she has not met Jada. After he explains about her mother's hospitalization, his mother understands. An appointment is set up to meet David's new family after Candy's funeral.

The last person he talks with is his long-term friend, Donald. They were college roommates and their friendship spans over two decades. He consents to be his best man. Donald's only concern is if the maid of honor is cute. "Not only is Tianna a knockout, but she is single," David shares with a laugh.

When they end their call, Jada enters.

"What is so funny?" she asks.

Still smiling, he dismisses her question. "Here is your breakfast, my queen. Micah, come eat," he calls.

The soon-to-be family all sits down, says grace, enjoys their meal while daydreaming and basking in the beautiful life-changing events of the morning.

CHAPTER EIGHTEEN

IT IS A SURPRISE

Your family will be there
As will the friends we share
It's a secret in disguise
It's our wedding day surprise
This day in front of everyone
Our prayer becomes, thy will be done
It's a secret in disguise
It's our wedding day surprise
Trying not to tell
Until the wedding bell
It's a secret in disguise
It's our wedding day surprise

After a marvelous night's sleep, Tianna wakes refreshed and prepared to begin her day. Awakened early by a text from David, she is ready to implement his strategy for a surprise wedding. Though she is wrestling with being happy and envious, she gets busy planning. *I am praying for a man like him. How blessed Jada is to find one who is romantic and loves her.* Locating a pen and paper, she outlines the many things necessary to ensure the ceremony is elegant, intimate, and unexpected. With the wedding less than four days away, she enlists the help of her sister, Tasha.

After placing a call to her, she assigns Tasha the tasks of handling the decorations, cake, and flowers. Together, they decide the color scheme as yellow, gray, and silver.

"Wow, how exciting! A wedding without the bride's knowledge is a first for me," Tasha states.

"Right, we are going to make this a day neither of them will ever forget. I think I will ask Mom to work on getting Nicke's outfit."

"Simone can be the flower girl if you would like. At six years old, this will be her third time. My daughter views herself as a professional," Tasha states while giggling.

"My beautiful niece will do a wonderful job. Just be certain her dress is long and flowing, and you curl her hair. You know how much she thinks she is a princess."

"Is Micah going to be the ring bearer?" Tasha asks.

"Yes, of course. I will advise David to buy a gray suit or tuxedo with a silver bow tie and cummerbund. Hopefully, he can find a pale-yellow shirt."

"Well, I should start my assignments. Contact me if you need any additional help," Tasha stresses before finishing.

Next Tianna calls the groom. "Can you speak freely?" she asks.

"Yes, I just left Jada's house. I told her I was leaving to complete the final paperwork for Candy's services."

"Wow, you are responsible for orchestrating both Candy's funeral service and your wedding. Those two things are on opposite ends of the spectrum."

"Tell me about it," he replies while sighing.

"Do not worry about anything. Tasha is going to help me. My sister is the most creative person I know. She will bring some flare."

"Good, I am glad because I do not have a clue how to pull this off. At first, this sounded like an exciting idea, but now I am not sure."

Tianna reassures him everything will be beautiful. She pulls her checklist out and gives him a recap of the items needing his attention.

"You can cross off contacting Dr. Maxey from your list. I spoke with Jim, and he secured the chapel at three o'clock. A friend of his is going to perform the ceremony. He also gave a medical clearance for Nicke to attend. All you must do is pick up the marriage license, rent yours and Micah's tuxedos, and of course show up on time." The humor used hoping to reduce his stress, fails and is not acknowledged. Moving past the attempt, Tianna continues through her schedule. "Make sure your best man is cute and available."

"Do not fear. This man was my elementary teacher who walks with a cane but is in search of a younger woman." This time, David laughs at himself.

Not sure if he is joking, she reframes from questioning him to avoid being disappointed. "Will your parents be in attendance?" she asks to change the subject.

"Yes, I arranged for them to join my bride-to-be and my new son at dinner tomorrow night."

Hearing this causes Tianna to flip into protection mode. "Did you explain you are getting married on Friday?"

"Sure," he replies, in an annoyed tone.

The phone line is silent for a few seconds as she awaits an update, and he tries to understand the meaning of her inquisition.

"What are their beliefs about you marrying into a ready-made family? I mean, do they object to Jada or Micah?"

"I understand your concern, but my mother and father always have and always will want what is best for me. They trust my decision. In fact, I told them about Jada and Micah from the start of our relationship. They cannot wait to meet them."

"Great," she says. "May I clone you?"

"No girl, God threw away the mold when he made me," he declares while he raises his shoulders back and sticks out his chest.

"Oh please, do not get the big head with me."

"Since we are speaking of parents, I wish Candy's family was half as understanding."

Eager to listen to the details, Tianna pulls the chair out and sits down. "What do you mean?"

"Her mother called me again and is threatening to sue if I go forth with her burial."

"What?" she exclaims with her hand covering her mouth.

"I spoke with my attorney, and he advised all my paperwork was in order. She is refusing to attend her daughter's funeral. Can you believe this?" he asks.

"Why?"

"Because not welcomed there is her husband."

"Gee, I feel bad for Candy. It seems she never had their support. Does her mother not comprehend a person who goes to the extremes of blocking him from attending their burial ceremony cannot be lying about their sexual abuse?"

"I know, right? All I can do is honor Candy's last wishes. I think both her mother and her husband are only concerned about the money."

"How can a parent choose a man over their child? I now understand why Candy tried to hang on to you and why she went to extraordinary lengths to get you back." After stopping to think, she wishes she could pull back this insensitive remark. "I am sorry David; I should not make such a callous statement."

"No problem, Tianna. As harsh as what you said may be, it is still the truth. I thought I was in love with Candy, but now I realize what I felt was a type of pity for her. I was busy trying to be her Superman. But what she needed and wanted was a Clark Kent kind of guy to return her affection."

This analogy causes Tianna to search deep into her soul. She wonders which one she is trying to find. Unsure, Tianna decides to revisit this topic when she is alone with herself and her thoughts. While doodling on her notepad, she draws a picture of a man with a red cape.

"Well, Tianna, I am just getting to the funeral home. I need to complete the details. Once I finish, I will pick up Micah, and the two of us will buy something to wear to my wedding."

"Oh, wonderful, while you are busy running around, I can pick up your bride, and we will also shop for the big day. One more question, though. Has anyone told Nicke?"

"No, not yet. Jada thinks we will go to the Justice of the Peace. Once we are married, we are going to stop by and share the news with her mother. So, we need a plan for her to arrive at the hospital beforehand."

Tianna snickers. "Leave this to my mother and me. We will make it work. Just make sure you, your teacher, and Micah come dressed in the color scheme."

"Understood. I will speak with you later."

As she ends the call, she considers ways to execute a fail-safe plan while chewing on the tip of her pen. As she figures out a strategy, she seeks help from her mother. She dials Lyric's number. "Hey Mom, what are you doing?"

"I am enjoying a cup of coffee with Judith."

"Who," Tianna asks.

"Officer Nelson."

"Oh wonderful, I can use your help in planning a surprise wedding on Friday for Jada."

"This Friday!" She shouts.

"Yes, All I need you to do is to make sure Nicke is aware, dressed, and shows up for her daughter."

While relaying this exciting news, Tianna's face flashes a Texas-size smile as she listens in on her mother conveying the information to Judith. "Mom, please invite Officer Nelson. With the way she has helped Jada and David, I think Judith should attend," she requests before hanging up.

***

Judith, "let's go shopping today. We have a surprise wedding to prepare for."

Judith's head snaps around. "You and Jim cannot get married until you are divorced," she jokes.

"Very funny. For your information, I spoke with my attorney this morning, and he stated that in sixty-one days it will be official. He filed the paperwork with the courts today."

"Wow, that is quick. I guess I will call Jim and cancel our date."

As Lyric sits down, she reaches out and touches Judith's hand. "I appreciate you are willing to turn down his invitation, but just because I am getting a divorce does not mean he and I will become a couple. I think you should attend the function with him."

Snatching her hand away, Judith says, "I am canceling. I consider you my new friend, and I will not allow you or him to use me as your cover. You both love each other. In fact, when I break the date, I am going to tell him that your divorce will be finalized soon."

"Please do not share this with him," she shouts. "I will let him know once I am single."

"Look, the only reason he asked me to attend was that he knew he would be safe with me. Many other women would love to accompany him. This man can care less about them or me. He wants you. I can understand the spiritual ramifications of adultery but consider giving him something to hold on to while he waits. He still thinks you and your husband are living in the same household."

Resting her elbow on top of the table, Lyric props her head up. How well does she understand Jim is the sort of man which will not be single long? One time he admitted to her he is tired of being alone. He confessed he needed a wife and family to grow old with. "Maybe you are right, but for now, I need some retail therapy to keep me from thinking about either of these men. Let's go," she declares while retrieving her phone, keys, and purse. They walk out the door with interlocked arms. Almost skipping, they head for the car.

The excitement returns to Lyric. Right now, she is thankful for the friendship developing between them. Her face radiates from the joy she feels inside.

They drive down the street giggling, laughing, talking, singing, and reflecting. Lyric teases Judith about which type of dress will hide their flaws and accentuate their curves but yet be sophisticated and flattering.

"Girl, as long as they make spandex, we have nothing to worry about," Judith states.

Lyric agrees as she pulls into the shopping center parking lot. "There is nothing like a pair of high heels to lift both you and your spirits," Lyric says as they exit the car and head for Neiman Marcus.

CHAPTER NINETEEN

PLANNING A WEDDING, FUNERAL AND A DATE

So much to do
Just for you
People to invite
To view us unite
This is the day
I will say I do
And let the world know
How very much
I love you

After completing all the items on his to-do list, David returns to his house to check on the status of the renovation. He and Jada have not talked about where they will live after they are married, but he is assuming Micah, and she will move into his house. To make sure the memories of her discovering Charles and Candy are not amplified, he is changing the previous decor. A contractor was commissioned to repair the walls, paint and update the flooring. For the furnishings, he ordered a new master bedroom set. The changing of his walls from white to sea mist green makes him think he is in a different house instead of the one he has lived in for the last four years. He wonders why he did not remodel before now. Even the artwork on his wall is new. The master bedroom door is open, and as he enters, he gasps as he soaks in the transformation. The focal point of the room is a built-in wall fireplace with flashing multicolor lightning. To David, the people on the television show 'The Property Brothers' or 'Love It or List It' commandeered his house or so it seemed. Every room received a makeover, ranging from painting, added molding, new drapes, hardwood floors, furniture replacement to the artwork. Delighted, he drifts from room to room. Once he sees what is to be Micah's bedroom, he cannot contain the joy whirling inside him. Life size football 'Fatheads' decals decorate the room and appear they are alive. My new family will love their home. *With all these changes, Jada will not recognize the house as the one where her nightmare ended. Everything is perfect.*

Unable to tame his excitement, he calls Jada. "Hey, what are you doing?"

"Tianna and I are out shopping for my wedding attire and her maid of honor dress."

"Really? Who is getting married?" He jokingly asks.

"I might if my fiancé behaves himself for the next few days."

"And miss the opportunity to marry and make love to the prettiest woman in my life? You can count on me being on my best behavior. Now, let me switch the subject while I still can."

"Yes, please."

"I am going to spend the night at my house. My parents will be in town this evening because they are attending Candy's services. They will stay here."

Without life in her voice, "Oh, I see."

"So, while you are out shopping, pick up a sexy dress for dinner tomorrow night. I would like them to visit with their soon-to-be daughter-in-law and grandson."

Sweat droplets fall from her trembling hands while repositioning the receiver. A sharp pain causes her to double over and sit in front of the dressing room. *What if they do not like me for David?*

"For them to meet you is a formality because they already understand their son loves you."

"How can you be so sure? They are coming to town to attend Candy's services and not to be introduced to me.

What if their preference is that they wanted Candy for their daughter-in-law?"

"My parents know everything about you. I made it very clear you are my choice."

Instead of David reassuring her, he causes further doubt.

"Did you say everything?" She repeats slowly.

"Yes, our entire story is known. My mom admires your strength. She shared that only when a woman comprehends and experiences the difference between pain and pleasure can she truly appreciate genuine love."

For a moment, she dissects his mother's statement while applying it to her life. Now understanding, she calms her initial primal urge to flee. "What time is dinner?"

"Is 6:00 PM too late?"

"No, that is perfect. By then, Micah will be home from school and should be finished with his homework."

"Good, I will pick you up at five thirty. It is time for me to return to work. We will speak later. I adore you."

***

David places a few other calls. He reserves the honeymoon suite at the Omni Hotel and advised them to deliver two dozen roses to the room. After completing his task, he catches up on emails from his job.

Being the Vice President of Marketing for Goldwater, Holmes and Williams affords him a decent salary, freedom, and a competent team. Though his work is fulfilling, he is cognizant that no matter the efficiency of his staff, there are situations which require his stamp of approval. Engrossed in his job, he works until time gets away from him. Before he knows it, his parents call and say they are only moments away from his house. Fast, he shuts down his computer and verifies all is tidy and in order. A splash of lavender scented air freshener provides the finishing touch. Aware that his parents may be hungry when they arrive, he places a delivery from the local Jamaican restaurant. He rushes to the door as the doorbell rings out and snatches it open. "Mom," he shouts while lifting her off her feet and swinging her around. After placing her down, he embraced his father.

Thrilled by their arrival, David steps back and invites his parents, Bryant and Frances Austin, inside. "I see somebody missed his mom and dad," Frances states while walking into the living room. "My, everything is so beautiful and completely changed. Did you decorate or is this Jada's artistic touch?"

After calming down from the excitement, he swallows the fullness he is feeling. "I guess I did not realize how much time has passed since we were together. Come on in here, Dad." David steps aside and follows behind Frances.

309 STAPLES / TEARS OF THE DEFLOWERED /

"After the deaths of Candy and Charles, I hired a contractor and an interior decorator. What you are witnessing, they're responsible for completing. Do you think Jada will approve?"

"I am sure she will agree with these lavish surroundings but do not get your hopes up too high. Due to the circumstances, she still could have problems living here."

His head drops. Even without all the upgrades, David recognizes he is attached to his house. Though his mother may be correct, he trusts he will not need to sell for her to be comfortable. Disappointment radiates from his face.

"Son, if you love her the way you continuously express, it does not matter if you live in a box under a bridge. I am certain she shares the same sentiments. Look at me, for the last forty years, I have followed this woman to the moon and back," Bryant boasts while pulling her into his arms.

Frances pushes him away. "The only reason you stayed with me was that you could not live without my food."

"Well, maybe so, but I like it more than your cooking skills, if you know what I mean," while patting her on her butt.

"Behave, Dad. Your luggage will be in the guest bedroom. I ordered out because I thought you might be tired after such a long drive."

"Son, when are we going to meet your bride-to-be?" Frances asks.

Huffing and puffing while unloading the last bag, David replies, "I am taking us all out to dinner tomorrow night."

"Instead, how about I cook us a big soul food meal right here, filled with the comforting aroma of simmering meats and spices?" Frances asks, as he returns to the living room.

"Mom, I would rather not put you through the trouble."

"Oh boy, you do not have to worry. I love cooking. Besides, eating here is a little more intimate and will provide us with the opportunity to get to know each other better. A fancy restaurant is too formal," she says while her nose wrinkles as she throws her head backward.

Before responding, he lightly taps his fingers on the coffee table. Turning toward his father, he asks, "What do you think?"

With his arm on David's shoulder, "Son, the first lesson you need to learn about marriage is the woman is always right." He releases a laugh before continuing. "Yes, dear, I think it is a wonderful idea," he states to his wife while winking.

David and Bryant share another laugh while Frances balls her fist up and shakes it in their faces.

"Then it is settled. Dinner will be tomorrow evening at six o'clock."

The doorbell rings. "I ordered us jerk chicken dinners with plantains," David says as he leaves his parents in the living room and heads for the door.

He returns and heads to the kitchen with three Styrofoam containers. "Come eat," he yells to his parents.

"Thanks, son, for the food. I am starving," she admits as she is tearing open the bag containing the plastic utensils. "Sit down, Bryant, before your food gets cold," she demands.

"Sure honey," he replies while winking at his son.

David says the grace before they eat. While sitting at the table, they talk for several hours about politics, marriage, Jada, the economy, sports, old friends, and family.

"If you two do not mind, I am tired and need my beauty rest. I am going to say goodnight." Frances kisses David on his forehead before retiring to the guest bedroom.

From the bar, David pulls out the decanter of brandy. "Dad, do you want a nightcap while we watch the news?"

"Sure, I will have just one," Bryant says, as he follows David to the media room.

David enjoys the bonding time until he and his dad begin to nod. Once they realize tomorrow is a packed day and exhaustion is setting in, they bid each other a good night and head for their respective bedrooms.

Before going to sleep, David calls his fiancée. "I lust you, Miss Jada. Three more nights of sleeping alone before we are husband and wife, and you become Mrs. Austin."

"Well, I love you, but if we do not make it to the courthouse, we may not make a Friday wedding."

"I know, baby. We can go tomorrow after the funeral."

"Do you think we should cancel for another week or so to allow you an opportunity to grieve properly, Jada ask."

"I am having a hard time waiting for three days. If it were up to me, I would marry you tonight," David announces while squirming on the bed. "But, to make you feel comfortable, we can pick up the marriage license on Thursday. All we are supposed to bring are our birth certificates and identification. This way, I can use Wednesday to shop for Micah and myself."

"Thank you for understanding. Are we still on for dinner tomorrow evening?"

"Yes, my parents are looking forward to meeting the two of you."

"Great! I, too, am excited, but I am trying to figure out what to wear. I have tried on five different outfits and cannot decide. The dress I bought, I am afraid, may have a neckline cut too low."

. "Will you please relax? My mother is preparing dinner at my house."

"Oh no," she bellows and flings the green ribbed lurex sweater dress on the bed.

"What is the matter?"

"The clothing I chose. I may be overdressed. I thought we were going out to eat."

He chuckles. "Trust me. By the time my mother finishes cooking, you will think you are in a five-star restaurant. If I know her, she will hire a butler to serve and a violinist to provide entertainment. Please, just wear what you bought. A paper bag on you, and you still would be displayed in Vogue as the beauty of the year. Although I hope whatever your attire is, it will help me fantasize about the things I plan to do to you on our wedding night."

"Sorry, but my dress is not sexy at all. It is quite the opposite. I chose a very conservative one which hangs to my ankles. I had a hard time finding one that buttoned up to my neck and yet was wide enough to conceal my hips, among other things. After all, I do not want your parents to think of me as a 'fast girl.' I will not show my arms, legs, breasts, or butt. My tent thoroughly covers everything," she laughs.

"It'd better not be, or you will need to slip into one of my starched dress shirts without the tie," he jokes.

"It is too late. You told me to put on what I purchased. Goodnight, my love," she states, ending their call before he has an opportunity to disagree.

Smiling, he hangs up and adjusts his pillow under his head. I sure hope she is joking, he thinks before falling asleep.

CHAPTER TWENTY

VALUE IN FRIENDSHIP

Some seek silver

Some seek gold

The more riches they possess

The more they sell their soul

Some seek houses

Some seek land

Collecting their acres

Like pebbles in sand

The more possessions of things

The more sadness it brings

Some chase wealth

While neglecting their health

Not understanding that true riches

Cannot be bought

But should be sought

In the value of

friendship

*A*fter a long day of shopping, body massages, manicures and pedicures, Judith and Lyric conclude at The Cheesecake Factory for a slice of fresh banana cream and coffee. "Now I know what people mean when they say, 'shop until you drop,'" Lyric says while kicking her shoes off under the table.

"Girl, I know what you mean. I had a wonderful day. The last time I had this much fun, I cannot remember. Because of being the police, many people do not care to deal with me socially. This is a lonely life."

"No, Judith, I am indebted to you. After the stunt Johnny pulled by inviting his girlfriend to our house, I needed to share my pain. You were there for me, and I thank you. I did not think about him or his shenanigans for at least twenty-four hours."

"For me, I did not worry about people killing others who is breaking the law, or carting someone to jail," Judith states as she folds her arms.

Lyric smiles as she detects the sincerity of Judith's words radiating from the bright sparkles which seem to dance through her pupils. "We will get together more often." She sips on her coffee, as she is not in a hurry to leave the restaurant. There is no need to rush home to an empty house, so she hopes to extend the company of being with another person. "Judith, is there a special man in your life?" Lyric asks.

"No, I have been single for a little over a year. My last boyfriend could not or would not give up smoking weed. It was all right as long as he kept it away from me, but he acted as though marijuana was for medicinal purposes. It came down to my money or my honey. I chose the dollars."

Lyric expels a boisterous laugh. Amid it, Lyric spots a couple across from her, glaring in their direction. She cuts her eyes toward them and tilts her head until they turn away from embarrassment. "I do not blame you for not allowing a man to jeopardize your career. You can either buy a toy or a dog; one only needs batteries, and the other only requires food and love. The point is that both come when you summon them."

Lyric joins Judith in a wild and riotous yell. Watching the burst from Judith with her eyes closed as her head falls back and every tooth exposed, is funnier to Lyric than Judith's comment. Lyric tries to speak, but the words get swallowed up as she alternates between giggles and chuckles. To ease the aching and strain on her diaphragm, she holds her stomach, and she manages to say, "Now that was funny."

In a more controlled form, Lyric holds back her chortle by covering her mouth even though her neck and shoulders shake up and down. The couple across the aisle continues to glare at them. Directing her conversation to the annoyed guests, "People need not take themselves so seriously and should enjoy life. Laughter is good for the mind, body, and soul. Often uptight people cannot release their cortisol and adrenaline hormones. Perhaps they could lower their stress levels by including fun in their lives." Now, turning back to address Judith, she says, "Are you in agreement?"

Still tickled, Judith falls over in the booth. "Yes, I think you are right," she squeaks out between her hysteria and while using the cloth napkin to wipe her eyes.

For the first time, Lyric is witnessing the fun side of her new friend. Until now, she did not know it existed. Even more, this revelation adds to the enjoyment of being in her company.

The server returns. "Would you care for anything else?"

Using a dignified tone, Lyric states, "Yes please, we would like the check."

While waiting for the bill, Judith changes the subject. "What do you think Jim will say when he sees you at the wedding in your yellow sleek silhouette dress?"

Turning away, Lyric squeezes her lips together while considering whether to offer a funny or earnest answer. "I am not sure. What do you think he will do?"

"When you step into the room revealing your statuesque figure, he is going to pant and beg you for both love and food."

This time Lyric cannot contain her emotions as she whoops it up, which invites the nosey patrons to again stare with disdain. She ignores their contempt. "I think I will call him and ask him to bring one of his single colleagues. Once you walk in sporting your gray, tight and plunging dress, his buddy will apply to become a replacement for your toys," she says while snickering.

"If he does, the first question I will ask before anything is set out in the trash is if he partakes in cannabis for recreational or medical usage."

The server returns and interrupts the friend's teasing. She picks up the bill with Lyric's credit card.

"I do not think Jim will even attend the wedding. Less than a dozen people are invited, from what Tianna says."

"Well, if he is not there, we are going to stop by his office for a surprise meeting. I need to respectfully decline his invitation to accompany him to the awards ceremony. Once he sees you, he will regret ever asking me to attend."

Lyric neatly folds her soiled napkin and places it on the corner of the table before fiddling with the empty coffee cup. Her once-light mood changes to a more dispiriting one.

"Are you okay?" Judith ask while touching the top of her hand.

"Yes, but I am unsure of what will happen to Jim and myself. I still have sixty days left before I can even entertain the thought of us being together."

She strokes her hand while offering Lyric some advice. "I suggest you call and tell him your marriage is over. The point here is you must be open and honest with him. To do that, the two of you should communicate with one another."

The server returns with the credit card. After applying the tip and paying the bill, they stand to leave.

"Enjoy your evening," Judith says to the couple that seemed disturbed by their laughter. They smirk as they head for the valet area.

While waiting for the car, Lyric smokes a cigarette. She uses the time to consider the advice given by her friend.

Once in the car, Lyric gets lost in her thoughts. Along with the radio, she hums but does not engage in conversation. When they pull up in front of her home, Judith collects her things.

"Once again, this was a wonderful day, and I appreciate you inviting me to spend the night." The shopping bags drop as she hugs Lyric. While Judith is walking to her vehicle, she yells, "Call me if you need me. I have a hairdresser appointment, but otherwise, I am free until time to go back to work. I am working from three to eleven."

"Please be safe getting home tonight," Lyric says as she waves goodbye.

After entering the house, Lyric hangs up her dress and the one she purchased for Nicke. Instead of turning on the television, she falls asleep to gospel music on the XM Radio. After saying her prayers, she climbs into bed and rubs her aching feet while reflecting on their venture. What a day this has been, she thinks.

CHAPTER TWENTY-ONE

MEET THE FAMILY

A tree has many branches, some old and some new
Their leaves turn many colors, giving all a sneak preview
Of the kind and type of tree the seed has produced
It may be weak or fragile and fall off in the wind
Or strong and mighty, and represent powerful warrior
men
This tree has existed for centuries before, and more are
yet to come.
With each branch, another member signals
where its roots are from

Known only by its name and the type of foliage that
appears
Some bright with color, with sepia hues
It is my family and represents everyone I hold dear

The blaring sound of David's alarm signals the beginning of a new day, one that is going to be filled with goodbyes to the past and hellos to the future. With his arms resting behind his head, he lays in bed. His mind races through the litany of things needing his attention. The most pressing is Candy's farewell service. He uses this time to rethink their relationship. His thoughts travel from their first meeting, the times they were intimate, and culminate at the funeral parlor where he approved her body for viewing. A part of him feels responsible for not releasing her sooner to find a man capable of saving her from herself. Today, he realizes that before entering a relationship with him or any man, Candy should have resolved the issues with her family. Even in death, she could not reconcile the wrong they did. The fact that she left him as her executor is a clear sign she died without forgiveness. A silent prayer of repentance, David whispers not only for her but also for himself. A Christian must encourage forgiveness. Instead, he felt sorry for her plight of molestation and should have demanded that she receive therapeutic and spiritual help. Now, since understanding, David resolves not to make the same mistake he did with Jada. Once they are married, he is going to insist she seek help to deal with the sexual abuse from Charles. Undoubtedly, he cannot be her source. His job is to be one of support. This situation requires Jada to do the work that it takes to become whole.

There is a tap on his bedroom door as he is pondering about his old life and future.

"Son, breakfast is ready," he hears his mother say.

"Okay, I will be right out after I wash my face and brush my teeth," he yells. Rolling out of bed, he slides down to his knees and prays for strength to make it through the day.

Afterwards, he returns from his bathroom and slips on a pair of sweatpants and slippers. Guided by his nose, he heads toward the kitchen to the sweet applewood-smoked scent. The smell is reminiscent of his childhood. His eyes behold bacon, scrambled eggs, fried potatoes and onions, biscuits, pancakes, and cinnamon apples. The delicious spread awaiting his arrival brings about a smile of sheer amazement.

"Good morning," he greets both his mother and father.

"Would you like a cup of coffee?" Frances asks.

"Wow, Mom. There is more food here than at the buffet at the International House of Pancakes. What time did you cook?"

At four this morning, I awoke because I couldn't sleep. I started dinner early by cleaning greens, seasoning a pot roast, mixing mac and cheese, prepping chicken, and fixing breakfast.

"She is just the Ever-ready Bunny," his father jokes.

"Bryant, if I am, then someone forgot your batteries. You are slower than a tortoise," she says while placing his plate in front of him.

From her cheek, Bryant steals a quick kiss. "I love you girl and thanks for fixing my food. Now, sit down so we can say grace and I can devour all this."

To keep from involving himself in their argument, David lowers his head and says the prayer.

"We need to hurry so we can be on time for the services," Frances demands while looking over her glasses toward her husband.

David laughs at how his father ignores his wife's slur, gripping his food as though he is afraid Frances is going to remove his dish and how Bryant shovels food into his mouth.

What joy David receives from observing his parents' playful bicker. For most of his life, they accused each other of one being fast and the other moving slowly. The one thing remaining apparent to him is regardless, they always respected and loved one another. The way Frances caters to him and how he coddles her is a sight to behold. Whatever they did seemed to work, because their marriage has remained intact for thirty-five years. Although he was sure they must have encountered problems, he was unaware of any specific issues. He hopes Jada and he will duplicate this type of love.

David leans back in his chair and rubs his stomach. "Mom, everything is heavenly. I am stuffed. After all these carbohydrates, I think I need to take a nap."

"There is no time. The wake begins in an hour and a half. Go get dressed," Frances demands. "I will wash the dishes and clear the table," she adds. "Bryant, move faster. You know how you like to sit on the toilet forever and how you take those long showers. Please limit this one to ten minutes."

"All right, darling, I will tell my bowels they are on the clock, so they better release quickly," he says while shuffling into the bedroom.

"Dad, that is too much information."

Both son and the mother laugh.

"That man of mine," she repeats while shaking her head and washing the dishes.

Just as David is about to exit the dining room, his cell phone rings.

"Good morning, my love," he says.

Jada replies. "I called to let you know I will pray for you today. I wish I could be with you but, I do not think it is appropriate for me to attend."

Before he can address her statement, Frances yells, "Is that my future daughter-in-law?"

Able to hear her in the background, Jada responds, "Aww, how sweet of your mother."

Frances tells David to ask Jada if she will attend the services.

Without relaying the question to her, he replies. "Mom, she does not think it is appropriate to be present even though I do not see anything wrong with her going."

Frances interjects her opinion. "I think her decision means your future wife possesses class and says she trusts her man. Sounds like a woman after my heart."

After Frances sides with her, he smiles. "Baby, I guess you are more like my mother than I originally thought."

An attempt to retreat to his bedroom for some privacy is delayed by her adding. "Tell Jada I am looking forward to meeting her and Micah. I hope they will enjoy my cooking."

"They will love you and your food, and you will feel the same about them," he replies while closing his door and flopping across his bed.

"Your mother sounds wonderful."

"Yes, everybody is magnificent. Are you still planning to marry me on Friday? I do not want you to be scared and leave me alone at the altar."

"Umm, let me think about it for a few seconds."

David waits for Jada's response. After considering she is taking too long to answer, he asks, "Jada, are you still there?"

"Yes," she responds.

"Well?"

"Well, what?" she snickers.

"You know what?" he says with an extra bass tone in his voice.

"Baby, this will be the day I become Mrs. David Austin, but that night I plan to fulfill your every fantasy. Now, consider yourself properly warned."

He shuts his eyes as he replays what she says in his head. Both his mind and body respond to her statement.

Because of the silence, it is her turn to check the connection. "Hello, did I lose you?" she asks while giggling.

"Girl, that was not fair. You know I need to shower and dress. Why would you put something like this in my thoughts?"

"What, did I do something?" she asks, using a coy tone.

"You know what you did. Why are you trying to act all shy and innocent?"

As he notices the clock, he decides he should hang up and prepare to leave. But before he can end their call Jada says, "I wanted to express my condolences for losing your friend. Losing someone is never an easy thing to accept. I can only imagine how difficult this is for you. At one time, she was an important person in your life. The strength and courage it is taking for you to honor her wishes, I admire."

Relieved because the funeral services did not appear to overshadow the pending nuptials, David relaxes. "Just understand, after the services today there will never be another place you cannot go with your husband. I appreciate your encouragement and love you for understanding."

"Make sure you are ready by five o'clock. After Micah gets out of school, I am going to grab him up from Tasha's house. He and I will be busy running errands. Once we finish, we will pick you up for dinner. Oh yeah, pack an overnight bag for him. He is going to spend the night with his grandparents and me. I want to show off my son."

Facetiously, she answers, "Yes sir, I will be ready as instructed."

After hanging up, he detects time has gotten away from him, leaving him twenty minutes to shave, shower and dress. To avoid being late, he rushes because his mother is a stickler for being on time.

Sweat drips down his face as he finishes. Out of his bedroom, he struts with only seconds to spare.

Frances' eyebrows are squeezed together, creating a two-inch fold in her forehead. With her purse, she walks toward the door.

Bryant follows behind her. "Son, you are almost as handsome as your old man," he states as he winks, then adds, "and we are all on time."

The ride to the funeral home is quiet except for a few words about the scenery, traffic, and the weather. The severity of Candy's plight is affecting everyone's mood.

David hopes Candy's stepfather does not attend. He considers how he will handle him if he does. Several scenarios run through his head before settling on doing and saying nothing. It is not worth causing a scene. "Mom, I am going to drop you and Dad off at the door. I will park the car and come inside shortly."

She nods in agreement as they step out with Bryant, grabbing his wife's hand.

After parking and walking in the corridor, David speaks to several hospital employees and co-workers of Candy. Once he reaches the entrance of the chapel, he holds his breath. Emotions that David did not expect flood his insides. Even though she lay peacefully, he cannot erase the picture of how she died. Tears form in his eyes and tumble down his face. He whispers, "I am sorry. You deserved better."

Frances steps up and rubs his back. He stares into his mother's eyes and acknowledges her concern with a forced smile. After collecting himself and preparing to stand at the top of the coffin to greet the guests, he hears a scream.

"Oh God, my baby is dead," Cleo Stevens hollers.

He turns in time to witness Candy's mother and stepfather acting as though their grief is going to kill them by the time they reach the casket.

Propped up by her husband, David watches as Cleo's arms are flailing about while her husband ventures to restrain her. Covered with dark sunglasses and an enormous hat, which David thinks at any second is about to fall off her head. He also considers that she must be attempting to disguise her appearance. The closer she gets to him the louder she cries.

Frances steps away and takes a seat.

Both David and his father move out of her path as David has no desire to take part in what he believes is her academy award performance. He prays for God to keep his mouth shut. The processional comes to a halt because of her theatrics. Searching the line, David locates the person who will help him remain calm—Tianna. Their eyes lock, and he watches her as she makes faces which he can interpret. She is staring at Cleo with her hands on her hips and throwing her head up.

From her gestures, David wants to bust out laughing. Sure, Tianna is saying with her eyes and posture, "Lady shut up. You did not do right by your daughter." He is thankful her presence provides a distraction to whom he decides is the new Catherine Hepburn. Cleo's 'Best Actress of The Year' trophy is going in the mail today.

Once she reaches the coffin, Cleo cuts her eyes at him, then touches Candy's hand and yells, "I am your mother, and no attorney can change that fact."

David shifts from one foot to the other but refuses to allow Cleo to egg him into an argument. With his eyes pleading for help, he looks at Tianna.

On cue, Tianna darts out of the line approaches Cleo and cuffs her arm. To David and others, it appears as though she is comforting the distraught mother as she leads her to a seat away from David. Once Tianna escorts Cleo and her husband, she retakes her previous position. After paying her respects, David hugs his friend leaning in for Tianna to whisper in his ear. "I told that faker if she did not sit down, I would kick her ass right here in the parlor." Then she extends her hand for David to shake as she states out loud. "I am sorry for your loss," before she sits behind Candy's parents.

David struggles to prevent his face from revealing his thoughts while pondering if she indeed did say that. Knowing her as he does, it is entirely possible she used those exact words. Whatever she relayed, it seemed to simmer Cleo down.

After the wake and the services are over, David introduces Tianna to his parents.

"What in the world did you say to quiet Cleo?" Frances asks.

With her question, David finally can expel the laugh he held since the Stevens' walked in the chapel. The laughter allows him a chance to let out his grief, fears, and anger.

A punch to his arm from Tianna still does not prevent him from expressing the humor he finds in her statement. "I just told her I was a reporter with the Texas Star newspaper and was doing a story on her daughter about why mothers do not believe in their children when they report their sexual abuse."

This time David doubles over because the answer by her is even funnier than what she told him. The harder he squeals, the more he must go to the bathroom. After he gathers himself, he just shakes his head. "Tianna, you keep me laughing."

"I will do whatever I have to do to protect my friends, family, and the people I love." Tianna then reaches over and hugs Frances and acknowledges Bryant with a handshake. "It is great to meet you both. I will see everyone at the wedding."

On the ride home, David is still snickering, although no one else is amused. Though they are thankful, Tianna managed to de-escalate a potential situation between their son and Candy's parents.

After they pull up in the driveway, David explains he is picking Micah up, and they are going to pick up their tuxedos and do a few other errands. "I will be back by dinner. Call me if you need anything," he shouts before pulling away.

Before the school bus returns, he arrives at Tasha's house. To use the restroom, he goes inside. While he is waiting, he tells Tasha about her sister's actions at the funeral services.

"That is my sister. The sad thing is Tianna probably said both things to Candy's parents. Tianna is very protective."

Next, they discuss his wedding plans. Once Tasha explains to him all the work she has completed, he is in awe. The decorations she handmade and purchased to decorate the chapel she shares with him for his approval. With everything shown to him, David is sure even though this is a small and rushed ceremony; it is going to be beautiful. To help defray her expenses, David offers her some money to which Tasha refuses.

As they are discussing the finances, Micah opens the door and runs into the house. He jumps into his arms. "Hi David, I mean," ... He stops mid-sentence.

"Hello, Son."

He greets him as his daddy.

The two left Tasha's house. David explains the surprise and all the things they must get done. Micah swears not to share any of the details with his mother. The two laugh, play, talk, shop, sing, and get haircuts, completing everything he set out to accomplish. They finish in time to pick up Jada for dinner.

As they approach her apartment, Micah runs toward the door. Instead of knocking, he bangs on the door. "Mommy, let us inside," he yells.

When Jada opens the door, Micah grabs her around the waist as tight as he can. "I have a secret, but I cannot tell you," He exclaims.

A grin brightens David's face as his eyes absorb the beauty standing before him. Jada's dress hugs her hips and accentuates her small waist. The front zipper reveals just the right amount of cleavage. David licks his lips and stares at her from head to toe. Her thick black hair is curled and pinned up on the side to allow a section of hair to lie on her shoulder. The lime-colored dress makes her green eyes pop, revealing their almond shape.

"Come inside," she states while stepping back.

"Mommy, we all have on the color green," Micah says as he glances at each of them. "Now we really look like a family. Did you notice my shirt is like my daddy's?" he rattles.

With her hand, she fans her face to prevent tears from falling and ruining her makeup. The excitement exuding from her son warms her heart and makes her emotional. "What a coincidence we all dressed in the same color," she acknowledges, giving David an understanding nod.

As David steps inside, he reaches for her hand. Into her eyes, he stares. "You told me you were wearing green. Simple as Micah said, we are a family." He pulls her into his arms, being careful not to disturb her hair, make-up, or dress. After inhaling her fragrance, he whispers, "You are beautiful. I am not sure I can wait until our wedding night."

What a man, Lyric thinks, and he pays attention to the details? Another glance at her engagement ring glistening on her finger signals her future looks bright.

"All right guys, it is time to leave. We have a six o'clock dinner date and my mother insisted we be on time. Besides, I cannot wait to show off my family."

Thankfully, David is ready. Jada turns to her son. Being sure to gaze into his eyes, she kneels. "Young man, you are quite handsome," she says. "I packed an overnight bag for you so you can spend the night with your dad and grandparents."

Micah quickly pulls back as though thinking about what his mother just says. He searches her eyes. "Are we going to move?" he asks.

"Yes, but not tonight," she replies.

"Okay, Mommy. Is my bag in my bedroom?" he asks as he is running down the hallway.

Jada turns her attention back to David. Careful not to explicitly mention Candy's funeral, she asks, "How are you doing after all the things you have been through today?"

"I am much better now, but your friend Tianna is something else," he says with a chuckle.

Agreeing with him, she shakes her head as Micah returns.

They lock up and head for the car. They say little during the ride. Perhaps, they are adapting to the roles they will play in the next two days.

As they are pulling into the garage, David turns to her. "Tomorrow is our errand day so do not allow my parents to keep you up all night."

Negativity threatens Jada's mind as she arrives. She tries to control her breathing, which seems to increase by the minute repeatedly. She swallows. Her insides squirm as a mixture of salty sweat and running mascara trickles down her face.

Once David realizes she is anxious about entering the house, he rushes around to her side of the car and opens her door. Extending his hand, he gently pulls her up. "Micah, run in and meet your grandparents. We are coming."

Obeying his request, Micah jumps out and darts inside.

"We can move if you will not be comfortable living here," he states to let her know he understands her unspoken fears.

Without responding, she steps in front of him, wipes her face and enters the home.

Immediately, the aroma of walking into a restaurant overtook her. There are candles lit, low music playing, silver chafing dishes lining the counter, a formal six-course place setting, and vases of fresh long stem roses adorn the front area of the house. Greeted by a butler holding a tray with glasses of champagne, he offers both Jada and David some 'Armand de Brignac.'

The newly renovated home paralyzes Jada as her eyes slowly move around and soak in the makeover. To her, nothing looks the same. In awe of the transformation, her mouth falls open.

David introduces his mother and father to their soon-to-be daughter-in-law.

Unable to respond, she fights to stop gawking at the changes. Even the furniture is new, she thinks.

Bryant is the first to speak. "Son, I did not think it was possible to find someone as gorgeous as your mother but let me tell you that you did."

Jada smiles and covers her face with her hands hoping her exposed ears are not red. "Thank you, Mr. Austin, for the wonderful compliment."

"Mommy, his name is Granddad, and that is Grandma," Micah says, pointing. He is comfortably sitting on Bryant's lap as if he knew him all his life.

"Micah is right. We are family now, so you must find a less formal way to greet us," Frances says.

As Jada sits down, she cannot stop the tears from falling. The house renovation, the extravagant dinner preparation, his parents' quick acceptance of both Micah and her, and all the extra things David is doing is overwhelming. Not considering ruining her makeup or what anybody may think, her cup overflows with the joy she feels.

Frances rushes to Jada and wraps her arms around her. Back and forth she rocks her as though she is a baby. "We have loved you since the first day our son fell in love with you and Micah. I can tell by your sweet spirit he chose the right woman."

Bryant commandeers his grandson's and his son's hands. He leads them to the back patio. "We need to let the woman get all those tears of joy out of their system while we menfolk do a little bonding of our own. Am I right, Grandson?"

"Yep, Granddad, women always cry when they are happy, but we boys and men only cry when we are sad."

They laugh as they agree with his assessment.

After about fifteen minutes, Jada summons the men and her son inside to eat. Keenly cognizant that her emotional breakdown sent them running for cover, she reassures them her mood is now ecstatic with the big grin on her face. Her alone time spent with Frances proved to be almost as valuable as a session with a therapist. Ringing in her heart is the words that Frances shared. She tells her that, "Life is a journey that leads to an end." Her ordeal with Charles led her to David.

As they all sit at the table, Jada takes the lead and says grace. She thanks them all for the role they share in her life. "Now let's eat this amazing spread," she says. Jada, Micah, Bryant, and David cannot stop complimenting Frances with each bite of food they consume. Although the chef is the major topic, the rest of the conversations with David's parents are relaxed and full of laughter for Jada. Together, this gives her a new meaning to the term 'one big happy family.'

CHAPTER TWENTY-TWO

WEDDING DAY

Some say they are tying the knot

Others call it getting hitched

I say it is my

Today

Tomorrow

And Forever

The plural

(2)

Becoming

The singular

(1)

As the new day dawns, it births a day that David and Jada will cherish. Today is the time they will announce to the world their relationship is public, official, and permanent. It is their wedding day.

Lyric cannot help but remember when she and Johnny were married. It was her second time going to the altar. Lyric vowed it was to be her last. She prayed she would not end up in this same position, but once again, in less than sixty days, she will wear the crown of a divorcee. *How funny it is that man proposes, but it is only God that disposes. Only he knows the plans he has for us.* She grunts as she dismisses thoughts of her old marriage and inhales the freshness of the couple's new merger.

The clock on the wall is fast approaching one o'clock. In the floor-length mirror, Lyric makes one last inspection of herself, not only visualizing her outward perfection in the reflection but the character deep inside. Turning completely around, Lyric twirls as she appreciates the three hours devoted to fixing her hair and make-up. Her A-line dress is a bright yellow canary with silver inlays. The fabric, made of French terry knit and chiffon silk, clings to her body. The show-stopping part of her semi-formal ensemble is the strapless, silver-beaded, and fitted bodice, featuring an elegant cascading skirt that stops just above her knees. She points her right knee forward while standing on her tiptoes. Staring back is her curvaceous bare legs. They are long and silky-smooth yet appear to glisten as they connect to her slim but stable ankles covered by the thick ankle strap from her five-inch Canter-S silver high heels. The shoes enhance the convexity of her pronounced upper calf muscles. "Okay, you are working it. Now it is time to go and get Nicke dressed," she says to the woman in the mirror. *The power that beauty once held over me is gone, and a sense of liberation washes over me. I am beautiful because I say I am and not because someone else says or does not say I am.*

While she is walking into the front room, the phone rings. "Hello?"

"Hey Lyric, this is Judith. Are you dressed yet?" she asks.

"I sure am. In fact, I was just about to go help Nicke."

"I was wondering if you wanted to ride together. I can pick you up in about ten minutes."

"Sure, I will be ready. Just blow your horn," Lyric says.

To be sure, she packed everything: Lyric rifles through the small bag. Once she is prepared to go, she calls Tianna. "Good afternoon, my wonderful daughter," Lyric says.

"Hey Mom, how are you today?"

"I am fantastic. Where is Jada?"

"Jada is in the shower. I am at her house helping her."

"Is everything set up?"

"Yes, I persuaded Jada to allow me to take her to the courthouse so we can stop by the hospital for Nicke to see her dress."

"Oh no, I am on my way there now. Once Jada sees Nicke, she suspects something."

"Calm down Mom. After you get Nicke dressed, take her down to the chapel. When we arrive, her room will be empty. Jada will think Nicke is in therapy. We will hang out in the room until about five minutes before three. David told her the time had changed and to meet him downtown at 3:30. Dr. Maxey advised the nurses to come to her room and tell Jada after Nicke's treatment that Nicke requested to go to the chapel. So, everything is set. Just make sure you are out of her room by 2:30."

"Sounds like a brilliant plan. What is Micah doing?"

"He is with David and his parents," she whispers. "Mom, I must go because Jada is out of the shower. Call me if anything changes."

A horn honks outside of Lyric's door. Lyric snatches the overnight bag and Nicke's outfit as she rushes out of the house. "Get out of the car and model for me, Judith."

"Oh my God Lyric, you are beautiful," as Judith takes the items Lyric is carrying from her arms. "Wow!"

Embarrassed, she covers her face and giggles. "I love your dress, too. I wish we could run into a single man because, girl there would be two weddings," Lyric says.

"I know you meant to say three. Wait until Jim beholds all that beauty. He just might forget you are married," Judith predicts while she is spinning Lyric in a circle.

"Stop now," Lyric insists while entering the car. "Let's go. Our time is short, and there is a lot to do."

On the ride to the hospital, Lyric shares the plan Tianna relayed.

"Jada is going to be shocked. Are you sure she is not aware of her having a surprise wedding?"

"I am sure she is clueless, but still I am scared for Jada and me."

"Why?" Judith asks.

"Well, after all the tragedies Jada is going through, I want everything to be perfect. The issue for me is my daughter asked me to perform a solo for the bridal march. I am nervous to sing in front of people."

"Wow, Lyric. I did not know you were a singer. What are you going to bless us with?"

"I am singing a BeBe Winans' song entitled, 'I Found Love.'"

Judith does not recall ever hearing this one. "Will you practice a little for me?"

Trying to find the correct key, Lyric clears her throat and hums while locating the instrumental version on her cell phone. Once the music starts, she snaps her fingers and bobs her head. With her eyes closed, a heartfelt melodious tune emerges.

By the time she completes the song, Judith parks the car. Her mouth drops in disbelief at the live concert shared. "Lyric, the words are perfect for them. Your voice is amazing. I wanted to cry."

"Aww, that is sweet of you. It takes a momentous occasion for me to perform in public."

The two exit the car and are discussing her apprehension for singing. Judith tries to convince Lyric of the importance of sharing the gift God gave her with the world. They banter back and forth until reaching the hospital room.

"Hey Nicke, how are you today?" Lyric asks as she plants a kiss on her forehead.

"I am a little tired but very excited for my daughter. Hello, Officer Nelson," Nicke says with her hand extended.

"Hi, but please call me Judith."

"Well, you ladies are stunning. I hope I am worthy of being in your presence." Nicke chuckles and continues.

"David's parents came this morning to meet me. They are sweet. Micah was with them, and he seemed very attached."

"How considerate of them to visit you; it shows what kind of stock David comes from. We must, however, hurry and get you out of here before Jada catches us." The pale-yellow sequined dress Lyric holds up and asks, "Nicke, do you like this?"

"Oh yes, I do. I love the color and the material. I lost some weight since I was forced to eat this bland hospital food every day, so I hope it fits."

"Well, like the rest of us, you could stand to lose a few pounds. Even with your weight lost though this dress is gorgeous on you. It is a perfect fit," Lyric states as she closes the zipper and while Judith applies Nicke's make-up and styles her dreads into a bun. They add the finishing touches with only minutes to spare.

Lyric suggests they go downstairs so Nicke can be sure everything is set up correctly.

Nicke's eyes sparkle as she agrees, while Judith pushes her in the wheelchair.

Transformed is the hospital prayer room into a magical wedding chapel. Two extravagant baskets of yellow roses tied with wide gray ribbons are placed on metal stands and frame the altar. In the center is a large crystal dish with a candle packed inside the gray and yellow sand. Aisle sconces line the pews with colored LED lighted candles.

"Tasha, everything is amazing," Lyric says as her eyes dart from one corner of the room to the other. "How in the world did you have time to put together such elaborate decorations?"

Nicke whispers, "Thank you, Lord." Using what little strength she can gather, she places both hands on the handrails and propels herself close to Tasha. "You have done a great job. You should become a professional decorator."

"Thanks, Auntie. I want everything to be perfect. Even if this is a small gathering, we worked to be sure it was memorable. I know Jada is going to be happy when she sees how beautiful you look."

Lyric sets up the microphone to play the music for her solo. As she completes the sound check the door opens. Jim enters wearing a tailored charcoal suit with a yellow and gray pinned striped tie. Accompanying Jim is an incredibly handsome, polished, and tall man whose debonair demeanor exudes from every pore. Lyric locks eyes with Jim even though she wants to turn away. Some type of power pulls her to him. It is like she is a sheet of metal, and he is a magnet. While she attempts to steady herself and fights her desires, she is gawking at the way his round shoulders fill out his suit jacket.

Judith approaches Jim and greets him and his guest.

Without breaking eye contact with Lyric, he introduces Judith to his friend and the Minister performing the services, Reverend Daryl Bates. To allow them to talk, Jim makes his way towards Lyric. "I have always known you are a beautiful woman, but today, may I say you surpass any words I can say?" as he hugs her.

The couple holds each other for several minutes. They forget other people are in the room. The only thing that matters to them is the electricity of their embrace.

Gently, Lyric releases his arms. "Thank you for the compliment. If I might add, you are looking very dapper yourself." She then leads him toward Nicke. "I think we need to check on your patient. She seems a bit out of sorts."

"Who is the stunning lady in this wheelchair? You resemble one of my patients by the name of Mrs. Nicke Smith," he states in jest.

Nicke smiles while lowering her head.

Although Nicke's mouth is turned up, both Jim and Lyric detect Nicke's smile does not seem to match her true feelings.

"Are you feeling, okay?" Her concerned doctor asks.

"Yes," Nicke replies as she flinches in the chair.

To allow him to address possible medical issues, Lyric walks over to Judith.

Giddy, Judith introduces her to, "Reverend Bates who will officiate the ceremony."

"Hello, sir. It is nice to meet you," Lyric states while extending her hand and sneaking a peek at his left hand in search of a wedding band. Lyric's eyes speak instead of her mouth as she glances in Judith's direction seemly saying, "He looks available and like dating material."

"The pleasure is all mine," Reverend Bates replies. They exchange a smile before Lyric makes her way toward David, his father and mother and an unknown young man Lyric assumes is the best man.

David kisses Lyric on the cheek with a grin spanning from one side of his face to the other. "My, everything is so beautiful," David says as he takes in the romantic ambiance of the room.

"My daughters are responsible for this setup. All of this is their doing."

After agreeing, David introduces his parents and his friend, Carlos, to Lyric, then excuses himself, stating he would like to thank Tasha.

Bryant and Frances acknowledge Lyric, but once they spot Nicke, they too step away.

Carlos admires Lyric from head to toe. "I am sorry for staring, but you are lovely," he says.

Lyric can feel her blood rising to her face. *Boy, I am old enough to be your mother. You better not be making a pass.*

"David tells me Tianna is the maid of honor, and there, pointing to Tasha, is your other daughter."

"Yes, you are correct," Lyric replies to him while rolling her eyes.

"Wow, after seeing you two, I am confident when David described Tianna as a knockout. He was not kidding."

"Yes, but more importantly, she is intelligent and caring," Lyric retorts as she turns and walks to the other side of the room.

"Excuse me, everyone. Please take your seats or head to your assigned places. Jada is on her way down," Tasha yells, motioning with her hands.

Micah runs to Lyric, jumping up and down and yelling, "Where should I go?"

"You are the ring bearer, and Aria is the flower girl," Lyric says.

"I want you two right here by the door," Tasha relays as she answers for Lyric. "When the doors open, walk down the aisle slowly and stand beside David."

Tasha also positions the photographer outside the room, advising him to capture Jada's emotions from start to finish. The moment Jada arrives, she instructs him to knock softly. "Mom, Mom, we are ready for you," Tasha adds as Lyric is transfixed and watches her daughter barking orders to everyone.

In the room's front, Lyric moves to the microphone. "Testing, 1,2,3," Lyric repeats while checking the volume.

Jim stations himself next to Nicke. Lyric suspects it is because he is concerned for his patient, although he still will not stop staring at Lyric. The frequent visitor in her dreams is causing her hands to tremble as she tries to calm her nerves and mentally prepare for her solo. Jim's attention to her every move is making it difficult.

The photographer knocks on the door.

Tasha motions for everyone to rise from their seats. She then points toward Lyric.

The music starts. Lyric removes the microphone from the stand and sings from the depths of her heart and soul. With eyes closed, she provides a rendition that modulates and floats like a feather in the air. The connection between the words and her melodious sound sends a ripple of goose bumps to the mesmerized audience. Every note is crystalline and piercing.

"When I found you,

I found somebody who cares.

When I found you,

I found my most intimate prayer.

When I found you,

I found what every heart dreams of.

When I found you,

I found love."

As Lyric reaches the second verse, the door opens. Still singing, Lyric marvels as a chapel bathed in exquisite flowers, striking candlelight, an array of gray and yellow decor and smiling friends and family is revealed to both Jada and Tianna.

Tasha must pry Jada loose from the death grip she has on Tianna before handing her sister an extravagant bouquet of vibrant yellow tulips and stepping aside for Tianna to march to the front of the room.

Lyric shoots a quick glance toward Carlos in time to see his knees buckle at the sight of her daughter, and also the maid of honor, Tianna. His eyes widen with every step she takes in his direction.

***

Once Jada steps inside the door, she comprehends she is the bride attending her surprise wedding. Stunned, her feet stick to the floor as though covered with cement. Tears overflow when she sees David standing at the altar.

Tasha hands her a tissue and sends Micah down the aisle, followed by Aria, who is dropping yellow and red rose petals.

When Jada must join her future husband in the front has arrived. Handed to her is an extravagant bridal bouquet filled with yellow and white roses, daffodils, tulips, and greenery.

Jada tries to move, but she still cannot make her legs cooperate. The tears will not stop flowing.

Then the strength she needs rolls toward her. God heard her heart's desire to have her mother present at her marriage. Jada stares into her mother's tear-stained eyes. How beautiful are her dress and her updo hairstyle adds a sophistication to which Jada had not seen since before she entered the hospital?

Nicke reaches her hand out to her daughter.

The bride bends down and plants a kiss on her cheek.

She wraps her arms around her daughter's neck while whispering, "You are exquisite. Your future awaits you. I can finally rest knowing you and Micah have a man who is God sent and one who loves you both."

Jada stands while her mother holds her hand and escorts her down the aisle.

With tears streaming down his face, David delights as she strolls toward him. Her beauty is undeniable and even more so, she is dressed in a low-cut sleeveless lace panel gown. He drools seeing her shape packed so neatly in the white satin underdress but covered by a flowing light gray sheer covering designed to play peek-a-boo with the sensual parts of her body. Although her physical allure seems to be all-encompassing, he moves past her radiant exterior to where her genuine beauty lies, her heart. His thoughts are on Proverbs 18: *"Whosoever finds a wife, finds a good thing and obtains the favor of the Lord."*

Nicke places both of their hands inside his. "Take good care of my babies all the days of your life," she says as she turns in her wheelchair and rolls back to the first pew.

There is not a dry eye in the place. Everyone recognizes the intimate emotional connection between this couple, their families, and friends.

Lyric throws her head back and belts out the last line of her song.

"When I found you,
I found love."

The chapel erupts in thunderous applause from the solo sung by Lyric and from Nicke, passing her daughter's and grandson's hands to David.

After a gracious bow, Lyric sits next to Jim.

"You are blessed with a voice I never want to see silenced." Then he cups her hand in his. "When I found you, I found love," he whispers before turning his attention back to the services.

Lyric listens and watches as the couple shares vows and commit to an everlasting love in both harvest and famine times. They promise always to allow God to be the head of their lives. Together, they agree to become one as they light the unity candle.

Reverend Bates asks the congregants to stand. "Ladies and gentlemen, I present to you, Mr. and Mrs. David Austin." He then tells the groom, "You may now kiss your bride."

David clutches Jada in his arms, and the couple shares an extended, passionate kiss as though no one is watching.

The preacher shares parting remarks. "I have married many couples during my tenure as a minister. I can honestly say, never have I felt more love radiating from the pew to the altar than I feel now. I challenge us all. If you do not have or know the type of love witnessed here today, find it, nurture it, guard it, then never let it go."

After he concludes, Reverend Bates walks over to Judith and pulls her close into his muscular arms. "Would you like to go to dinner with me this evening?" he asks.

Everyone hugs the person they are with or the one they wish to have in their life. In the room, the tears of the deflowered are healed through love, understanding, and the presence of God.

Congratulations, Mr. And Mrs. David Austin
May God bless your union

<<<<>>>>

www.ingramcontent.com/pod-product-compliance
Lightning Source LLC
Chambersburg PA
CBHW021438240626
47153CB00001B/198